FADE

Also by Robert Cormier

THE CHOCOLATE WAR
BEYOND THE CHOCOLATE WAR
I AM THE CHEESE
AFTER THE FIRST DEATH
THE BUMBLEBEE FLIES ANYWAY
EIGHT PLUS ONE
TAKE ME WHERE THE GOOD TIMES ARE
A LITTLE RAW ON MONDAY MORNINGS
NOW AND AT THE HOUR

FADE

Robert Cormier

Delacorte
Press

Published by
Delacorte Press
The Bantam Doubleday Dell Publishing Group, Inc.
666 Fifth Avenue
New York, New York 10103

Library of Congress Cataloging in Publication Data

Cormier, Robert.
  Fade.
  Summary: Paul Moreaux, the thirteen-year-old son of French-Canadian immigrants, inherits the ability to become invisible, but this power soon leads to death and destruction.
  [1. Supernatural—Fiction. 2. French Canadians—United States—Fiction] I. Title.
PZ7.C81634Fad 1988   [Fic]   88-3540
ISBN 0-440-50057-5

Manufactured in the United States of America

September 1988

10 9 8 7 6 5 4 3 2 1

BG

To my wife, Connie, with love

PAUL

At first glance, the picture looked like any other in a family album of that time, the sepia shade and tone, the formal poses, the men in solemn Sunday suits and the women, severely coiffed, in long skirts and billowing blouses. It was a portrait of my father's family taken before World War I on the front steps of the house in Quebec on the banks of the Richelieu River.

The family moved to New England shortly after the picture was taken, my father along with my grandparents, my five uncles and four aunts, among them my aunt Rosanna, whom I would love all the days of my life.

I discovered the photograph when I was eight or nine years old and was told immediately of its mystery by my cousin Jules, who swore me to secrecy. I found out eventually that the mystery of the photograph was not really a secret, although it provoked various reactions among members of the family. Some dismissed the mystery not as a mystery at all, but as a failure of the camera's mechanism or the result of a childish prank. Others spoke of the mystery in hushed tones, with raised eyebrows, as if even the mere mention of the picture would bring terrible consequences. My grandfather refused to talk about the photograph altogether and acted as if it didn't exist, although it occupied a place in the big family album in the mahogany desk in the parlor at his house.

My father was amused by it all. "Every family has its mysteries," he said. "Some families have ghosts, we have a picture."

The mystery?

In the space that was supposed to have been occupied by my uncle Adelard, at the end of the top row, next to my father, there is simply a blank space. Nothing.

My uncle Adelard had disappeared at the moment the camera clicked and the shutter opened.

My uncle Adelard was always disappearing, going away and coming back again, a drifter whom I regarded as a glamorous figure, an adventurer, although he was thought of as a hobo and a tramp by some of the others in the family.

The family had settled down in Frenchtown on the east side of Monument in Massachusetts along with hundreds of other French Canadians, living in the three-decker tenements and two-story houses, working in the shops producing combs and shirts and buttons, sending their children to St. Jude's Parochial School, and attending mass at St. Jude's Church on Sundays. They shopped every day in the stores on Fourth Street, although they made regular excursions to Monument Center, the downtown shopping district.

I was puzzled by the way the people of Frenchtown accepted the daily grind of the factories, week after week, year after year. My father, for instance. A handsome man who was quick to laugh, he enjoyed a great reputation as a ballplayer in the Twilight Industrial League, swift and daring as a base runner and hitting dramatic home runs in the clutch. He danced the quadrilles at weddings with the same kind of quickness, whirling my mother around dizzyingly on the dance floor with whoops of delight while she hung on for dear life. The next morning he trudged his way back to the Monument Comb Shop, where he worked for forty-five years, enduring the layoffs, the lean years of the Depression, and the violence of the strikes.

My uncle Adelard escaped the shops—the daily drudgery and the layoffs and the walkouts—just as he had escaped the photographer's lens in Canada. That was why I felt a kinship with him. In that summer of 1938, I was thirteen years old, timid and shy and sometimes afraid of my own shadow. But in my heart I was brave and courageous like the cowboys in the Saturday afternoon serials at the Plymouth Theater. I felt that I, too, could become a hero if the opportunity presented itself or if I were tested. But there were no opportunities in Frenchtown. I longed to explore the outside world I saw in the movies or heard about on the radio or read about in books. Uncle Adelard was the only person outside my books and movies who had the dimensions of a hero, who dared to be different, who wandered the earth.

And that was why I hounded my father with questions whenever I got the chance. I waited while he listened to the radio and the news of Hitler gobbling up countries in Europe, felt guilty because the photograph was more important to me than the marching armies overseas. But this did not deter me from my purpose. I would gauge his disposition after he snapped off the radio, and if he seemed in a talkative mood, brought up the subject of the photograph.

Sipping the beer he brewed in the porcelain crocks in the cellar, smoking his Chesterfields, he often smiled in resignation and said: "Okay, what do you want to know?" As if I had never asked these questions before.

"Okay, it was a Sunday afternoon, right? And you were all on the front steps up in St. Jacques . . ."

"That's right," my father said, lighting another Chesterfield with a kitchen match scratched on his pants. "We were dressed in our Sunday best in shirts and ties and wool jackets. It was a hot summer afternoon so there was a lot of moving around, a lot of squirming."

"And Uncle Adelard was standing right beside you . . ."

"He sure was," he said. "It was impossible not to notice him. He was restless, refused to stand still. Until your Pépère turned around and gave him a look. He could shrivel your bones with that look.

"So at last Adelard became quiet, although he still managed to give me a pinch, daring me to flinch or jump."

"And then what happened?"

"Well, nothing. The photographer, Mr. Archambault, snapped the picture when we were all settled down. Rosanna was a baby in your Mémère's arms and had been fussing a bit. But she fell asleep, dozing nice and quiet. And, bang, the picture was taken."

"Now, tell me what happened when Mr. Archambault brought the picture to the house," I said.

The smell of celluloid clung to my father, a sweet acid smell that emanated not only from his clothes but from his skin as well, even when he emerged from a bath. It was the smell of the material from which combs and brushes were made at the shop. It was the smell of work, the smell of weariness, even the smell of danger because celluloid was highly flammable and sometimes spurted into flame without warning.

Sighing, he said:

"Well, when we looked at the photograph, there was no Adelard. Instead of Adelard, there was a blank space. He had disappeared. . . ."

"Did he really disappear?" I asked, as if I hadn't asked the question a thousand times before.

"Well, Adelard was a trickster, you know. I think he might have ducked out of sight at the last minute, just as the photographer took the picture. . . ."

"Wouldn't you have seen him do that?" I asked. "He must have made some kind of movement."

"I don't know, Paul. I was concentrating on the camera. Mr. Archambault told us to smile, told us not to move. It was hot in the sun, my collar was tight. I didn't really care what the others were doing, especially Adelard. He was a pain in the neck most of the time anyway. So I didn't see him move."

This delighted me because if my uncle Adelard had simply disappeared, there would have been no movement at all, of course.

"Now, the photographer, Mr. Archambault. Didn't he see anything unusual?"

"Who knows?" my father asked, his eyes flashing as he prepared to make his usual joke. "It's hard to see what isn't there."

I laughed, not only to be polite but because I enjoyed this ritual of question and answer, and my father and I in the kitchen together, the cigarette smoke curling in the air and everybody else off somewhere.

My father went on: "Mr. Archambault, poor guy, was more mystified than we were. He swore that Adelard had been posed like the rest of us but he also admitted that he was not looking at anyone in particular when he snapped the picture. Mr. Archambault offered to take one-twelfth off the price since one of the twelve wasn't in the picture. But your Pépère paid him the full price. He said the family was his responsibility, not the photographer's."

"What did Uncle Adelard have to say about it?"

It's funny that even when you know the answer to a question, you wait for it eagerly anyway. Is it because this time, *this time*, the answer might be different, that some forgotten piece of information might come forth? Or is it that the answer will confirm what you hope to hear?

"Did anybody ever get a straight answer out of Adelard?" my father asked, a question he didn't expect me to answer. "Anyway, he always said that if he told us what really happened, we'd have nothing to talk about anymore, except the shop and time studies, dull stuff."

"So he never admitted that he ducked down and was hiding, did he?" I asked, triumph in my voice.

"That's right, Paul. He only smiled when we asked him. Still does. And then he changes the subject. . . ."

We sat there a moment in silence, each with our own thoughts about my uncle Adelard and the photograph, I guess.

"Where is he now, Dad?"

"Who knows?"

My father pulled back the white ruffled curtain and stared out the window at the other three-deckers along Sixth Street, clotheslines looping from house to house, hung with clothes like flags of many colors, some bright and vivid, some faded and sad.

It thrilled me to think that my uncle Adelard was out there in the big world beyond Frenchtown and Monument.

* * *

"He's back," my father announced as he entered the kitchen in a cloud of celluloid and banged his lunch pail on the table.

I leapt from the chair where I had been reading the latest issue of *Wings* magazine, eager for details.

"When did she arrive?" my mother asked, turning from the table where she had been supervising my twin sisters, Yvonne and Yvette, as they laid out the knives, forks, and spoons.

She?

"Last night, late as usual, knocking on Pa's door after midnight," he said, shaking his head in mild disgust. "That's Rosanna for you."

I realized that my ears had fooled me into hearing what I wanted to hear—that my uncle Adelard had returned—instead of what my father had actually said.

"Poor Rosanna," my mother said.

My father snorted and went to the kitchen sink to wash up.

I had not seen Aunt Rosanna for at least five years, which is a lifetime, of course, when you're thirteen years old looking back to the age of eight. I had almost forgotten her existence and retained only a vague image of red lips and shining black hair and clothes that sparkled and shimmered when she walked. Whenever her name came up, a hush always followed and people in the family averted their eyes from each other. She was not like Uncle Adelard, who was always the subject of speculation and curiosity and sent postcards home from places like Boise, Idaho, and Billings, Montana, and Waco, Texas. No one ever heard from Aunt Rosanna.

A few days later my mother sent me to my grandfather's house with an apple pie she had baked. The steaming pie in my hands, I knocked awkwardly at the door with my elbow. A moment later I found myself in the presence of my Aunt Rosanna.

She stood near the kitchen window in a purple skirt and white blouse, the black hair even blacker now and glinting in the afternoon sunlight, her lips still full and red, redder even than the brightest McIntosh. And her eyes. What eyes. Brilliantly blue but not the blue of the sky or the blue of my mother's fancy goblets she put out only on holidays. Her eyes were a brimming blue as if on the verge of tears, and the light danced on that blue the way the sun dances on the surface of a lake.

There are moments that stop the heart, that catch the breath, that halt the beat of blood in your veins, and you are suspended in time, held between life and death, and you wait for something to bring you back again. And what brought me back was my name on her lips:

"Paul. You've grown up. It's so good to see you."

Somehow the pie was out of my hands and I was in her embrace, her arms around me, her perfume invading me, spicy and exotic, and I was aware of her breasts crushed against me, and I couldn't breathe and my blood pulsed wildly and my skin itched and my head whirled.

"Let me look at you," she said, thrusting me away but her hands gripping my shoulders, and I was both reluctant to leave the circle of her embrace and yet eager to get away, to run and hide, to gather this moment to myself, burn it into my memory, and I also wanted to sing a song or write a poem or leap with joy. I did nothing but stand there, stunned.

"What's the matter, Paul? Aren't you glad to see me? You haven't said a word."

Was there teasing in her voice? Was she enjoying the effect

she had on me? I felt that I was turning all colors before her, that I appeared awkward and ridiculous. My pants were too tight and trickles of sweat rolled down my ribs from my armpits.

I stammered and swallowed and gulped and didn't know what to do with my hands as she laughed a wonderful laugh, full-throated and raucous while her eyes told me without words that she understood what was happening to me, that there was something special between us.

"I remember picking you up as a baby and kissing you all over," she said. "And now you're almost a grown man . . ."

I almost dissolved in ecstasy there in the kitchen in front of my grandparents. I ached to tell her that I loved her, instantly and forever, that she was the most beautiful thing I had ever seen, lovelier than Merle Oberon and Margaret Sullavan in the movies at the Plymouth, more beautiful and enticing than any of the women in those magazines at the back of Lakier's Drug Store that I feasted upon with hot eyes when Mr. Lakier had his back turned.

My grandfather coughed explosively and my grandmother bustled about, and I sensed that they wanted to end this meeting of my Aunt Rosanna and me.

"I'm glad you're back," I managed to utter as I fumbled for the doorknob. Fleeing the kitchen, I slammed the screen door behind me, clattered down the stairs and across the yard, scurried through the rows of tomato plants in my grandfather's garden, streaked along the sidewalk down Eighth Street, running, running, heart pounding, thoughts in a frenzy, wondering what was happening to me, happy and sad, hot and cold, all at the same time, my heart filled to bursting with—what? what?—I couldn't put a name to it. Someone called my name as I hurtled past Dondier's Meat Market and it might have been Pete Lagniard but I didn't stop, couldn't stop, wanted to run forever, alone but not alone, because my Aunt Rosanna ran with me— *Paul . . . you've grown up   I remember kissing you all over*

That night in bed, curled up like a child, I erupted into ecstasy.

"What the hell are you doing?" Armand, my older brother, asked from the other side of the bed. My younger brother, Bernard, lay between us and I was glad he was sound asleep.

"Nothing," I said, voice low and muffled, strangling with shame and remembering Father Blanchette's whispered warnings in the confessional about such practices.

Yet, could it be a sin if you did it out of love, if you surrendered to a terrible longing, if, by surrendering, you ended the torture, sweet as it was, that made you run the streets with no destination, that took away your appetite, that kept you tossing in bed, that made you so happy one minute that your body sang like a violin and so miserable the next that you wanted to cry?

"Go to sleep," Armand said, his voice surprisingly tender for someone concerned mostly with baseball and skipping school and hanging around the comb shop.

I lay there in the bed, listening to the sleep sounds of my brothers and sisters. The bedroom was large enough to accommodate two beds at right angles to each other. While Armand, Bernard, and I occupied the bed nearest the kitchen door, my twin sisters, Yvonne and Yvette, who were eleven, slept in the bed near the window. The sounds of the night were everywhere around me—the melting ice dripping from the pan beneath the icebox in the pantry, the sounds of my brothers and sisters softly snoring, turning in their sleep, sometimes uttering small sharp cries in the night.

The baby, Rose, slept in a small bed close by my parents in their bedroom and she sometimes wakened, whimpering, and I would hear my mother crooning softly to her.

I pondered the mysteries of life as the minutes passed. How did I manage to be born in Frenchtown in Monument at this moment of history? I thought of the poems I had written that were hidden away in the closet, poems full of my longings and loneliness, my fears and desires. I wrote my poetry in secret, lying beneath the bed with a flashlight or in the shed behind an old and useless black stove. But I did not know if I was a poet. I wondered why I tossed and turned in my bed at night instead of plunging into sleep the way my brothers and sisters did. I sometimes envied the way they lived their lives without asking questions or pondering the mysteries that surrounded us. Or did they, too, have secrets they shared with no one?

I sometimes longed to be like them, a star ballplayer who was always chosen first for a team, like Armand, or handsome like Bernard, almost too beautiful to be a boy, some people said. I even envied my twin sisters, who were all giggles and laughter, got good marks in school, and were never scolded by my parents or the nuns. Most of all I envied Pete Lagniard, my best friend, who ran faster and climbed fences quicker than anyone else, knew a thousand secrets—all the uses of corn silk, how to make a slingshot that never failed, the best hiding places in the neighborhood. I considered my lack of talent at schoolyard games, my thousand fears, the loneliness I could not explain that threw a shadow across my life even during happy moments.

I pulled the sheet around my shoulders even though it was a hot night, and I brought forth in my mind the image of my aunt Rosanna and all her beauty, the scent of her and the feel of her as she held me in her arms. Her face was a beacon shining in my mind, a glowing light that led me with sweet caresses into sleep, deep and dark and, because of her, utterly beautiful.

The photograph was not the only mystery in my life that summer. There were rumors of strange happenings on the shores of Moccasin Pond on the outskirts of Monument. Rumors of bonfires and pagan rituals and the appearance of ghosts. Like all rumors, they were difficult to pin down. Some brave people actually went to the pond to investigate and found nothing. Others reported that they were driven away by phantoms breathing fire on their necks. Those fires were nothing but their own whiskey breaths blowing back on them, my father scoffed. As July burned on, Moccasin Pond became a part of the summer's lore, a topic to pass away the hot and humid days and evenings. Until Pete Lagniard came with proof that the rumors were not rumors at all.

Pete told me of his proof one Saturday afternoon as we were on our way to the Plymouth Theater, where the latest episode of *The Ghost Rider* was playing along with a Charlie Chan mystery.

Pete always was the first to know what was going on in

Frenchtown. He was the youngest of a family of nine and his older brothers and sisters carried home the gossip of the shops where they worked. Pete was an expert eavesdropper and he reported all that he heard to me. We both loved drama and movies and mysteries and this cemented our friendship. He lived on the first floor of the three-decker on Sixth Street and I lived on the second. We rigged a pulley system between our windows at the rear of the house so that we could send messages to each other in a Campbell's soup can. It was easier to shout out the windows, of course, but not so dramatic.

Pausing in front of the Acme Upholstering Company, Pete said he overheard his brothers talking about strange meetings taking place at Moccasin Pond.

"What's so strange about them?"

"These are meetings with masked men. They carry torches. They meet Friday nights . . ."

"Who are they?" I asked, doubtfully. Masked men and flaming torches were far removed from Frenchtown and belonged on the screen at the Plymouth.

"Nobody knows yet but my brothers are going to find out," Pete bragged, strutting a bit. "I heard them say they were going to the pond with a gang next Friday night. My brother Curly said: if these mutts are looking for trouble, they're going to find it." Curly, a giant of a man who worked in the shipping department at the comb shop, was capable of lifting huge crates that ordinarily required the strength of two or three men.

"Are you sure of all this, Pete?" I asked, wondering if his imagination was working overtime as usual.

"Well, there's one way to find out," he said, his eyes dancing with excitement.

"How?" I asked, although I knew how.

"Friday night," he said. "We'll be there. You and me. At Moccasin Pond . . ."

A shiver rippled through my body, a shiver of dread and foreboding and danger. Yet I couldn't deny the excitement that also ran just below the shiver. How often I had longed for adventure, thinking that I could only find it beyond Frenchtown, far from Monument, in the distant places of the globe. But here was drama and mystery only a few miles away, attainable, waiting for us.

On Friday night, when darkness had inundated the streets of Frenchtown, Pete and I made our way toward Moccasin Pond, after slipping out of our tenements. We cut through the back alley between the Monument Comb Shop and the sheds of Boudreau's Bottling Works and ghosted through Alphabet Soup, that area of streets with letters for names where transients lived in disreputable shacks and shanties. We streaked down Water Street, where the houses were few and far between and the streetlights equally sparse. We glanced at each other occasionally, nighttime conspirators, thrilled to be out so late together. The night was filled with unidentified fragrances, as if it produced a smell of its own, musky and dark and pungent, that the day kept hidden. When an occasional car passed, we drew into the shadows and became a part of the night and its mysteries.

We struggled up Ransom Hill, out of breath as we reached Pepper Point, a spot from which we could see the lights of downtown Monument winking in the distance. As we paused to rest for a moment or two, Pete asked:

"What time do you think it is?"

"After eleven," I said, guessing.

The words sounded beautiful. *After eleven.* And Frenchtown dozing below us, most of the people asleep in their beds.

"Let's go," Pete said, and we groped our way into the woods. A dog barked somewhere, the sound emphasizing the stillness of night. Insects buzzed around our heads. Stars wheeled in the sky and a full moon emerged from drifting clouds. We passed under the branches of towering trees and squeezed through clumps of bushes. We bumped into each other, blundering our way forward, tripping and sometimes falling, heard our own desperate grunts and groans. Finally, gasping for breath, we emerged into a clearing and followed an irregular path that led to the shores of Moccasin Pond, the surface shining in the moonlight, the water as calm and unruffled as the white bedspread in my parents' bedroom.

Across the pond stood the pavilion where dances were held on Saturday nights, its white clapboards gleaming ghostlike in the darkness.

"Listen," Pete said, turning his ear to the pond.

The sound of automobiles reached faintly across the water, then grew louder, the pond acting like an amplifier. Squealing brakes and the honking of horns mingled with the roar of racing engines. Headlights flashed across the water like searchlights in a prison movie, and we ducked our heads.

We circled the pond, keeping to the shadows, following the curve of the shoreline, low to the ground. We snaked our way to the picnic area and took up positions behind a table that had been upended and stood on its side.

Peeking above the table's edge, I saw that fifteen or twenty cars had formed a circle, their headlights focused on a central point, the motors quietly idling, the drivers shadowy figures behind the windshields.

As the men began to emerge from the cars, slamming the doors and calling to each other in muffled voices, Pete whispered in my ear a single syllable of awe and wonder: "Wow."

And I echoed the word silently as I saw instantly what he had seen.

The men wore white shrouds with peaked hoods, their eyes dark caves where holes had been cut into the material. One hooded figure carried a huge wooden cross, taller than he was, the horizontal bar wider than a man's outspread arms. He made his way to the center of the lighted area.

He raised the cross above his head, like an evil priest in a pagan ceremony, defying God himself as he thrust the cross toward the sky, the hooded figures gathering around him, cheering and yelling.

"The Ku Klux Klan," Pete whispered in my ear.

"They belong down south," I said.

"But they're here."

Pete's hand gripped my shoulder sharply, his fingernails digging into my flesh. "Duck," he commanded.

As I lowered my head I glimpsed a hooded figure walking in our direction, holding a rifle in one hand, a whiskey bottle in the other.

Pete's voice trembled in my ear: "A guard."

The guard passed so close to us that we heard his feet crunching on pine needles and, after a pause, the gurgling sound of whiskey being swallowed as he went on his way.

When I raised my head again, the cross had become a fiery torch, angry flames biting at the darkness, the cross brandished high as the Klansmen leapt and danced, shouting, clapping each other on the back in a terrible kind of jubilation. The air blazed not only with the leaping flames of the cross but with an aura that was difficult to define. Words rose to my lips but I could not say them aloud. They were lodged in my throat. *Hate. Malice. Evil.*

Sudden silence fell as the hooded men formed a circle around the crossbearer.

"Get rid of the niggers!" he yelled.

An answering shout from the crowd: "Get rid of the niggers!"

"Get rid of the Papists!" the crossbearer yelled again, his voice higher and shriller, the cross still aflame above him.

Pete turned to me with an inquiring glance.

"That's us," I said. "Catholics."

"Get rid of the Papists!" the crowd echoed, their voices accompanied by the thumping of fists on car hoods.

"Get rid of the Jews!" The words rang out with a terrible kind of splendor.

"Get rid of the Jews!" the crowd echoed.

"Where the hell is Curly and the gang?" Pete whispered in my ear.

A surge of movement in the darkness beyond the pavilion, vague and undefined, caught my eye. As I squinted in that direction there was an explosion of lights. Headlights and spotlights and flashlights focused on the hooded figures. At the same time, war whoops and screams of delight blazed in the air and, at last, I saw the invaders streaming into the parking lot carrying clubs and baseball bats, yelling and screaming as they ran toward the Klansmen.

For a long moment the hooded figures stood frozen in surprise, mute, obviously stunned and unprepared for the attack. Then, as if on cue, they began to run, panic-stricken, tripping and falling, encumbered by the flowing robes.

Pete leapt to his feet and hooted with glee. "Kill the bastards," he yelled.

The fight was not really a fight but a furious chase as the Klansmen scurried for their cars, gathering the skirts of their shrouds like frantic women while their pursuers swung their weapons, missing their targets more often than they hit them. Shouts and cries and bellows of pain filled the air. Pete's brother Curly stalked through the smoke and dust, without a weapon, grinning wickedly, as if he were taking a casual stroll on a Sunday afternoon. Suddenly, a hooded figure leapt on his back with a fierce cry and Curly spun him around effortlessly, twisting swiftly for someone so big, and his attacker went flying through the air, striking the side of a car with a dull thud.

As I shouted "Hooray" I turned to see the wooden cross, flameless now, abandoned, on the ground, pathetic and charred.

"Watch out, Paul," Pete cried.

The hooded guard was coming our way, waving his rifle at us.

"I see you," he shouted, "you little shitters."

We scrambled to our feet. Pete pushed against the table and sent it flopping to the ground with a *whomp* that made the guard jump back awkwardly, almost tripping on the hem of his shroud.

Dashing for the protection of the woods, we zigzagged, keeping low to make ourselves smaller targets, imitating the movie heroes we had seen in a thousand getaways. Pete plunged into low bushes but I tripped and fell forward onto the beach, my face mashed into the sand. Sputtering and spitting sand, wiping frantically at my face, I tried to get up as I heard the oncoming footsteps of the guard.

"Come on, Paul," Pete called from the shadows.

I attempted to stand but my breath went away as if someone had struck me in the chest and a flash of pain went through me, from the top of my head to my toes. I collapsed on the sand, fighting to regain my breath, thankful that the pain at least had passed as quickly as it came. As my breath returned I saw the guard advancing, a grotesque silhouette in the moonlight.

Cold invaded my body as I stared helplessly at the nightmare figure lurching toward me, rifle in hand.

"Where are you, Paul?"

Where did he think I was?

The guard came closer, closer, and stopped only a few feet away, the rifle aimed in my direction. Shivering, I began to pray, knowing that I was about to die. *Je Vous salut, Marie* . . . I asked forgiveness for my sins, looking up at the guard who stood almost directly above me.

The rifle wavered in his hand and he looked around, swaying a bit, his hood bobbing up and down.

I felt a surge of hope. He's drunk, I thought, drunk as a bat and doesn't see me.

He took a step backward, as if he had lost all sense of direction. Behind him, in the parking lot, the skirmish continued, shouts and cries, and he swiveled toward the sounds, unsteady on his feet, the rifle lowered. I was still shivering, although the night was hot.

He glanced my way again, muttered, "The hell with it," and let out a war whoop as he charged back toward the battle, holding on to his hood with one hand, waving the rifle with the other.

Wasting no time in getting to my feet, I hurled myself into the woods, groping blindly forward. I finally stumbled into a clearing and flung myself to the ground, exhausted, drenched with sweat. No longer cold with fear.

Pete found me there a few minutes later.

"What happened?" he asked. "I've been looking all over for you."

"I tripped and fell down. I thought he was going to kill me."

"I couldn't see you, I thought you ran the other way."

"He was drunk," I said. "I was right in front of him and he couldn't see me. He ran back to the fight. . . ."

Pete gave me a handkerchief to wipe my face and we slithered through the woods, following patches of moonlight that guided our footsteps. The sounds of the battle diminished, growing fainter behind us until we were aware once more of the woods surrounding us, the presence of things, small scatterings, sensations of flight and movement.

At last we collapsed at the base of a huge spreading tree, gasping for breath, bones aching. Pete closed his eyes and fell asleep almost instantly. After a while I yielded myself up to exhaustion and fell into a deep, dreamless sleep.

When we awakened, dawn was spilling blood across the sky, and we drifted out of the woods and made our way like weary phantoms down Ransom Hill and through the streets of Frenchtown to Sixth Street and home.

The next afternoon, as I arranged oranges in precarious pyramids in the vegetable section of Dondier's Market, Pete brought me the *Monument Times*. We ducked out of sight and knelt on the floor near the potato bin.

"Look," Pete whispered, spreading the front page of the newspaper before me on the floor. I heard the ringing of the cash register as Mr. Dondier rang up the order of Mrs. Thellier of the eleven children.

The headline in the top right-hand corner of the *Times* said:

KLAN, LOCAL GANG
CLASH AT POND

And below:

> Comeback efforts of the Ku Klux Klan were
> thwarted here last night when a gathering of
> Klansmen at Moccasin Pond was disrupted by a
> group of men reported to be residents of the
> Monument area.
>
> Unofficial reports indicated that several inju-
> ries occurred but no one sought medical treat-
> ment.
>
> Klan activity, last reported here in the mid-
> 1920s, has been on the increase in recent
> months.
>
> Police Chief Henry Stowe said today that "we
> will not tolerate the existence of the Klan in our
> city."

"Isn't that great, Paul?" Pete whispered in my ear. "We
were there. We made the headlines."

As I read the story once more, my thoughts went back to
the beach, and the hooded guard who had stood above me
with his rifle, and the pain and the fear, and how I prayed
and waited to die. But didn't. In the stuffy heat of Dondier's
Market, my knees on the sawdust floor, I shivered at the
memory of my narrow escape.

I did not know that on the beach at Moccasin Pond on that
Friday night I had faded for the first time.

I became a spy that summer, searching for more mysteries, carrying on a bittersweet espionage, a solitary watcher and an eavesdropper as well, hanging around corners, listening to conversations, stalking shadows that existed only in my imagination and settling at last on the sweetest of targets —my aunt Rosanna.

I focused my attention on my grandfather's house on Eighth Street because she had taken over the spare bedroom in the front that was usually reserved for visitors from Canada. My grandparents' kitchen was seldom empty or silent. Someone usually occupied the chairs around the big table, my grandfather presiding in the rocking chair near the big black stove while my grandmother, a sparrow of a woman who flitted here and there and everywhere, kept busy pouring coffee, slicing pies, serving suppers and dinners. No wonder she took a long nap every afternoon.

I lingered in that tenement, keeping my ears alert to conversations, drifting off to other rooms. Once, when my aunt was out, I slipped into her room and shamelessly opened one of her bureau drawers, saw a pair of her silk panties lying on top of other underwear. I held the pink panties to my cheek while her perfume assailed me and I was weak and half sick with love and longing.

I schemed to obtain glimpses of her and drank in her loveliness whenever I could, feasting on the marvels of her body. It was torture to be in the same room with her because I tried to look at her and not look at her at the same time, my eyes skittering anywhere and everywhere but coming back to her finally, my heart accelerating, my body fevered, my eyeballs hot and stinging. Whenever our eyes met, I was held there as if hypnotized. Sometimes I tore my eyes away, afraid that she could see right into my soul and knew the terrible and wonderful thoughts I had of her.

One evening after supper as I sat in the bedroom reading, I heard my father and mother in conversation and Aunt Rosanna's name flashed in my ears.

"She should have stayed away," my father was saying. One minute the radio had been playing *Amos 'n' Andy*, the next moment those gravelly voices had faded and my father's words came from the kitchen.

Getting up cautiously from the bed, I glided to the doorway in my stockinged feet.

"But Frenchtown's her home, Lou," my mother said. "Why shouldn't she come home?"

"She always causes trouble," he said, his voice stubborn in a way I seldom heard.

"People make trouble for her," my mother replied, voice soft as always but with her own kind of stubbornness. "You know what her problem is . . . ."

"I know, all right. She can't resist anything in pants."

"No, Lou, you're wrong. You're not being fair. She's got a

heart as big as the world. But she falls for the wrong people and gets left in the lurch."

"Why can't she be like other girls? Like her sisters? Work in the shop, find a good man. Instead, she acts like a bum."

"She's not a bum, Lou. And you know it. All right, she's not a saint but—"

The sentence was not completed as Armand and the twins arrived home in a rush. Conversations in our family seldom ended of their own accord; they were always interrupted by an arrival or a departure or a sudden eruption of activity. The worst part of eavesdropping was all the incomplete conversations you heard.

I went to my grandfather's house one humid afternoon and heard no answer to my soft knock on the kitchen door. Holding my breath, I tried the doorknob. The door swung open without a sound. I paused, peeking in, feeling as though I were committing a sin. Walking softly across the kitchen floor, I listened at the door of my grandparents' bedroom and heard the soft snores of my grandmother rising and falling. I slipped through the dining room and parlor, glad for the soft carpets, on my way to my Aunt Rosanna's bedroom at the front of the house.

I paused before the desk that contained the family album with the photograph from which my uncle Adelard was absent. On the wall next to the desk was another photograph, in a black frame, of my uncle Vincent, who had died long ago and was buried in St. Jude's Cemetery. He had died in his sleep, found dead in his bed, at the age of ten, a gentle boy who, my father said, had loved birds and small animals.

Although my father always defended my uncle Adelard when my uncle Victor and others criticized his wandering ways, he was bitter toward Adelard for having left French-town so soon after Vincent's death.

"A family should stick together when tragedy strikes," I heard my father telling my mother after a high mass on the anniversary of Vincent's death. "Adelard had no business leaving like that, on the day of the funeral. . . ."

"Maybe he was so sad he couldn't bear to be here," my mother said.

"Maybe," he answered, but the tightness of the muscles in his face showed that he was not convinced.

I made the sign of the cross in front of my uncle Vincent's picture before walking slowly, carefully, to my aunt's bed-room.

Her door was slightly ajar, and I paused, all my senses alert. Her spicy perfume scented the air. Was she inside? Should I knock on the door? I ached to see her and had gathered enough courage to show her the poem I had writ-ten especially for her. I had carried it around in my pocket for more than a week. The poem would speak for me, say the words I was too shy and self-conscious to say. Now, standing in the parlor, breathless and apprehensive, I lost my nerve.

Turning to leave, I heard a sound I couldn't identify. Was she crooning a song? Approaching the door, I inclined my head, taking a deep breath. And I realized at once that my aunt Rosanna was softly crying in the bedroom. Like a child, sniffling.

"Who's there?" she called suddenly.

"Nobody," I said. Then: "Paul."

I heard the rustle of her clothing as she approached. The door swung open to reveal her in all her loveliness. She wore a blue robe of filmy material and, unbelievably, as in my dreams, the robe was not buttoned all the way and her breasts almost spilled out. But I was immediately stricken with guilt when I saw the tears on her cheeks.

"Paul," she said, and, as always, my name on her lips made my body quiver like the string after the arrow has flown.

"I'm sorry," I said. Sorry for sneaking up on her like this, sorry for seeing her in such distress and yet made all warm and itchy at the sight of her and my pants again too tight.

"There's nothing for you to be sorry about, Paul," she said, pulling her robe around her, hiding those objects of my lust.

"Is there anything I can do?" I asked even as I knew the futility of that question.

"Do you know how to pound some sense into a person?" she asked. "That's what I could use. A good dose of common sense. About men. About everything." She wiped her cheeks with a lace handkerchief and managed a small smile. "Then maybe I wouldn't be so stupid. . . ."

"You're not stupid" I protested. "You're . . . you're . . ." And hesitated, the words stuck in my throat. For weeks I had been wanting to declare my love for her, to tell her of the storm she had created in my heart and the sweetness she had brought to my life. But I couldn't even open my mouth as I stood before her.

"What am I, Paul?" she asked, and I searched for the sound of teasing in her voice but it wasn't there.

With trembling fingers I groped for the poem in my pocket, saw to my dismay as I drew it out that it was wrinkled from being folded and refolded so many times and soiled from my sweating fingers.

"Here," I said, thrusting it at her, unable to utter more than one word.

She unfolded the sheet of paper and after a glance at me,

soft and full of tenderness, she began to read, her lips form-
ing the words. I recited the words to myself as she read
them.

> *My love for you is pure*
> *As candle flame,*
> *As bright as sunshine*
> *As sweet as baby's breath.* . . .

Yet even as I said the words I knew they were a lie. Because my love for her was not pure and sweet. It was hot
with desire for her body. I wanted to caress her, to gorge
myself on her.

> *My love for you*
> *Is a whisper in the night*
> *A silent prayer at vespers* . . .

This was the worst of it, I saw now. Bringing church and
prayer into the poem, a sacrilege, and yet I needed to show
her that I was not like the others, the men I pictured groping
for her in saloons, the men who whistled at street corners. I
wanted to assure her that I was different from the others.
Despite my shameless thoughts and my desires. Underneath
all of that was something pure, unsoiled, chaste.

She sank onto the bed as she read the poem, and I could
see by the movement of her lips that she was reading it
again. Her robe had fallen open once more and the tops of
her breasts were again visible, round and full and white as
milk. She had crossed her legs and I saw the red garters on
her thighs, a sight that made my eyes bulge and my heart
pound and a terrible hotness race through my veins.

"It's beautiful," she said, her voice gentle as she held the poem in her hands, her eyes liquid blue as always but the liquid now resembling tears.

My own eyes were fastened on her breasts—it was beyond my power to look elsewhere—and for a glorious moment I feasted on them while I squirmed before her, face flushed, juices thick in my mouth. Then I felt the surge of ecstasy developing and struggled, bringing my knees together, stricken, as she looked at me, the poem still in her hand, her expression soft and tender. I bent forward, trying to make myself small and, at the same time, to hold back that quick beautiful terrible spurt but unable to do so. As our eyes met, my body quivered with delight. I had never known such piercing happiness, such an explosive moment of sweetness. I trembled, shivered, as if strong winds were assailing me. And then, as always, came the swift shame and flush of guilt but this time worse than ever before because it had happened while she watched and I had seen her eyes grow puzzled and then alarmed and then—what? I could not read her expression—surprise, disgust?—I saw her mouth shape itself into an oval and heard her voice.

"Oh, Paul."

Could she see the stains on my trousers?

"Oh, Paul," she said again. Such a sadness in her voice but beyond sadness. Accusation, maybe, or betrayal.

For a split second I could not move, stood pinned and fixed before her in my shame and disgrace, feeling the terrible stickiness in my trousers, trying to swallow and almost choking on the juices that had turned sour in my throat.

"I'm sorry," I cried, backing away, tears blinding me so that I could not see her through the blur they created. Then I was out the door, sobbing my tears away as I ran through the parlor and the kitchen to the back hall and the piazza. Down the steps and into the street I ran, past the three-deckers, the stores, the church, the school.

Why did I always seem to be running from her?

Omer LaBatt.

There on the corner of Fourth and Mechanic, waiting for me in front of the First National Store, his feet planted firmly on the sidewalk, hands on his hips, the visor of his green plaid cap tilted over his eyes.

Bad enough that I had probably lost my aunt Rosanna forever, but now on the very next day I was confronting my enemy, my nemesis. Although he was across the street, I saw his dark scowl and, as he pushed up his cap, the dull, luster-less eyes without a flicker of mercy in them.

Omer LaBatt always appeared before me this way, like a phantom, without warning, out of nowhere. Sometimes I'd burst out of the alley between the two five-deckers on Second Street—the tallest buildings in Frenchtown after St. Jude's Church—and find him waiting for me, hands on his hips. Other times he stationed himself near places he knew I would visit sooner or later—Dondier's Market or Lakier's Drug Store—and confront me as I came out the door.

Like at this moment.

I gulped, preparing to make my getaway.

He was older than I was, yet seemed to have no age at all—was he fifteen or nineteen or twenty? He was not tall, which accentuated his wide shoulders and broad chest. His legs were stumps and he wasn't a good runner. I could easily outrun him and that was my saving grace. But I had night-mares about tripping, falling down and lying helpless on the ground as he approached.

Because I was so miserable about the loss of my aunt Ro-sanna and figured I had nothing more to lose in the terrible place my world had become, I called out:

"Hey, LaBatt, why don't you pick on somebody your own size?"

I had never spoken to him before. He didn't answer, but continued to glare at me. Then he grinned, a vicious grin that revealed jagged teeth.

I pondered my chances. My chances, of course, depended on what he did. Omer LaBatt didn't always chase me. Some-times he was satisfied if he merely forced me to change direc-tions, to cross the street, giving him wide berth, letting him dominate whatever piece of the planet he stood on. Other times we engaged in a wild chase through streets and alleys and backyards.

Made a bit bolder by having spoken to him and not having the earth crumble at my feet, I yelled: "Why me, LaBatt? Why pick on me?"

This was a mystery I had long pondered and never solved. He had been the bully in my life for at least three years and I couldn't figure out the reason. He was a stranger to me. I had never done him harm. I didn't know his family or friends, if he had any. He had simply appeared in my life one day, in front of Lakier's, our eyes meeting in a fatal deadlock, and I knew in that instant, looking into those pale yellow eyes, that here was my enemy, someone who had the power and the desire to hurt me, maim me, to destroy me, maybe.

I never talked to anyone about this, not even Pete Lagniard. But shortly after that first encounter, I pointed him out to Pete one day and asked: "Who is that guy, anyway?"

As usual, Pete had the answer.

"That's Omer LaBatt," he said. "A tough guy. He just moved here from Boston. He does things for Rudolphe Toubert."

This information was enough to cause me shivers because I had an idea what he meant by "does things." Pete wasn't finished, however.

"He quit school," he continued.

"Everybody quits school," I said, pointing out the truth. Most of the boys and girls of Frenchtown ended their education at fourteen, the legal age for going to work in the shops.

"Yeah, but he quit in the fifth grade," Pete said. "Fourteen and still in fifth grade."

This knowledge sealed my doom. You could reason with someone who was halfway educated and appeal to his intelligence, but I felt helpless in the face of utter stupidity. Trying to approach Omer LaBatt to make some kind of peace would be like coming face-to-face with an animal.

I was face-to-face with him now as he called out:

"You're a dead man, Moreaux."

He came after me.

Hurtling himself toward me, leaping over the curb and into the street, legs pumping away, huge shoulders looking even broader and bigger as he came closer.

Off I went, as if shot out of a cannon, my feet barely touching the pavement, proud of my single athletic accomplishment, running. Something else in my favor: the ability to hide, to find places in doorways or on piazzas, behind bushes and fences and banisters.

I cut through Pee Alley between Bouchard's Hardware and Joe Spagnola's Barber Shop, hustling over the ground that was littered with broken bottles left by drinkers who gathered there for quick gulps of booze or to pee against the brick wall. In Mr. Beaudreau's tomato garden, I crouched behind the plants, the smell of the tomatoes making my nostrils itch. Peering through branches heavy with tomatoes, I saw Omer LaBatt standing indecisively near some rubbish barrels. He looked my way, squinting, and I ducked my head.

But not quickly enough.

"Dead man," he raged as he galloped toward me.

I leapt up and the chase was on again. I ran along a warped wooden fence that I knew contained a loose slat through which I could squeeze. Protected from exposure by the outlaw bushes that sprouted in empty lots, I scurried forward, hearing Omer's curses—*son of a bitch, dirty bastard*— as he thrashed through the tomato patch. My hands found the loose board and I inhaled, trying to make myself thinner as I slipped through the opening. Omer LaBatt would have a bad time, I figured, sliding his wide shoulders through that slender space. Panting furiously, drenched with sweat, I paused as I found myself in the widow Dolbier's backyard.

Mrs. Dolbier supported herself and her brood of children by taking in washing and doing ironing and sewing. Her backyard was an unending series of sagging lines always filled with clothing of all shapes and sizes and colors, like a small tent city. I crouched down low so that I could scoot beneath the clothes as I made my way toward the front of the house. But I tripped over the wooden crate in which she

carried the clothing. When I scrambled to my feet, I found
myself mixed up with a long pink nightgown. As I fought to
free myself, I heard Omer LaBatt grunting and swearing his
way through the slat in the fence. Panicking, grabbing hold
of a pair of overalls, I found my face covered with a lumber-
jack shirt while the nightgown clung to my body.

Omer charged into the hanging clothes with a ferocious
scream while I flailed desperately, overcome momentarily by
my exertions, trying to catch my breath, my body flashing
with pain, fear turning my blood cold. As I tugged at the
clothes, a blue shirt draped itself around me as clothespins
flew through the air and I fell down. Looking around, I saw
Omer LaBatt had blundered into the same trap, desperately
fighting the shirts and blouses that entangled him.

"Son of a bitch!" Omer cried.

Suddenly, there was a third presence among the billowing
clothes. Mrs. Dolbier's voice, shrill as a factory whistle, tore
at the air.

"Out of here, bum," she cried, vaulting into the melee,
wielding a broom that she swung at Omer with passion. I
ducked away on all fours.

"Bum," she screamed again. "All my hard work . . ."

I looked up and saw her pummeling Omer LaBatt with the
broom. He tried to get away but was trapped in an assort-
ment of shirts and trousers, at the mercy of her blows. In an
effort to protect himself, he raised his arms, a movement that
brought down an entire line of shirts upon him.

I howled with glee and the widow's head popped out of
the confusion of pajamas and nightgowns. She looked in my
direction, paused, frowned, and then attacked Omer again
with the broom, her voice rising to a dangerous pitch. "Bum
. . . thief . . . sinner."

She had looked straight at me, and then had turned back to

her assault on Omer LaBatt. Safe from her now, I untangled myself from the clothes, glad to be rid of my disguise, trying to catch my breath, enduring the pain brought on by my fall, still shivering with cold.

Free at last, I ran through the yard, across her front lawn, down the street, streaking to safety. I rested in the shaded doorway next to Dondier's Market and waited for my heart to resume its normal beating, my breathing to become regular.

Trudging homeward, I took solace in acknowledging that Omer LaBatt's pursuit of me that day had served one purpose, at least. For a little while I had not been thinking of my aunt Rosanna, my pain and anguish absent as I ran for my life through the streets and alleys and backyards of Frenchtown.

What I did not know was that I had faded for the second time.

Women never wore high heels in Frenchtown on weekday afternoons. Except my aunt Rosanna. I spotted her one day hurrying along Seventh Street in bright red high-heeled sandals with straps that wrapped around her ankles like thin fingers caressing her flesh.

I ducked behind the big oak tree across from the Lachance Steam Laundry as she passed and, after counting to fifty, began to follow her.

Once or twice she glanced over her shoulder as if suspecting a follower, but I was too quick for her to spot me. I slipped from tree to tree, skittered between houses, hid behind banisters on piazzas, crouched behind bushes in my hot pursuit, feeling clever and resourceful, trying to ignore the small sense of shame that grew within me as I dogged her footsteps. Shame at following her like this, shame at how I had betrayed her in the bedroom.

She approached the corner of Fourth and Spruce, where men and boys on short time at the shops hung around, and I grimaced, knowing the remarks the men would make as she passed. Watching from a piazza across the street, I silently cheered as she held her head high and paid them no atten tion. But this didn't prevent them from whistling and yell-ing at her. "Hey, baby, want some company?"

At the intersection of Mechanic and Third where St. Jude's steeples climbed to the sky, she paused. Would she go into the church? Confess herself, maybe? Confess what? But she continued on her way. She went toward Fourth Street again, walking aimlessly, more slowly now, head down, as if deep in thought. She didn't glance behind anymore and her movements were not at all furtive. It was easy to follow her now without much risk of being spotted, but I still took pre-cautions as she turned at Fourth and Mechanic.

She stopped suddenly in front of the three-decker at 111 Fourth, bent over to straighten the seams of her stockings, then patted her hands around her waist as if to make certain her blouse was still tucked into her skirt. She fluffed her hair and the rings on her fingers caught the sunlight. I knew who lived at 111 Fourth and my spirits sank as I crouched behind the bushes across the street.

Make her walk away, I prayed. Make her change her mind.

But my prayer wasn't answered.

She marched into the driveway, her high heels kicking up small pieces of gravel. She passed the steps leading to the back door and headed toward the garage at the rear of the three-decker. A sign on the garage proclaimed: TOUBERT EN-TERPRISES.

Not him, I cried silently as I watched her knock on the door, tilting her head like a child about to ask for candy. Even in my despair, she melted my heart with that tender inclination of her head.

The door opened and she stepped inside and I caught a glimpse of waiting arms.

Of all the people in the world, I thought, why did she have to choose Rudolphe Toubert?

Rudolphe Toubert was the closest thing to a gangster in Frenchtown and yet no one ever spoke that word aloud. He was known as "the man to see." The man to see if you wanted to place a bet on a horse or a football game. The man to see for a loan when the Household Finance Company downtown rejected your application. The man to see if you needed a favor. It was well known in Frenchtown that if you were faced with trouble of some kind—at the shop, on the streets, even in your family—Rudolphe Toubert was the man to see. Of course, you paid for his services in more ways than one. For instance, people still changed the subject when the name of Jean Paul Rodier came up. Jean Paul was found bruised and bleeding in Pee Alley one morning and it was said he had not paid back a loan he had taken out with Rudolphe Toubert. But there was no proof. And no witnesses.

Rudolphe Toubert was a dashing figure who commanded instant attention. Tall and slender with a movie star moustache on his upper lip, he always wore a suit with a vest and drove a big gray Packard that rolled majestically through the streets of Frenchtown, a pretty girl sometimes at his side. My mother said he was cheap-looking with his slicked-down hair and his pinstripe suits, like someone in a B movie at the Plymouth. My father said it didn't matter whether he looked cheap or not—he was a success at what he did. My father bought a lottery ticket every week from the runner at the shop who worked for Rudolphe Toubert. A twenty-five-cent ticket of hope, my father called it. Old man Francoeur on Ninth Street had once won fifteen hundred dollars on one of Rudolfe Toubert's tickets, and Mr. Francoeur's name was still spoken with awe and wonder by people who remembered his good fortune and had memorized the winning number: 55522. But it never came up again.

Rudolphe Toubert controlled all the newspaper routes in Frenchtown, including the delivery of the Boston newspapers—the *Globe, Post,* and *Daily Record*— as well as the Monument *Times.* He paid the boys a flat fee for each route instead of a commission. As a result, Frenchtown newsboys earned far less than the boys who delivered papers in other sections of town. He arranged the routes to suit his own purposes, giving the best routes to boys he favored. The routes everyone wanted were those that covered a small territory of three-deckers where papers could be delivered quickly and the customers always paid on time and gave big tips.

My younger brother, Bernard, was struggling that summer with the worst of the routes, the longest, least profitable, and spookiest route in Frenchtown, which Rudolphe Toubert always gave to the newest and youngest boy. Although the route consisted of only twelve customers, it stretched more than two miles from the railroad tracks at the edge of downtown Monument along Mechanic Street to the small cottage of Mr. Joseph LeFarge at the gate of St. Jude's Cemetery. Mr. LeFarge was the parish *bedeau,* which meant that he was the church janitor as well as in charge of the cemetery, where he dug the graves and cut the grass. He was a silent, forbidding man with thin lips that never softened into a smile and eyes that seemed to contain secrets. He could have stepped out of a Boris Karloff movie, although my father claimed he was actually a gentle man who wouldn't harm a fly.

But then my father didn't have to deliver papers to Mr. LeFarge's house day after day, especially during the fall and winter months when darkness had already descended or was threatening by the time you arrived there, the tombstones visible from his front walk. Not only was his house isolated, a quarter mile from the nearest three-decker, but it was located across the street from the city dump, where clouds of smoke from smoldering rubbish rose like pale ghosts against the sky. The worst time of all was Friday, collection day. Instead of flinging the rolled-up newspaper to his piazza and hurrying away, you knocked on the door and waited an eternity for him to respond, while trying not to look toward the cemetery and those lurking tombstones. He never hurried to answer your knock and he never gave a tip.

I sympathized with Bernard when he set off each day on the route because I had undergone the same ordeal a few years before.

Bernard was only eight years old. I, at least, had been ten. He wanted to quit after the second day but knew he couldn't. Every penny was important to the family. I worked afternoons packing potatoes and doing errands at Dondier's and Armand did odd jobs at the comb shop.

"I don't mind the long walk and the dogs," Bernard said as we sat on the piazza steps after supper. He was trying not to cry. "But it's . . ." And his voice faltered.

"Mr. LeFarge's house, right?" I asked.

"It's summer, for crying out loud," Armand said. "It's not even dark when you get there." Armand spoke with the bravery of his 145 pounds, the strength of his muscled arms and legs. He did not believe in ghosts and never woke up at night from bad dreams.

Later, when we were alone, I struck a bargain with Bernard. I told him I would deliver the paper to Mr. LeFarge's house every day after I finished my chores at the market. I bragged that I was the master of shortcuts and assured him I could easily do the delivery and be here in time for supper.

"What about my part of the bargain?" Bernard asked.

There was nothing Bernard could offer me. "I'll think of something," I said.

His smile was beautiful to see, almost like a girl's. It was no wonder my sisters Yvonne and Yvette envied his good looks and his hair that curled without the touch of a comb or a curling iron.

So, every day that summer, I delivered the Monument *Times* to Mr. LeFarge's house. Bernard left the newspaper at the market and I raced after work to Mechanic Street, cutting through backyards and across empty lots, avoiding houses with dogs in their yards and always on the lookout for Omer LaBatt. Despite my thirteen years and all my experience, I was still uneasy as I approached the *bedeau's* house, averting my eyes from the cemetery and trying not to inhale the fumes of burning rubbish from the dump across the street.

Now I stood across from Rudolphe Toubert's house, thinking of my aunt Rosanna inside the garage with him. I tortured myself with images of his long, tapered fingers caressing her flesh, his lips on hers, their mouths opening to each other the way it happened in the movies.

Scanning the windows of the three-decker, I searched for the figure of his wife lurking behind the curtains. She was confined to a wheelchair and never left her tenement and spent her days, they said, wheeling from one window to another. Sometimes I caught glimpses of her thin pale face as she peered out at the street or watched people in their comings and goings as they did business with Rudolphe Toubert. Women visited him at odd hours as my aunt was doing now, and this flaunting of his love affairs seemed to me the worst thing about him.

Finally, my aunt Rosanna emerged from the garage, closing the door slowly behind her, lingering a moment in the yard. Did she look disheveled? Was her hair a bit mussed and her orange lipstick hastily put on? Or was jealousy feeding my imagination? How could I be certain of anything as I crouched miserably behind a hedge across the street, worried that a dog would find me there and bark me out of my hiding place?

As she left the driveway, tugging at her skirt, she surprised me by turning left instead of right, which meant that she was not going to my grandfather's house. She was heading in the direction of the Meadow down at the end of Spruce Street. The Meadow was a place for family picnics on the shores of the Moosock River, which meandered without design among stands of birches and pines, in the shade of elms and maples, and on through the long, open fields. The Meadow remained unspoiled despite constant rumors that the city's rubbish would be carted to the place once the city dump was filled. The kids of Frenchtown frolicked there on occasion, building bonfires at night, swimming naked in the river, playing games. Boy Scouts often pitched their tents on the grounds and pursued their merit badges in camping and nature studies and such. I often visited the place with pad and paper and tried to write poems as I sat with my back against a tree trunk or dangled my legs on the banks of the river, watching the changing colors—red or green or a murky brown, depending on which dyes had been used that day in the shops.

I remained safely behind my aunt as she left Spruce Street and walked quickly across the narrow footbridge that led to the Meadow. It amazed me that a woman could move so fast on high heels without wobbling or tripping. I was glad for my rubber soles as my feet glided over the wooden bridge with barely a sound.

As she made her way toward a picnic bench under a cluster of birches, I paused, watching her, struck as always by her beauty. The sounds of summer filled my ears, birds scattering in the trees and the high buzzing of the sewing needles, which I used to believe could sew up a person's lips before you had time to cry out. A dog barked, but far away, too far to be a threat.

The Meadow shimmered in the sunlight, my aunt and I alone in that vast expanse, and I felt exposed suddenly, wondering if I could find a place to hide before she realized I was there.

Suddenly, she turned.

And saw me.

She didn't appear surprised as our eyes met. As usual, whenever I was in her presence, I blushed and grew flustered and didn't know what to do with my hands. And now it was worse than ever, because I was racked with guilt, from having both followed her and spied on her but most of all for that other day when she had seen me in my shame, my pants stained, my lust exposed.

She beckoned to me, her expression inscrutable.

And I went to her, helpless to resist, although a part of me wanted to run away again.

"Why are you following me, Paul?" she asked.

"I don't know," I said, the blood rushing to my face, my temples throbbing. Then in desperation: "Are you still mad at me?" And cursed myself for asking that question because it was a reminder of that other day.

She sank to the picnic table, her arm trailing along its surface. "I'm not mad at you, Paul. Mad at myself, maybe. Are *you* mad at me?"

I wanted to cry out *yes*. Because she had visited Rudolphe Toubert of all people, had probably made love to him while I waited outside and his wife watched his office from the window. And I wanted to shout *no*. Because my love for her forgave everything and anything.

Shaking my head, I said: "How could I be mad at you?"

She motioned me to the bench.

I sat down carefully, as if my body would fall apart if I moved too suddenly. I was immediately caught up in the scent of her, made almost dizzy by the closeness of her body.

"I was wrong from the start," she said. "Flirting with you like that. Ah, not flirting, really. Since you were a baby, Paul, you were special to me. You always had a kind of shyness about you. A gentleness. I always loved to pick you up and cuddle you." She blew air out of the corner of her mouth as an errant strand of hair brushed her cheek. "You still are special to me, Paul. But sometimes I forget that you aren't a baby anymore, not someone to toy with. . . ."

"It was my fault," I cried out, not wanting her to take the blame for anything between us. "It's still my fault. I was the one who was wrong. . . ."

"Wrong? About what?" she asked, puzzled.

"Wrong because I spied on you. Sneaked into your room when you weren't home. Followed you today. It's none of my business what you do." And then I plunged. Like leaping from the highest steeple of St. Jude's Church, not caring if I crashed into a million pieces. "I love you. . . ."

"Oh, Paul," she said, her voice catching as if her throat hurt. "It's not love—"

"Yes, it is," I said, ready for her. "I know I'm only thirteen, but it's love. It's not a crush. It's not puppy love. I know all about those things from books and movies. I love you. With all my heart. I will love you forever."

The confession freed my spirit and my soul. I wanted to run and shout to the sky, join the birds in their singing. But then I saw the sad look on her face, and I drew back.

She reached out, touched my shoulder and my shoulder burned sweetly.

"That's the nicest thing anybody ever said to me," she whispered. "And I'll never forget those words, Paul. But you mustn't love me. I'm your aunt. I'm too old for you. You're going to love a dozen girls before you finally find the right one. Then you'll look back on your old aunt Rosanna and wonder: What did I ever see in her?"

"Don't say that," I cried, tears springing to my eyes, my chin beginning to tremble, the chin that always betrayed me. "I'll always love you. I'll never love anyone else."

She reached for my hand, and I hesitated, drew away a bit, because my palm was wet with sweat. She took my hand in hers anyway, didn't seem to notice the embarrassing moisture, locking my fingers with hers. I felt so close to her that I took my courage in my hands and asked the question that had always been on my mind.

"Why did you leave Frenchtown, Aunt Rosanna?"

She looked away, toward the far horizon where old barns, hazy in the heat, seemed like ancient animals pausing to rest.

"A lot of reasons," she said absently.

"Please. You said I wasn't a child anymore. So don't talk to me like I'm a child." My boldness surprised me, but her hand still clutching mine gave me courage.

"Okay," she said, looking directly at me, a challenge in her eyes. "I left Frenchtown because I was pregnant."

I had never heard that word said out loud before. Once in a while I overheard my mother and other women describe someone as being "in the family way" or "expecting" and even those words were spoken in hushed tones. On the street corners, girls got "knocked up." *Pregnant* was almost a street corner word, a shocking sound on my aunt's lips.

"Does that shock you?" she asked.

"No," I said, trying to hide my shock.

"I wasn't married, Paul, but I wanted to have the baby. I knew I would have to give it away but I wanted it to be born." She breathed away the wisp of hair that had fallen again across her cheek. "Oh, I suppose something could have been arranged so that I didn't have to have it. But I could never do that. I always loved children. . . ."

I knew at that moment that I would love her forever.

"So I left town before I began to show."

"Where did you go?"

"Canada. To my aunt Florina and my uncle August. They were very good to me. They asked me no questions and I told them no lies. They still live in St. Jacques, on a small farm there. They took good care of me. They arranged everything. With the doctor, an old man from the parish. But the baby was born dead."

I did not say anything. Everything was silent around us, as if the birds and the small animals in the woods were holding their breath.

"A girl. I saw her only once," she said. And then, with a small laugh: "You know, all the new babies I've ever seen, Paul, have been red and wrinkled, but not my baby. She was like a rose, all pink. I held her for a few moments and then they took her away. She's buried in the cemetery at St. Jacques. I never go there."

Her voice was a whisper now and it was as if she were not talking to me at all but to herself. "The plan was for me to give her up. The doctor would see to it, place the baby with a good family. I agreed, although I wondered as she grew inside me if I could do that. And then she died . . ."

She shook her head and slapped the bench. "Enough of that, Paul. It's past and gone."

We sat for a while without saying anything, so close that I could smell the peppermint of her breath.

"Did you stay in St. Jacques all the time you were gone?" I asked finally.

"I'm not the farm type," she said. "I got to Montreal, worked in a beauty shop there. Then, last year, to Boston. Know what's the matter with me, Paul? I don't belong anywhere. I don't belong here in Frenchtown. Your Mémère and Pépère took me in when I came back because they never shut the door on anyone. They let me live there but I'm like a tenant who doesn't pay rent. The girls I knew at St. Jude's are married now, have children. Those who aren't married work in the shops. I don't fit in. I'm not the shop type anyway." She said this last with a kind of pride in her words.

"But why did you come back?" I asked.

"Good question," she said, frowning. "I came back because I got tired of rooming houses, cheap hotels, being picked up by strangers. Even my closest friends were strangers. . . ."

I ached for her loneliness, for all the things that had gone wrong in her life.

"Let me tell you something, though, Paul. Strangers sometimes treat you better than your relatives. They judge you by what you're doing today, not what you did yesterday. So, I'm ready to go again. To leave Frenchtown. There's nothing here for me anymore."

But I'm here, I wanted to shout in protest even as I knew that I could only offer her a thirteen-year-old boy's love and nothing else. No protection from the pickups. No money to dress her in the fancy clothes she loved.

"When are you going?" I asked, even though it was better if I did not know when.

"It depends," she said.

The afternoon began to alter, changing almost imperceptibly, glowing rather than shining, pewter suddenly instead of silver. The trees were limp and weary now, leaves closing on each other, branches bending as if in genuflection. The birds had fled, leaving an emptiness in the air.

"I knew you were following me this afternoon, Paul," she said. "And that's why I almost didn't go to Rudolphe Toubert's. I didn't want you to see me going there. But I had made up my mind to see him and it was too late to change. It took a lot of courage for me to see him and I was afraid that if I changed my mind, I wouldn't go again."

"Does your going away have something to do with him?" I asked.

She nodded. "I asked his help. This time, when I leave Frenchtown, I want to do it the right way. With prospects. I'd like to start a small business . . ."

A business? My aunt Rosanna a businesswoman?

"What kind of business?"

"Hairdressing. I'm good at it too. I worked as a hairdresser in Montreal. I'd like to open a small shop there. That's why I went to see Rudolphe Toubert. To arrange for the money."

I thought of Jean Paul Rodier and the beating he took in Pee Alley. Would Rudolphe Toubert send his goons all the way to Montreal?

"Did he say he'd lend you the money?" I asked, hoping he had refused and she would remain in Frenchtown.

"It's not a question of lending," she said, and then pressed her lips together, a small frown creasing her forehead.

Suddenly I knew, the knowledge coming to me the way

blood spurts from a wound, the way pain is absent one moment and agonizingly present the next.

"Was he the one?" I said, my voice sounding far away, as if someone else were speaking. "The one who . . ." I couldn't say the words.

"Yes, Paul. He was the one who got me in trouble." Shy suddenly, the words *in trouble* instead of *pregnant*, delicate and almost prim on her lips. "The baby—it was his."

A pang tore at my heart. She had slept with him, after all. Had carried his flesh and blood in her body. Had let him caress her, kiss her—I did not let my thoughts go further.

"Not many people know this, Paul. Your Pépère would kill him if he knew. So would your father. They think it was somebody passing through Frenchtown. Which made them think worse of me but . . ." And she shrugged, her shoulders lifting and falling as she sighed.

"Will Rudolphe Toubert give you the money?" I asked.

"I think he will. He likes to keep people dangling on a string. That's what he did the first time. He gave me the money to go away but only after he kept me waiting. He said he had doubts the baby was his. . . ."

Again, she read what was in my eyes and on my face. "Oh, the baby was his, all right, Paul. And he knew it, too. I liked a good time in those days, still do, I guess, but I didn't sleep with just anybody at all. He said if he gives me something this time, it will be out of the goodness of his heart."

"I don't think he has a heart," I said. Again, I plunged. "When you saw him this afternoon, did he . . . did you . . ." But I couldn't bring myself to finish the question.

She shook her head. "No." Emphatically. "Oh, he wanted to. He . . . touched me. Felt me up. But I took his hand away . . ."

My blood raced at her words—more street corner words,

felt me up— and the words inflamed my lust again and despite my hate for Rudolphe Toubert and my horror at what he had done to my aunt Rosanna and what he had tried to do only an hour or two ago, despite all this, I felt my body getting warm again and I was caught between pleasure and agony, between sin and desire.

My hand had been in hers all this time, and she had alternately pressed and caressed it and entwined her fingers around my fingers as we talked. And now she took my hand and placed it on the white blouse, on her breast, and my fingers cupped her breast, caressing instantly and instinctively, as if they had been born for this, as if *I* had been born for this moment, what all my days and nights had been preparing me for. I was stunned by the softness and the firmness of her breast—how could it be both at the same time?— the way it yielded to my touch and filled my hand so beautifully. I had never held a breast before, either a woman's or a girl's, except in my hot dreams at night. Its weight was gentle, light and heavy, both at once, as I caressed it in the silkiness of her blouse.

Raising my eyes to hers, I saw a terrible sadness in them. "Do you like that?" she asked, covering my hand that covered her breast.

And I knew then that I was no better than Rudolphe Toubert and all the others in her life who had wanted only her body, her flesh, not caring about her, who she was, her needs, her desires, her ambitions. I had never inquired about her hopes and dreams—had not even known she was a hairdresser, for crying out loud—had not known until today why she had left Frenchtown. Yet, I loved her. Love? Did I even know what love was? Rudolphe Toubert had not loved her. We both wanted the same thing from her. In my shame, my body went limp and all desire left me.

I withdrew my hand and it trembled, a thing apart from my body, like a leaf detached from a branch, pausing in the air until the wind takes it away.

"I'm sorry," I said, wanting her even as I denied myself the touching of her, the caressing.

The shop whistles blew in the distance, five o'clock, the end of the workday. The whistles of Frenchtown always blew at once, the deep bellow from the Monument Comb Shop, the piercing tones of the Wachusum Shirt Company, and the short blurts, like someone in agony, from the Royal Button Company. Carried on the summer air, the whistles created a strange kind of harmony, harsh and out of tune yet blending together, like the cries of all the workers down the hallways of the years, protesting the long hours, the blistering heat, the aches and the pains, the frustrations and the losses. The whistles were the sound of Frenchtown and I sometimes hear them in my dreams.

I looked at my aunt and said: "Why did you do that? Why did you put my hand there?"

"Because I love you, Paul. In my own way. You mean more to me than Rudolphe Toubert. If he can touch me there, then why not you?" There was a hint of a smile at the corners of her mouth. "I wanted to give you something to remember me by. Even though it was wrong, of course. But then I'm always doing the wrong thing, I guess. . . ."

A blue jay's cry pierced the stillness of the afternoon, as if to coax the factory whistles back.

"It's time to go, Paul," my aunt Rosanna said.

I followed my aunt Rosanna across the narrow bridge. She walked barefoot, carrying her shoes in her hand, her stockings in her purse. We walked home slowly, nodding to the weary, sweat-soaked workers as they returned from the shops, their shadows long on the sidewalks, their movements languid in the failing heat of the day.

At the corner of Mechanic and Sixth, my aunt and I parted. She smiled tenderly at me, touched my cheek with her hand.

When I reached home, my mother greeted me with the news that my uncle Adelard, that elusive traveler, had returned to Frenchtown and was waiting for us to visit that night at my grandfather's house.

My uncle Adelard's homecomings were always a treat for the family, even for those who, like my uncle Victor, didn't approve of his wanderings and thought he should settle down in Frenchtown, marry and have children. When he arrived, excitement spread through the family and everyone gathered at my grandfather's house to listen to his stories and pepper him with questions. I sat on the floor, at my aunt Rosanna's feet, enthralled to be in his presence, thrilled to be so close to my aunt yet barely able to raise my eyes to hers when I thought back to that moment with her in the Meadow.

My uncle Adelard stood in the doorway, tall and thin, in old clothes that seemed faded from the sun and worn out with use. His face was the same as his clothes, pale and faded, eyes sunken into deep sockets. Listening to him intently, I realized after a while that he did not so much tell stories as answer questions, patiently and dutifully, as if this were some kind of debt he must pay, an ordeal he must endure.

"Yes," he said, answering my cousin Jules, "the West is like what you see in cowboy pictures. The rolling hills and the plains. But what the movies don't show is the cold. It's always hot in the movies and the cowboys gallop over the prairies in the heat, and the sun is always shining. But last year in Montana on the Fourth of July, it snowed—sure, melting as soon as it hit the ground—but snow all the same."

"Were you a cowboy?" I asked, the question popping out as unplanned as a hiccough.

Everyone laughed and I blushed and my aunt Rosanna reached out and tousled my hair, her touch like a caress.

Uncle Adelard looked down at me and smiled, his eyes crinkling as he did so. "Well, I rode a horse a few times and we had cows where I worked for a while so, yes, maybe I was a cowboy, Paul. I did carpenter work, though, fixing the fences in the corrals. You've heard of chuckwagons? Well, we had a chuckwagon but the food was so bad that I had the runs one whole summer. . . ."

We all laughed, and I was delighted that he remembered my name. I wondered if I ought to press my luck and ask him about the photograph. Then decided not to, afraid to appear foolish in front of the family, knowing my uncle's reputation for avoiding straight answers.

As he continued to ponder other questions—"Did you see the Golden Gate Bridge?" and "Is it true the Mississippi is so wide you can't see across it?"—I studied him closely and noticed the way he held himself apart from all of us between the piazza and the hallway, as if he needed space around him. He talked in matter-of-fact fashion about his travels without exhibiting any excitement over great cities like Chicago and Los Angeles. "They're like Monument, only bigger," he said. Was he joking or was he serious? If he did not seem charmed by the places he visited why did he keep going, year after year, always moving on, moving on?

There comes a moment when evening passes into night-time and people begin to stifle yawns and stretch their legs. The shops waited tomorrow and the workers never stayed up late in the middle of the week.

My father finally stood up, my baby sister, Rose, sleeping floppily in his arms, a doll with dangling limbs. "Well, Del, we're glad you're home. It's good to have you back. . . ."

The others murmured assent as they rose and prepared to depart. My uncle Victor flung his arm around his younger brother's shoulders and pecked him on the cheek. "I can get you a job at the shop anytime you say," he said, but there was good humor in his words and it was evident that he did not expect Adelard to take him up on the proposal.

"Time for confession," my mother proclaimed one Saturday morning.

I flinched at the dreaded words but had known they were inevitable. During the school year the nuns marched us once a month to the church, where we confessed our sins. The confessions were torture. You whispered your sins to the priest, your lips close to the screen, conscious of the priest listening intently, inches away. You were aware of your classmates in the nearby pews, waiting their turn, afraid your voice would float through the trembling curtain, carrying your words of disgrace to their ears.

During vacation, those agonizing confessions were suspended, although at least once during the summer my mother dispatched us to the church. Armand and I always protested. Summer Saturdays were busy with baseball and movies and chores around the house, too busy for confession. My mother was adamant. "Bad things happen in the summer. People get struck by lightning. The LeLonde boy drowned last year. Do you want to go straight to hell if, God forbid, you missed confession?"

I looked out the kitchen window as Armand carried the argument. I was aware of the sins piling up inside me, staining my soul. The worst sin had always been that sly act at night in bed when I summoned the visions that brought me both ecstasy and shame. I had routinely confessed them, enduring the humiliation of the priest's scolding—"God does not love the impure of heart"—as well as the entire rosary to be recited as a penance. But now I carried with me a sin beyond all my others. I had held a woman's breast in my hand. This was more than impure thoughts in the dark and the touching of my own body. Surely, a mortal sin.

Armand and I trudged to the church that afternoon and stepped into the shadowed stillness, our sneakers padding over the cement floor.

"We'll never get out of here," Armand whispered, pointing to the people kneeling patiently in the pews. "What a crowd."

Actually, there was not much of a crowd.

The thought struck me: Did he also have sins he did not want to confess?

"What happens if we skip confession?" I asked, aghast at my boldness.

"Nothing," he said. "That's not a sin."

"But we'll have to lie if Ma asks us if we went."

"We'll just confess it the next time," he said with complete logic.

We huddled indecisively in the corner, inhaling the scent of incense and burning candles. I'll save my money and light a twenty-five-cent candle next week to make up for it, I promised silently. A new thought intervened: "How about tomorrow morning?" I whispered. "We won't be able to receive communion."

Armand shrugged. "We'll get up early and go to the seven o'clock mass. Ma and Pa always go to the ten . . ."

More deception. More sins.

"Come on," Armand urged over his shoulder as he headed toward the doorway. Outside, in the sunlight, I watched him as he galloped away whooping with delight. While I stood there, conscious of my soul blackened with sin, yet limp with relief at having postponed that terrible moment in the confessional.

A few minutes later I was back in church again, kneeling in a remote corner, reciting an entire Rosary—a total of five Our Fathers and fifty Hail Marys—hoping this might spare me hell if somehow I did not survive the summer.

On the way home, I recited an extra ten Hail Marys. As insurance.

In the next few days, my uncle Adelard visited the homes of his brothers and sisters, taking a dinner here or a supper there, and everyone brought out the best silverware and served a Sunday kind of meal. At my house, my mother made *tourtière,* that French-Canadian meat pie usually reserved for holidays, even though it was summer. The pie was my uncle's favorite and he said my mother made the best *tourtière* in the world.

We sat at the big table in the dining room, reserved usually for holidays and special occasions, and my uncle ate like a starving man, the food disappearing so fast that it seemed he swallowed without even chewing. He glanced up once to see us all watching him in awe.

"You learn to eat fast on the road," he said, "because you never know when you'll be interrupted."

I felt his eyes resting on me once in a while and I looked shyly away, pleased that he had noticed me. My mother said that he always inquired about me in the occasional letters he wrote. "He says you are the sensitive one," she explained when I appeared puzzled by his attention.

During the meal, Uncle Adelard directed questions to each of my brothers and sisters, inquiring about school and such, polite queries that drew ordinary responses although Armand said defiantly that he couldn't wait to quit school and work in the comb shop, as my father shook his head. It was an old family argument because my father wanted Armand to continue with his schooling. No one in the Moreaux family had ever graduated from high school—all my cousins had ended their education at the age of fourteen to enter the shops—and my father was adamant that his sons and daughters would break that pattern. Much to Armand's dismay.

Finally, Uncle Adelard's eyes fell upon me and lingered.

"And you, Paul," he said. "Do you still write your poems?"

I squirmed and blushed and found my food impossible to swallow. I was stuck with a mouthful of *tourtière* but managed to nod my head and somehow utter one word, "Yes." Although my brothers and sisters seemed to be enjoying my discomfort, I was secretly pleased that my uncle Adelard knew about my poetry.

"Just think, Lou," Uncle Adelard said to my father. "A Frenchtown boy who's a writer. Someday, we'll be proud that he's one of us. Can you imagine what it will be like, to go to the library downtown and see a book there written by Paul Moreaux?"

By Paul Moreaux.

The prospect dazzled me and I spent the rest of the meal unable to eat—food was unimportant, even the apple pie and whipped cream for dessert—envisioning myself as a famous writer traveling the world and coming home to Frenchtown, where I would be greeted by cheering crowds when my train pulled into the depot downtown.

"Ah, Elise," Uncle Adelard said to my mother as he pushed his empty dessert plate away from him. "This is what I miss when I'm away, and worth traveling a thousand miles for. . . ."

A thousand miles. How I envied him, the sights he had seen, the people he had met, the secrets he must harbor in his heart.

After the meal, he and my father sat near the kitchen window while my mother cleared the table and washed the dishes with the help of my sisters. My father asked my uncle about working conditions in other parts of the country. "Not very good," Uncle Adelard said. "But it would be worse without F.D.R. in the White House." My father raised his glass of beer. "To Roosevelt, the greatest president of them all," he proclaimed. "Abe Lincoln wasn't too bad either," my uncle said, clinking his glass against my father's.

Not interested in politics, I went to the bedroom and picked up *The Adventures of Tom Sawyer*, which I had already read several times. I could not keep my mind on that exciting and terror-filled chase through the caves because I kept wondering whether I would have the courage to ask my uncle about the photograph while he was here in our house.

A few minutes later, his shadow fell across the bedroom doorway. I put down the book and looked up at him. Did I dare?

"I have something for you," he said, reaching into his pocket. "A letter. From your aunt Rosanna . . ."

His expression told me that the letter contained the news I dreaded to hear. "She's going away," I said.

He nodded. "You are very special to her, Paul. She didn't leave a letter for anyone else."

I felt somehow that he knew of my burden—the burden of love, the burden of departures, the burden of not having what you wish most in life to have.

He touched my shoulder, his hand lingering there for a moment, and then he left, sensing perhaps that I wanted to be alone, needed to be alone at that moment.

Carefully, I slit open the envelope with my scout knife, although I had never been a Boy Scout, and unfolded the sheet of lined paper inside. Blue lines, a few blots of ink.

Dear Paul,

By the time you read this, I will be gone. I don't like goodbyes. Keep up with your writting. Stay as sweet as you are, like the song says. Forget me not.

Love,
Aunt Rosanna

I was surprised at the childish scrawl, as if a third-grader had laboriously written the words with a scratchy pen. The two *t*'s in writing. The inky smudges. I would keep this letter forever, read it faithfully every day even when I was old and gray.

You opened the door of the Rub Room at the comb shop and a blast like purgatory struck your face. The workers sat on stools, huddled like gnomes over the whirling wheels, holding the combs against the wheels to smooth away the rough spots. The room roared with the sound of machinery while the foul smell of the mud soiled the air. The mud was a mixture of ashes and water in which the wheels splashed so that they would not overheat at point of contact with the combs. Because the Rub Room was located in the cellar of the shop where there were no windows, the workers toiled in the naked glare of ceiling lights that intensified everything in the room: the noise, the smells, the heat, and the cursing of the men. On the coldest day of the year, the temperature in the Rub Room was oppressive; in the summer, unbearable. The workers there were exiles from the rest of the shop: newcomers from Canada and Italy eager for any job at all, troublemakers who needed their spirits broken, and workers who had lost favor with the superintendent, Hector Monard.

Hector Monard had greeted me at the shop's entrance that morning. My father had forgotten to take his lunch to work and my mother had dispatched me to bring it to him. I felt myself shrink as Hector Monard hovered over me. He was tall. And thin. But a lethal thinness, like a knife's. And as dangerous as a knife, the workers said.

Gulping, I held up the paper bag. "I have my father's lunch."

He inspected me as if I were a piece of lint that had defiled his Sunday suit.

"What father?"

"Louis Moreaux." Finding it difficult to swallow.

"The Rub Room," he said, jerking his hand over his shoulder.

My father in the Rub Room? Impossible.

"What?"

"Are you deaf, boy?" he said, scowling. "The Rub Room." And turning away: "Take it to him there. We don't run errands here."

I walked tentatively down the hallway leading to the shop's interior, conscious of entering foreign territory. I had always been curious about the shop that for so long had dominated our lives, the subject of so many conversations at the supper table and on the piazzas as men gathered in the evenings to smoke and drink beer. It was on our piazza that I had learned about the Rub Room and the other departments, the threat of fires, the lack of safety measures, and the actions of Hector Monard. My uncle Victor made a big speech about him one evening—Uncle Victor was always making speeches—as he sat on the banister. "He's worse than the owners," he said. "They're Yankee—what can you expect from Yankees? But Hector Monard is a Canuck, like us.

You'd think a Canuck would help his own kind. But not Hector Monard."

I made my way through the departments, the wooden planks trembling under my feet as machines vibrated somewhere in the building. The sweet acid odor of celluloid stung my eyes. A thousand fingers moved insect-like at the benches while the workers did their jobs.

Moving through the shop, I saw the combs and brushes in all stages of production: cutters slicing into sheets of celluloid; small stoves heating the stock so that it could be bent into the desired shapes; punchers driving holes into combs for rhinestones and other fancy stones to be inserted; bristles pouring down on brushes. An eye-dazzling array of operations that made my head spin. But more than the machinery, the workers. Men and women, boys and girls. Concentrating on their work, glancing up sometimes as I passed. Did I see resentment in their eyes? Did they feel I was not only an outsider but an enemy entering their private territory, violating the camaraderie of their departments?

My sense of alienation grew when I received a gruff reply from a boy almost my own age after I asked directions to the Rub Room. "Down there," he pointed, turning away abruptly, the corners of his mouth pulled down in contempt.

As I descended the wooden steps to the cellar, the roar of machinery increased, the stairs vibrating beneath my feet. I knocked on a closed door, expecting it to buckle and crash open from the pounding of the machinery behind it. I knocked again, louder, then pounded with a closed fist. I finally jerked the door open—and that was when I saw the Rub Room for the first time, felt the blast of heat and smells, and, horrified, saw my father in his black rubber apron, his hair mussed and his face streaked with the mud, bent over the wheel like a slave in a horror film, as if he had been beaten and whipped.

Rubberman Robillard loomed above me instantly, blocking my view, a giant of a man, covered with mud, a wide grin displaying broken teeth. I had heard of the Rubberman during those evening talks on the piazza. He was the opposite of Hector Monard. The Rubberman was a Canuck who helped his countrymen, a man who respected the job, a foreman who worked right along with his men at the machines.

He saw the lunch bag in my hand.

"For who?" I couldn't hear his voice above the noise but managed to read his lips. Not waiting for my answer, he stepped out of the Rub Room and slammed the door behind him. The sound of the motors receded, although the floor continued to vibrate under my feet.

"Are you Lou Moreaux's boy?" he asked, squinting at me, wiping his face with a mud-streaked hand.

I nodded, speechless, still dumbfounded by the sight of my father at the wheel.

"That bastard Monard," the Rubberman said. "He sent you down here, right?"

Again I nodded. My father had always avoided trouble at the shop, which had often made my uncle Victor unhappy. Why had he been demoted, then?

"It's not bad enough he put your father down here, he wanted you to see him at the wheel," the Rubberman said. He exploded into French, the old words of the province that men used for swearing.

"Why?" I managed to utter. "Why is my father down here?"

"These are bad times, kid," he said. "A lot of bad stuff going on. Union stuff. They're making an example of your father. But he's a tough one and stubborn. He knows how it is in a shop. You take the good times with the bad." He coughed mightily, cleared his throat, spit a huge gray blob onto the floor. "Your father will be okay," he said, pronouncing the word the way so many Canucks did: *Hokay.*

Stumbling up the stairs, pushing open a side door that led to the outdoors, I burst into the world of fresh air, the sounds of the factory muted behind me, the gathering heat of the summer morning benevolent after the heat of the shop. Standing across the street, I studied the building where my father and so many others spent a third of their lives and where my brother, Armand, wanted to work. The shop was four stories high, dirty gray like the mud in the Rub Room, clapboards charred by fires and never replaced. I thought of how my father and the other workers resembled the place where they made their living, their skin pale from all the hours spent indoors, the smell of celluloid in their pores, their flesh scarred from burns and injuries suffered during the long years.

I thought of my brother Armand, now attending vocational school to learn the printing trade but neglecting his classes because he wanted to work in the shop.

Handsome Armand, swift on the bases, never afraid of the dark, swinging through his days and nights with never a doubt, bold and dauntless.

I wondered if he would someday become like the shop—blemished and battered. And I wondered, too, if long ago my father had been a boy like Armand. My father, my brother, and the shop.

For the first time that summer, it rained. Bursting from the skies in the middle of the night but gentle and tender by the time morning arrived. The rain brought such fresh breezes that people threw up their windows and kids ran in the streets, barefoot, hooting with glee.

By the middle of the morning I was ready to write. The chores were done and the family had dispersed, charged with energy by the fresh air the rain had brought. My mother took the girls on a shopping trip downtown after spending a half hour looking for hats to wear as protection from the rain. Armand went off to a Boy Scout meeting in the school hall and Bernard was scheduled for altar boy practice at the church.

Pad before me on the kitchen table, pencil in my hand, I prepared to put down the emotions churning within me, feeling as though I would explode if I could not express them. A face swam before me, my aunt Rosanna's. More than her face. The breast I had held in my hand for that fleeting moment. Could I capture that moment on paper?

And what of my father and the sight of him bent over the wheel in the Rub Room like a stranger I did not recognize? I pondered the paradox of trying to remember every facet of that moment with my aunt Rosanna and trying to forget the terrible sight of my father at the wheel, yet finding the reverse happening: haunted by my father, unable to wipe away the memory of my glimpse of him, and finding the memory of that time with my aunt fragmented, dissolving, even as I tried to capture it again.

Finally, I began to write. But not a poem. Until this moment I had always fashioned poems out of my emotions. This time, however, I wrote a story, letting the words flow easily and smoothly, not having to search for words whose most important function was to rhyme. I wrote about a boy and his father, the visit to the Rub Room, getting the words down quickly, not worrying about where the story was heading but trying to capture on paper that visit to the shop. Maybe, I thought, if I can rid myself of this anguish on paper, then I will be free to write about my aunt Rosanna.

I wrote until my arm and shoulder sang with pain.

And the words dried up.

I felt exhausted, as if I had run long distances. I counted the words I had written. Two thousand three hundred and three.

I stepped onto the piazza and held my face to the cool breeze the rain had brought. Leaning over the banister, I called out, "Pete . . . Pete . . ." No answer came from below, my voice echoing faintly in the quiet neighborhood. The rain fell steadily, mistily, splashing softly like small fountains in the yard below, running off into rivulets toward the gutters.

Footsteps crossed the first-floor piazza downstairs and paused at the bottom of the steps.

"Pete?" I called again.

Still no answer, but someone was climbing the stairs.

The rain was a whisper in my ears and the footsteps grew closer.

"Come on, Pete," I said.

But Pete did not come into view. Instead, my uncle Adelard appeared, wearing a dusty soft hat spotted with raindrops pulled down low on his forehead so that his eyes were hidden in the shadow of the brim.

"There's nobody home, Uncle Adelard," I said. "Only me."

He drew up the chair my father always sat in after work in the summertime while waiting for supper, removed his hat and placed it on the floor. He wore a blue bandanna around his neck, the kind that cowboys wore in movies. Or hoboes. Or bums, as my uncle Victor would say.

"That's all right," he said. "I came to talk to you, anyway."

"Me?" I asked incredulously, but thrilled at this attention.

"Yes, Paul," he said, settling back in the chair, gazing at the rain.

I thought of the story I had begun to write and wondered whether I had the nerve to show it to him, whether he would understand what I had tried to put down on paper.

Hitching myself up onto the banister, I perched gingerly on the soaked wood. We sat in silence for a while. The wetness of the banister penetrated my pants. The neighborhood was so still, except for the whispering of the rain, that it seemed like a movie sound track that had been shut off.

What did he want to talk to me about?

I had always found it hard to endure silences with people and I began to swing my legs, sitting precariously on the banister, flirting with the possibility of losing my balance.

A way to break the silence occurred to me. Did I have the nerve to bring up the subject?

Astonishingly, he brought it up himself.

"You know the picture, Paul? The one they took up in Canada before we came to the States?"

I nodded, not trusting my voice.

"I have to talk to you about that picture," he said, looking at me with those penetrating eyes. "That's the reason I came home this time."

"I've looked at it a thousand times," I said, studying his face, the lines of weariness enclosing his mouth, the dark pouches like bruises under his eyes. "I've always wondered about it."

"Tell me what you've wondered about, Paul."

"Well, you're supposed to be in the picture. Mémère and Pépère are. And my father. And all the uncles and aunts. Everybody except you . . ."

"Yes," he said. "All except me." His voice sad, wistful.

Gathering my courage, I said: "It's a big mystery, Uncle Adelard. Everybody wonders about you and the picture. I mean, were you there or not? Or were you just playing a prank?"

"It was a prank, Paul," he said.

"Oh."

"What's the matter?" he asked. "You look disappointed."

"It's crazy, Uncle Adelard," I said. "But I always hoped that you hadn't played a trick, that you hadn't just ducked out of the picture, that you . . ." My words dribbled away, sounding foolish suddenly.

"That I'd disappeared?" he asked. "Into thin air?"

I nodded, my cheeks flushed, feeling ridiculous.

"But I did," he said.

Blinking, I asked: "Did what?"

"Disappeared."

"But you said it was a prank."

Or was he still playing a prank at this moment but this time on me alone?

"It *was* a prank, Paul. I had found out only a day or two before the picture that . . ." Now it was his turn to give up on words, to frown and look again at the rain slanting down.

"What had you found out, Uncle Adelard?"

My voice echoed strangely on the piazza. Did I already know?

The rain began to fall harder, hissing as it struck the ground. I looked away from him, at the steeples of St. Jude's shrouded in mists, barely visible above the three-deckers. I listened for other sounds in the rain—a car horn, a dog's bark, bird's cry, footsteps, voices, anything—but there was nothing. My uncle and I were alone in a world of our own.

"Paul," he called.

I continued looking at the steeples as they wavered in the wet gray sky.

"Paul," he called again.

Reluctantly, I turned to him.

He was not there.

I stared at the chair in which he had been sitting. It was vacant. His hat was still on the floor beside the chair. The piazza was empty but I had not heard his departure, had not heard his footsteps going across the floor and down the stairs. Yet I didn't feel as if I were alone on the piazza. I felt his presence there, as if he were hiding, just out of sight, a small distance away. Felt also that his eyes were upon me, studying me, watching me.

I blinked and he was there again.

Sitting in the chair, legs crossed, hands folded in his lap, the bandanna around his neck.

In the moment before he appeared, the air in the vicinity of the chair shimmered, as if a thousand stars had congregated, clashed, and dissolved in a burst of brilliance. Out of the brilliance, my uncle Adelard emerged.

He was looking at me with the saddest eyes I had ever seen.

The strike at the Monument Comb Shop began during the dog days of August, in weather so hot and humid that we were warned by our parents to avoid dogs, which might go on a rampage, mad with the heat, and attack not only complete strangers but people they knew, especially children.

We learned about the strike when my father came home an hour late from work and announced, after he had washed his face and hands at the kitchen sink: "We walk out tomorrow. If they don't meet our demands."

My mother looked up sharply.

"No, I didn't vote to strike," he said as we gathered at the table. "But you have to go with the majority. We agreed to that. I don't think this is the right time to strike but I'll do what the others voted. We have to show we're united."

This was the longest speech my father ever made about the troubles at the shop, unlike my Uncle Victor, who never stopped talking about it.

I wanted to say to my father: At least you won't have to work in the Rub Room during the strike.

Excitement crackled in the air when the men gathered in the streets and marched to the shop in the first days of the strike. Everyone was good-natured, shouting and joking, and there was a lot of clowning around—Mr. Landry, who called the quadrilles at the Saturday night dances at St. Jean's Hall, led the parade with a baton like the kind used by drum majors. But the atmosphere changed as the heat intensified in the next few days and men began to realize that there would be no paychecks at the end of the week. The sun was merciless during the daytime when the men picketed the shop, and nightime brought little relief, as if the three-deckers and the pavement had stored up heat all day long and released it after dark.

The absence of paychecks gradually showed its effects, particularly in the Frenchtown stores. Mr. Dondier told me that my services were no longer needed, that he would do without extra help sweeping the floors and delivering orders and packing potatoes into peck bags. He touched my arm, his face long with regret. Miss Fortier, who operated the Laurentian Gift Shoppe next door to Lakier's, would close her doors "temporarily" at the end of October and never open them again. Someone said she went back to Canada.

When my uncle Victor dropped in to visit, the strike was the big topic.

"We'll never make up what we're losing," my father insisted. "Depression is no time for a strike."

My mother sighed, knowing the inevitable argument that would follow.

"It's never the right time," Uncle Victor said. "But we have to think beyond the moment. We have to look to next year, ten years from now. Look at your kids, Lou. Do you want them on short time, no job protection, no vacations?"

"My kids aren't going to work in the shops," my father

said, determination in his voice. Which made my brother Armand look away in dismay. "Education, Vic. That's the key to the future, not strikes."

"But there'll always be shops, Lou. And people working in them. What we're doing will help people in the future, whether or not they're your flesh and blood. . . ."

My father joined the picket lines, carrying a banner that read UNFAIR TO LABOR, and I watched him as he paraded in front of the shop with the other strikers, both men and women, my aunts among them. My father's face was grim and he walked stiffly, as if his legs ached. Many of the picketers laughed and joked as they paced back and forth, while others scowled or swung their shoulders belligerently, yelling "scab" and swearing at the foremen and office clerks who reported for work as usual when the whistle blew. My uncle Victor did not yell or curse. As a strike leader, he did not walk the picket line, either. He stood to one side, never alone, others clustered about him as he gave orders and answered questions, chewing his cigar. Armand hung out nearby, ready to run errands, eager, panting for action. He did not look at my father and my father did not look at him.

When Hector Monard reported for work a few moments before the whistle blew, a deadly silence fell. No one yelled or screamed curses at Hector Monard. The strikers regarded him in grim silence as he went by, eyes full of hate, more chilling to me than screams or shouting. There was murder in that silence. He walked with head high, looking neither right nor left, his lips curled into a sneer, the same sneer I had seen the day I brought my father's lunch bag to the shop.

Snow fell early that year, before Thanksgiving, followed by a cold wave that brought sharp winds that took the breath away and rattled the windows of the three-deckers. The strikers never stopped walking in front of the shop, holding their signs, stamping their feet on the frozen ground, bundled now in heavy mackinaws and overcoats, breathing white clouds when they spoke. As the cold intensified, they built small fires in trash barrels and huddled around them.

The strike lasted 121 days, ending on a Wednesday, a week and a half before Christmas. The end came after a night of violence during which my father was taken, along with three other men, to Monument Hospital, with blood gushing from his wounds.

But before the strike even began back in August, I had learned that I had become a fader.

First of all, the pause.
Then the pain.
And the cold.
The pause is a moment in which everything in your body stops, the way a clock stops. A terrible stillness that lasts only the length of a drawn breath—although it seems longer than that, almost an eternity—and then, at the onset of panic, the heart beats again, blood rushes through your veins and sweet air into your lungs.

After that, the flash of pain, like lightning, pain that darts throughout your body, so intense that you gasp at its brutality. But the pain is merciful in its quickness, gone as quickly as it comes.

The cold begins when the fade begins and remains all the time you are in the fade. It has nothing to do with the time of year or the seasons of the weather. The cold comes from inside, spreading under the surface of the flesh, like a layer of ice between skin and bone.

"The cold is a reminder that you are in the fade," Uncle Adelard had said dryly. "In case you should forget."

* * *

I stood on the sidewalk in front of my house in the deepening evening, darkness obscuring the three-deckers and the steeples of St. Jude's Church, although its white stone held on to the vestiges of daylight.

In the fade.

I can do anything, I thought, go anywhere, cross oceans, reach mountaintops.

But at this moment, what do I do?

No mountains to scale in Frenchtown.

No oceans to sail.

The cold invaded my body, causing me to shiver in the August heat, and I wrapped my arms, which I could not see, around my chest, which I could not see. I did not move, absorbing the cold, and then it became less intense, muted, bearable.

I walked toward Spruce Street heading for Third, where the streetlights shone brighter and the store windows splashed lights on the sidewalk. Kids had gathered in front of Lakier's, and I spotted David Renault licking an ice-cream cone as he watched Pete Lagniard and Artie LeGrande matching cowboy cards on the sidewalk, on their knees, flipping the cards expertly. Theresa Terrault, who giggled and pressed herself against boys and wore tight sweaters and skirts that displayed her budding breasts and rolling hips, leaned against a mailbox, the only girl on the street. Other girls quickly made their way home to the tenements when darkness fell before their brothers came looking for them. Theresa was only thirteen but she did not go home.

I approached with caution, not trusting the fade altogether, wondering whether it would abandon me without warning. Pete Lagniard cursed softly as he lost one of his favorite cards, a Ken Maynard.

Theresa's giggle lit up the night with merriment and I paused, looking at her, my eyes sweeping her face, her flashing eyes, round cheeks, dimples deep enough to dip your tongue into. Then to her small breasts. I drank in the sweetness of her body. I realized that I could never do this before. I could look at the movie screen or pictures in magazines but always had to avert my eyes when looking at a girl or woman in real life, the way I had agonized in my aunt Rosanna's presence, not knowing where to look. So now I filled my eyes with Theresa Terrault, staring deliciously, realized that I could, if I wanted, walk up to her and actually touch her.

I shivered as a wave of cold swept my body.

"What's that?" she cried suddenly, looking around, hugging her arms across her chest.

"What's what?" Andre Gillard asked. He had been showing off in front of Theresa, doing a fancy dance step, and now glanced up at her.

She shrugged, looked around as if a wind had suddenly risen to chill her.

"I don't know," she said, her lips turning downward in a pout. "Something . . ."

Shivering in the heat, she looked directly at me, six feet away, standing at the edge of the group.

I recoiled, leapt back a step or two, risked exposing myself by making a sound. But a sound wouldn't matter, would it, if she couldn't see me? *Could* she see me? Had I begun to lose the fade? I looked down, saw nothing, only my absence, and remembered what my uncle had said: *You will be there but not there. They will not see you but they will feel you there, know your presence.*

The moment passed and Andre Gillard kicked his heels as he leapt in the air and Pete Lagniard yelled to him to cut it out, Andre was spoiling his concentration, and Theresa Ter-

rault looked admiringly at Andre once more, giggling behind a hand with blood-red fingernails while I beheld her
loveliness, the slenderness of her body, her softness.

Andre and Theresa began to walk away together, away
from the glow of the streetlight. Andre's arm circled her
shoulder and she leaned against him, and her giggle carried
on the night air.

Pete and Artie paid no attention to the departure as they
concentrated on their game while David Renault finished his
ice-cream cone, the last piece disappearing into his mouth
with a satisfied smack.

Andre and Theresa continued down Third Street, in and
out of the shadows, caught in the glare of a streetlight for a
moment and then becoming lost in darkness. I saw them
duck into an empty doorway.

Should I follow?

Should I watch them wherever they went and spy on what
they did?

I looked around, at the three-deckers on the other side of
Third Street, opposite the stores, saw the lights in windows,
glimpses of people sitting on the piazzas in the cool evening
air.

I could go anywhere, I thought. Into any of those tenements. Spy on whomever I chose. Watch them talking and
arguing and making love. See the women take off their
clothes as they went to bed. Stand close enough to touch
them. I could slip into parlors and bedrooms.

I was lifted on a wave of possibilities and thought of all the
possible heavens at my fingertips.

Why was my uncle always so sad when he talked about the
fade?

The cold was still with me as I left Pete and Artie to their
card game with David Renault as their solitary audience. I

walked in the direction Andre and Theresa had taken, uncertain of my destination.

At Dondier's Market, I saw a light burning inside and Mr. Dondier at the cash register tallying the day's receipts with pencil and pad, touching the tip of his pencil to his tongue as he always did, so that his tongue had a permanent dark spot at its tip.

Mr. Dondier, such a serious man, seldom a smile. I wondered if I could make him smile.

Better yet, could I play a trick on him, among the fruits and vegetables and canned goods, something I never had the courage to do until this moment?

The fade now gave me courage.

I opened the door and closed it carefully. Mr. Dondier looked up, pencil poised at his lips, the overhead bulb shining on his bald head. He looked at his watch.

The store smelled, as usual, of coffee and oranges and pungent odors I could not identify, odors that clung to Mr. Dondier himself the way the smell of celluloid followed my father.

His pencil leapt across the pad as he resumed his work, and I advanced stealthily. Moving closer to him, amazed at my boldness, I watched as he tabulated the figures, his lips moving with his calculations. I shivered a bit.

He raised his head.

"Who's there?" he called.

He looked directly into my eyes and for a frantic moment, I was again afraid that the fade had failed and I was visible, standing directly in front of him. Then I reasoned that he would not have asked "Who's there?" if he could see me.

Wetting his lips, he bent again to his work, small beads of perspiration on his forehead, like dew on a melon. He looked up again, eyes slitted, scrutinizing the store, trying to see into all corners, muttering words under his breath that I could not understand.

He looked so apprehensive, so weary and haggard, that I knew I could not play any tricks on him.

Finally he placed his pad and pencil in the little box next to the cash register and walked to the front of the store, peered out at the street through a window, and then snapped the lock in place. Glancing over his shoulder, he walked urgently through the narrow aisles of the vegetable section to the back room. I waited a moment near the meat counter before following him. I was barely aware of the cold now.

In the back room, he had turned on the gooseneck lamp that threw a flood of light on the clutter of account books, papers, and pencil stubs on his old desk. Taking a small key from his vest pocket, he inserted it delicately in the bottom drawer. He pulled out the drawer, reached inside and brought forth a quart bottle of whiskey. He lifted the bottle, drank from it in huge gulps, gasped, wiped his eyes with the back of his hand, and placed the bottle on the desk top.

Looking around, he called out again: "Anybody there?"

He uncapped the bottle and drank again, his eyes watering from the sting of the whiskey. Shuddering, he sat down on the old piano bench that served as his office chair. He replaced the bottle in the drawer and sat with head bowed. He did not move for several moments and my legs began to ache. I turned as someone rattled the front door and knocked on the window.

Mr. Dondier leapt to his feet and made for the doorway, so swiftly that I had no time to draw back and he almost brushed me as he passed.

I watched his progress to the front door, saw a slender figure faintly through the windowpane. Mr. Dondier unlocked the door and drew it open.

Theresa Terrault stepped inside, hurriedly, glancing over her shoulder as she entered.

"I thought you weren't coming," Mr. Dondier said, locking the door behind her, "so I closed up a few minutes ago."

"I couldn't help being late," she said, her voice like a little girl's. She *was* a little girl, despite the flashy sweater and the budding breasts.

"I heard some noise in here," he said. "I thought you sneaked in early and was playing a trick. . . ." As they came toward the backroom he touched her cheek, then her breast. "You wouldn't play tricks on me, would you, Theresa?"

"No, Mr. Dondier," she said shyly.

I stared at Mr. Dondier and Theresa in disbelief. His daughter, Clara, was in my class at school, a happy girl who laughed quickly and easily, and blushed as often as she laughed. She was the same age as Theresa, but Theresa was a poor student who hated books and homework and had been kept behind. Now my cheeks burned as I saw Mr. Dondier, who collected at the ten o'clock mass on Sunday mornings, pull Theresa to him and run his hand over her breasts.

"Wait a minute," she said, drawing back, extending her hand.

Mr. Dondier fumbled in his trousers, took out his wallet and extracted a bill whose denomination I could not see. One dollar, five dollars? He placed it on the desk, his hand trembling. "It's yours," he said. "After . . ."

She giggled as he raised her up, lifting her under the arms and setting her on the desk, facing him. She pulled back her skirt, revealing knobby knees.

Mr. Dondier sat down on the piano bench, his face red and sweating and his eyes strange and staring, as he raised her legs onto his shoulders and plunged his face between her legs. He moaned and his shoulders jerked violently as he burrowed between her thighs. Theresa looked down at his bald head, still moist in the light of the gooseneck lamp. Her eyes were vacant, lusterless, as if she were not really there, as if Mr. Dondier were using someone else's body.

"Oh, Theresa," Mr. Dondier moaned, his voice muffled as he gasped her name and reached around now to clutch her buttocks.

Vomit rose in my throat, my heart pounding so dangerously that I backed away instinctively, my cheeks hot and pulsing.

I had to get out of there.

As I headed for the front of the store, the image of Mr. Dondier and Theresa Terrault burned in my mind, like the dancing spots that linger after you've stared too long at a bright light. Blinking away the image, I made my way through the aisles, careful not to upset the displays of merchandise.

I opened the door quietly and slipped out, hugging the shadows of the entrance, waiting to see if the street was empty. A car passed, headlights dim, the driver a shadow behind the windshield. The cold was intense again. I hurried down the street, my sneakers gliding over the sidewalk, trying to outdistance my thoughts.

Later, in the shed at home, I endured the pause and the flash of pain as I forced the fade away and saw, to my relief, first the vague outlines of my body and then my bones and flesh. Then the clothes I wore. I stayed there a while, sitting on the floor, knees drawn up to my chest, exhausted, body limp, as if I had traveled long distances.

Glancing out the small, dusty window, I saw the moon hanging remotely in the sky. I concentrated on the moon, filling my mind with it to blot out the memory of what I had seen in Mr. Dondier's back room. But what about the others

I had spied on earlier? David Renault and Artie and Pete Lagniard, my best friend. And the people in the three-deckers carrying on their lives behind the walls of their tenements. If I had followed any of them, spied upon them, entered their homes, would their private lives have also revealed secrets? Dark and nasty secrets it was better not to know about?

Finally, the moon was gone and I slipped into the house, past my father dozing in his chair near the radio, my mother already in bed. I stood for a moment in the doorway to my bedroom, looking at my father, listening to the small sounds of the tenement, and I seemed like an alien to those sounds, a stranger to this place that was my home. I was filled with guilt and shame, as if I had committed a terrible sin. I undressed and slid into the bed but did not sleep for a long time.

That was the second time I summoned the fade.

The first time had been in the presence of my uncle Adelard in my grandfather's house on a Saturday afternoon when everyone was gone and he tilted his chair back against the wall, and gave his command:

"Do it."

He had given me careful instructions. Told me to lean against a wall that was not there, to close my eyes to shut off distractions, concentration coming easier in the darkness. Told me to expect what he called "the pause."

Now I closed my eyes and leaned against the invisible wall, body taut, elbows bent, legs stiff, prepared to withstand strong winds, hurricane, rain, sleet, thunder.

Suddenly, there was nothing.

I was in that pause he had mentioned, all sensations gone, breath caught and held, my entire being a void, a blank in space. Was this what dying was like? I wanted to scream, cry out in terror, but before I could do anything at all, pain flashed throughout my body, a stinging, savage pain that found its way into every part of my being. I heard a moan, like the sound of a wounded animal, and knew the sound came from me although it was not like any sound I had ever made.

I opened my eyes and saw my uncle on his chair at the same moment that the cold invaded my body, exploding from inside and spreading through the same bones and sinews that were singing with pain.

Then, without warning, the pain stopped. Did not recede gradually or diminish in its impact but simply stopped. And the cold was balm after the searing pain.

My eyelids fluttered and I realized I had not actually opened my eyes to see my uncle—I had seen through my eyelids. My eyelids were gone, not there. Just as the rest of me was gone.

"How do you feel?" my uncle asked. There was an abundance of sadness in his eyes, the sadness I had seen that first day on the piazza.

I was surprised to find my voice normal when I spoke. "Fine, now. It was terrible for a few minutes, all those sensations."

"Seconds," he said. "Three seconds, maybe."

"That all?"

He nodded.

I lifted my hand, held it in front of my eyes, and could not see it. Studied the space where my hand should have been, where my hand actually *was*. Not there.

Uncle Adelard squinted at me, then nodded his head in satisfaction. "Perfect. A perfect fade."

"Why do you call it 'the fade'?"

"Because you have faded away. Like color gone from an old piece of cloth . . ."

I shivered with the cold. As I hugged my arms to my chest for protection, I could feel my shirt, the cotton fabric and the buttons.

"My clothes," I said. "They're in the fade. You can't see them, can you?"

"No. Anything within the immediate energy of your flesh, even a wristwatch or a ring, goes into the fade with you. But anything you touch or pick up will not be affected, will still be visible." His eyes narrowed. "You're cold, aren't you?"

"Yes," I said. "As if it's suddenly winter."

"The cold remains with you during the fade. But after the first few minutes, you adjust to it, get used to it. And remember this—it won't always be hard to go into the fade. Yes, there will always be the pause and the flash of pain—but this happens so quickly that sometimes you'll slip into the fade easy, the way a knife slips into a sheath. . . ."

"How long does the fade last?" I asked.

"As long as you want," he said. "Until you force it away."

"I'm afraid, Uncle Adelard."

"Of what?"

"Everything. Moving. Walking. Right now, I'm afraid I might lose my balance and fall down if I try to walk. Does that sound crazy?"

He shook his head, smiling. "It's what happens the first time. Trying to walk on legs you can't see. How do you know they are really there? But trust me, they are. Trust yourself, too."

I looked down and saw nothing. Only space. Although my body retained its weight, I felt a sensation of lightness, as if my body could soar through the air.

"Take a step or two," he suggested.

Those steps were like a child's first steps, faltering, wobbly, my body unbalanced, in danger of falling, as if I were walking a tightrope and could not see the rope. I placed my hand on the back of a chair for support, surprised at the solidity of wood in my grasp. As Uncle Adelard promised, the chair remained visible.

Walking tentatively across the room, I gained confidence. Went to the window and looked out at the world of Eighth Street, a world that seemed very far away. I made my way cautiously, dragging my feet a bit, toward my uncle. Stood a few feet away from him.

"Some precautions, Paul. Sometimes, the fade comes without invitation. There'll be a warning—your breath will suddenly become short, which means the pause is about to begin. You won't have much time before the fade begins. If you are in public, you must get away, seclude yourself as soon as possible.

"The fade will also take away your energy. After the fade, you will feel wrung out, tired. Not so much at your age, perhaps, but as you grow older. The longer you are in the fade, the bigger toll it will take on your body."

He held up his hand, as if to detain me, perhaps sensing the panic that was growing in me.

"One more rule," he said. "Stay away from cameras. Avoid having your picture taken when you are *not* in the fade. Cameras will not capture your image. Other times you will appear on film. There are many things I can't explain to you about the fade, Paul, and this is one of them. This camera thing is maybe something to do with light and how it affects film. I don't know. So, you must avoid having your picture taken. . . ."

"That picture in the album, Uncle. You told me you played a prank," I reminded him.

"Yes, I did. That time. I forced the fade just before the photographer took the picture. But I found out later, by accident, that I did not emerge on film. . . ."

Standing before him in that strange new state, present but absent, transparent, my head spinning with his rules and precautions, I wanted to cry out: Get me out of this, take away the fade, let me wake up from this dream, this nightmare.

As if he heard my silent plea, he said: "Come back, Paul. Leave the fade."

I pressed forward against the invisible barrier, my hands curled into fists at my side, felt a force pushing against me, held my position, and I was in the pause again, caught in that strange place between darkness and light, my breath taken away, panic racing along my flesh. And then the flash of pain, as if my body were a taut wire through which bolts of electricity passed, unendingly, excruciatingly. At the point where I had gathered myself to scream, the pain fled, the pause ended, air filled my lungs and the cold vanished.

I was suddenly whole again, restored, intact, visible, *here* and *now*, Paul Moreaux, in the second-floor tenement of my grandfather's house on Eighth Street. Everything the same as before.

But not really the same again.

Never to be the same again.

"Why did you choose me?" I asked as my uncle Adelard and I walked the streets of Frenchtown, nodding hello to people as they passed, pausing to watch Mrs. Pontbriand hanging shirts and pants on her clothes reel, as if putting invisible children—children in the fade—out to dry.

"I didn't choose you, Paul," my uncle said as we crossed Seventh Street.

"But you said you came home this time because of me," I pointed out with whatever logic I was able to summon. For a week, since his first revelation on the piazza, I had been in turmoils of thought and emotion. He had told me that day to be patient, that he would explain it all in due time. He asked me to trust him completely, to keep the fade a secret between us.

During that week, I had kept to myself, reading books, taking long walks to the Meadow, avoiding Pete Lagniard especially, afraid my secret would burst out of me if we talked. I stayed away from our usual hangouts, ignored the urgent messages he sent me in the soup can on the pulley. My final insult had been my refusal to go to the Plymouth that afternoon for the final chapter of *The Ghost Rider* when we'd learn the identity of that phantom cowboy who galloped across the prairie. Incredulous and then angry, he cried out, "The hell with you." He stalked away without looking back while I watched his departure with regret, knowing I had had no choice but to let him go.

Uncle Adelard had chosen that afternoon to initiate me into the fade, borrowing the apartment of my uncle Octave and aunt Olivine in my grandfather's house while they went on a picnic to Lake Whalom.

Now we turned into Mechanic Street, past the houses to which I had once delivered papers whose tenants were now Bernard's customers.

"I came back because I knew it was your time for the fade," he said.

"How did you know?"

He sighed, placing his arm around my shoulder. "Something in the blood. Something that passes through the generations. I look at you, Paul, and see myself as I was back on the farm in St. Jacques. I asked the same questions of my uncle Theophile, who revealed the fade to me the way I revealed it to you."

My shirt was damp with perspiration from the heat and my overalls clung to my body.

"Theophile was a commercial traveler, a fancy name for salesman in those days. He made his home in Montreal and visited us once in a while on the farm for the holidays. *Les fêtes.* But he arrived this time in July and stayed a few days. One afternoon he followed me to the outer fields and showed me the fade. . . ."

Dust danced in the sunlight, rising from the street that had been tarred and covered with gravel earlier in the week.

"My uncle Theophile told me all that he knew about the fade. He said it passes from one generation of the Moreauxs to another, always from an uncle to a nephew. And how it all began a long time ago. . . ."

Anticipating my question, he asked: "How long? Who knows? Back to the time of Christ, maybe. Uncle Theophile traced it for me as far as his knowledge took him. He was initiated in the fade by his uncle Hector when he was eight years old. That was in 1878, I figured later. And Uncle Hector learned about the fade from *his* uncle, a man named Philippe, back around 1840 or so, according to my calculations."

We left the paved section of Mechanic Street and headed down the hill toward the city dump and the cemetery.

"I spent only that one afternoon with Theophile and the poor man tried to tell me all he knew, which wasn't much. There were big gaps he couldn't fill in. He said Hector told him of a peasant in France, a Moreaux, who was a fader. This Moreaux sailed on a ship to New France, which is what Canada was called then. This was sometime in the middle of the seventeenth century. Do you see how far back the fade reaches, Paul?"

Arriving at the house of Mr. Lefarge, we paused in the heat and glimpsed the desolate tombstones in the cemetery. I followed my uncle as he traversed the narrow road barely wide enough for funeral processions.

"So what we know of the history of the fade starts with that peasant who came to Canada. We can guess the rest, of course. He settled in Quebec, farmed the land, raised a family, had descendants. You and me. Philippe and Hector and Theophile before us. He instructed his nephew in the fade as he had been instructed, as I'm instructing you."

We rested on a stone bench, the heat of the sun passing through the fabric of my overalls, stinging my skin. Uncle Adelard leaned back, thrust out his legs, and closed his eyes. Lines of weariness were in his face, like old claw marks.

"I wish I had a lot more to tell you, Paul. More history, more rules and regulations. Answers to all the questions that must be in your mind. But that is all I have to offer, sorry to say."

He opened his eyes and looked at me. "Maybe you'll find out more about the fade yourself in time to come. Maybe you'll write about it. Not for others but for people like us, faders, as a guide for them. We do not have many consolations. . . ."

The sadness I had come to identify with him was there in his eyes. Where was the sly trickster my father had told stories about? This wan, weary man did not resemble my father or my other uncles. Had the fade done this to him? Would the fade do this to me?

"Come on," he said, rising.

I followed him across grassy paths, between tombstones of all shapes and sizes, crosses and angels, some ornate and others merely slabs of slate.

He stopped at a corner lot where an impressive granite

stone stood, the name *Moreaux* chiseled on its front. A small square of granite had been planted beside the big stone. Daisies surrounded the square, fresh and bright. The name *Vincent* had been carved into the stone.

Uncle Adelard knelt down, made the sign of the cross, his lips moving in prayer. I also knelt, and prayed for the soul of my uncle Vincent. It was strange to think of him as Uncle Vincent. He was only twelve years old when he died. I remembered my father's anger because Uncle Adelard had left town before Vincent's funeral.

We rose to our feet. When I glanced at Uncle Adelard, his face looked misshapen.

"The grass is nice here," I said, needing to say something.

"Vincent died because of me," Uncle Adelard murmured, his voice so low that I barely understood him.

"Let's leave this place," he said wearily, his hand on my shoulder as if my body were a cane to support him as we walked away.

"**B**less me, Father, for I have sinned," I whispered in the darkened confessional, the words hissing against the screen that separated me from Father Gastineau. I had chosen him for my confession because he was the youngest of the three curates at St. Jude's. "It has been June since my last confession. I received absolution and made my penance."

The old formula completed, I hesitated, unsure of myself despite my careful plans. To gain time, I called upon my usual "start-off" sin, the venial sin to ease my way into the more important transgressions. "I lost my temper, three times."

One of the church's huge doors closed gently, almost with a sigh. Otherwise, all was silence.

I had chosen late afternoon, the final moments of the confessional hours, to make my move, waiting in a distant pew for the penitents to thin out. I had also argued silently with myself, wondering why I was there in the first place. Since Armand and I had been successful in deceiving our mother about confession earlier in the summer, she had not brought up the subject. Yet, as August dwindled, the sudden cool nights hailing the imminent end of summer, I felt a need to confess and had made a total of all my sins. The total was overwhelming. Get rid of them and die in peace if you are struck by lightning, I told myself.

Father Gastineau cleared his throat and I swallowed painfully, bringing my lips within an inch of the screen, and said:

"I have touched the breast of a female, Father."

"A female?" the priest asked, his voice muffled, as if he were trying to strangle a cough.

I had thought long and hard about how I would confess my sin. I could not say that I had touched a *girl's* breast since that would be a lie. Priests had an uncanny way of knowing whether the penitents were young or old. How could I confess that I had touched the breast of a grown woman without opening the door to a lot of questions? Finally, I had settled on *female*.

"Yes," I said, feeling my Adam's apple jumping. "A female."

"And this female, how many times did you touch her breast?"

It was always "how many times," the inescapable arithmetic of confession. "Once," I said.

"Only once?"

"Yes."

"What happened then?"

"Nothing."

"You did not go—further?"

"No." My lungs burned. I had been holding my breath.

"If you see this female again, do you plan to touch her as you did before?"

"No," I said fervently.

Pause. My fate hanging in that pause, teetering as if on a high wire.

"Anything more?" he finally asked.

My first instinct was to say no and end this torture, but I had come this far after all these agonizing weeks and did not want to turn back.

"Yes." I lowered my head as I said the words I had rehearsed countless times: "Father, I must confess a sin that I'm not sure is a sin."

A sigh, almost a moan, came from the darkness on the other side of the screen. Had I made a mistake, waited too late in the day for confession? Was he too tired after hours of being besieged by sins to deal with a complicated question? But what else could I have said? I did not know whether the fade was a sin. In the shed or in the cellar, I had practiced fading, learned to endure the frightening limbo of the pause and the excruciating flash of pain. I had learned to absorb the cold, as well. After a while I was able to slip in and out of the fade easily, staying unseen for longer periods of time, my body becoming accustomed to it, the way eyes become accustomed after a while to the dark. The experience of the fade was always disappointing, however. The fade did not provide the freedom it promised. I had the power to pass through the streets unnoticed, to spy on people, listen to private conversations, enter stores and homes and public buildings, unseen, undetected. But for what purpose? Steal from Lakier's or the five-and-ten downtown? Sneak into the Plymouth without buying a ticket? These acts were too petty for the fade. I did not want to steal. Anyway, how could I take anything from a store when the thing I took remained in sight? And where would I hide it later? I was not a thief, did not plan to be one.

"Tell me about this sin that you are not sure is a sin," Father Gastineau said.

I tried to gauge his attitude. Did he sound impatient, angry, tired? Or receptive?

"Don't be afraid," he added, more gently.

"Is it a sin to spy on people?" I asked. "To watch them when they don't know you're there?"

"Are you a peeping tom?" His voice cracked, like a piece of wood snapping.

"No," I said. But perhaps I had been. "Yes," I amended. "I spied on people. Saw them . . . doing things they should not be doing. . . ."

"Listen, my boy," he said, so close to my face that I felt the breeze of his breath. "I will not ask you what you saw. If you saw a sin being committed, then you have the necessity to remain quiet. If you tell others about it, then you become a part of that sin. The privacy of people is sacred to them. If what they do in private is a sin, then it is up to them to confess. You must do no further spying. Do you understand?"

"Yes," I said. But I did not understand. Was spying a sin or not? It seemed to me that he had avoided the issue, had not given me an answer. I sagged with relief, however, had escaped an explosion of anger, and I dropped my chin to my laced fingers on the small confessional shelf.

"Anything more?" the priest asked, brusque suddenly, stirring in his chair.

"No," I said. Hadn't he heard enough?

"For your penance, you will recite one rosary. For the rest, you will keep away from this female and not touch her again. And you will stop spying. Now, say a good act of contrition. . . ."

Only later, running homeward, face lifted to the cool

breeze of a waning summer afternoon, did I realize that I had forgotten to confess my other great sins: the impure thoughts at night and the spasms of ecstasy they brought.

Would the sinning never stop?

"Hey, Pete," I called. "Pete . . . are you coming out?"

No answer from inside his tenement.

"Aw, come on, Pete," I cried, listening to my voice echo back at me in the twilight, the neighborhood caught in after-supper stillness.

Again no answer, although I knew Pete was home and so were most of his family.

I kicked at the bottom step and drifted aimlessly toward the street. Twilight was smoothing the harsh edges of things, bringing with it an aching loneliness. I thought of the fade and how it had set me apart from the rest of the world, my world, Frenchtown. From my family. From Pete. He and I had barely communicated in the past two weeks. I had purposely avoided him at first and then he had stayed out of my way. At the beginning, I had been relieved that there were spaces between us. I had been dazzled by the fade, had had to find a way to live with it.

"What do you want?" Pete yelled, suddenly appearing at the window.

I shrugged. "Want an ice cream?" I called back. Lakier's still sold two-for-a-nickel cones and I had eight cents in my pocket.

"I'm not hungry," he said, his face disappearing from view.

I strolled down Sixth Street, without destination in mind, and came to a halt at an abandoned garage, its doors torn off, next to the Luciers' house, one of the few bungalows on the street. Melting into the shadows of the garage, I thought of the fade and the pause and the flash of pain. Piano music drifted from the house. Yolande Lucier, who was in my class, was singing "All alone by the telephone," her voice sweet and plaintive in the evening air.

I, too, was all alone but no telephone at our house. Who would I call on the telephone, anyway? No one I knew had a telephone, either. Call my aunt Rosanna in Montreal? Impossible. No one had heard from her since she left Monument.

If only my aunt Rosanna were here in Frenchtown, still at my grandfather's house . . . but I turned from the thought. It would be a sacrilege to consider the fade for such a thing, especially so soon after my confession. I thought of her far away in Canada, men waiting outside her shop when she closed for the day. If love was so wonderful that they wrote poems and songs about it, why was I so miserable?

"Are you in there?"

Pete's face was dim and pale as he peeked into the garage. "What the hell are you doing?" Curiosity diluted the anger in his voice, however.

"Nothing," I said, an answer that was always accepted, even by your parents, although they'd look annoyed.

"Do you want to hear the last chapter of *The Ghost Rider?*" he asked.

Armand had already told me that the phantom cowboy had turned out to be the storekeeper in town. But I said: "Sure," responding to his gesture of friendship, glad that we were pals again, even for a short time.

On the cement floor of the garage, our backs to the stuccoed wall, the sounds of Yolande's voice in endless repetition of "All Alone" like a poignant soundtrack, Pete told me, scene by scene, the events of that final chapter.

Then we sat in silence as Yolande began her piano exercises, the notes harsh and discordant.

"School starts next week," Pete said, disgust in his voice.

He had expressed the thought that was on my mind and the main reason why I had called to him earlier. I knew that our friendship was nearing its end. Although Pete and I were the same age—we were born exactly a month apart—he was two grades behind me in school. School was enemy territory to Pete. He became sullen and brooding, arrogant to teachers, failed tests, started fights in the schoolyard, a sharp contrast to the carefree summer adventurer. And he often looked at me with the eyes of a stranger.

"Junior high for me," I said. The Silas B. Thornton Junior High School downtown in the center of Monument near City Hall and the public library. A quiver of anticipation— and apprehension—went through me as I thought of the school term that lay ahead and the drastic changes it would bring. My class had graduated from St. Jude's in June, the boys in blue serge jackets and white flannel trousers, the girls in white dresses, wearing delicate crowns to match the dresses. There were tears in Sister Angela's eyes as she looked at us standing at attention. "You will never be this pure again," she had said, her rosary in her clasped hands.

Her words had been prophetic, at least for me. Turning to Pete, I was seized by an impulse to tell him about the fade and the night I had watched him matching cards with Artie LeGrande and what I had seen in the back room at Dondier's Market. We had shared a thousand secrets—why not this, the greatest secret of them all?

"Pete," I said.

"Yeah?" Brooding, chin almost touching his chest.

Yet, if I could not tell a priest in the darkness of a confessional, how could I tell Pete Lagniard? I wanted to say: Pete, I can make myself disappear. Become invisible. Like in that movie you saw a while back where the man wrapped himself in bandages.

"Remember that movie you saw, the one I missed because I had a toothache?" I asked.

"What movie?"

You must never tell a living soul, my uncle had warned.

"Never mind," I said.

Yolande was no longer practicing her exercises and the garage was spooky with silence.

"Will we always be friends?" Pete asked.

"Always," I said.

But the word sounded hollow and empty in the stillness of that Frenchtown evening.

There were three courses of study available at Silas B. Thornton Junior High School, but Sister Angela had ordered everyone in our eighth-grade graduating class to sign up for the commercial course.

"No one for the classical course," she said. "That's for the rich ones on their way to college."

"How about the general course?" my cousin Jules asked. Jules was never bashful about asking questions.

"The general course is for good-for-nothings," she said. "If you sign for the general course, you might as well quit school and work in the shop."

So it had been settled and I found myself with courses in bookkeeping and mechanical drawing and shorthand, all dull and dry and deadly, preparing me for—what?—a job in an office?

But when I arrived at Silas B. Thornton Junior High School on the first day of school, the courses suddenly did not matter. The corridors were filled with activity and excitement. Teachers in suits or dresses, not the black-and-white habits of the nuns, stood at their classroom doors and talked and joked with students as they passed. Bells rang, doors slammed, laughter burst from classrooms, and the sunshine splashing through the windows was brighter than any sun that ever shone through the windows of St. Jude's Parochial School.

My homeroom teacher, Miss Walker, took my breath away. She wore a red dress and lipstick to match. Her high heels clicked rhythmically as she walked to and fro in front of the class, checking off our names.

Every forty-five minutes bells signaled the changing of classes, and this was the most exciting part of the day. Hustling into the corridor, finding my next classroom, I thought of the interminable days in Sister Angela's class, from eight in the morning to three-thirty in the afternoon, monotonous, suffocating, and wondered how I had endured such a terrible routine. Here at Silas B. (already I had learned to call the school by its popular name), we changed classes seven times a day, new teachers, new subjects, and—marvel of all marvels—a daily study period in which to do nothing but read or daydream or glance surreptitiously at the new people I was encountering who, I could tell by their names—Buchanan, Talbot, Weidman, Kelly, Borcelli—were not French but Yankee and Protestant and Jewish and Irish and Italian. My head danced with color and light and laughter and voices and ringing bells as I stumbled down the stairs that afternoon to meet my cousin Jules across the street.

Of all my cousins, he was the closest to me in age and interests. If Pete Lagniard was my summertime conspirator, Jules was my closest friend during the school year. We usually parted company in the summer because he played baseball in the Neighborhood League and was a patrol leader in St. Jude's Scout Troop 17. Pete and I were renegades, with an aversion for organized fun, preferring the Plymouth or roaming the streets and fields, making up our own games, raiding gardens in the evening and distributing the tomatoes and cucumbers to the families of Alphabet Soup and galloping off on our imaginary horses.

When summer ended, my cousins and I were brought together again and I was always drawn to Jules. Jules and I loved to read. On crisp fall nights or wintry afternoons, we journeyed downtown to the Monument Public Library and borrowed books. There was a limit of five books per patron and by going together we doubled our quota and swapped the books back and forth. We read everything and anything from Tom Swift to Penrod and Sam, books on travel, pirates, explorations, books with pictures and without pictures. Pete Lagniard and I gobbled up comic books in the summertime and marveled at Superman and Terry and the Pirates. But Jules and I found literary treasures in the library, and we ran down the street whooping with glee and spilling the books in excitement the day Miss Wheaton, the tiny, whispering librarian, issued our adult cards. Which gave us permission to invade the stacks containing grown-up books that had always been forbidden to us.

Jules showed no evidence of glee at this moment, however.

"I hate that place," he declared, handsome face suddenly pinched and sour as he tilted his chin at red-brick Silas B., through whose doors hundreds of kids were pouring.

When I didn't reply, he said: "Don't you?"

I merely shrugged, not wanting to betray him.

"We don't belong there," he said. "We'll never catch up." By this he meant that we were joining the school in the ninth grade, and would be leaving at the end of the year for Monument High. "These kids have been together since the first grade. My homeroom teacher called Raymond LeBlanc a Canuck. But not in a nice way. Said it like it was a dirty word."

"My homeroom teacher is beautiful," I said. "She likes the movies. She saw every chapter of *The Ghost Rider*. Cripes, Sister Angela thinks going to the movies is a sin, a venial sin on weekdays, a mortal sin on Sunday."

"I'm sitting behind a Jew," Jules said. "Her name is Stein. Her father owns the Vanity Shoppe where women buy all their fancy clothes. She looked at me and wrinkled her nose. Like I was a piece of shit. . . ."

"Changing classes is great," I offered. How could he possibly find fault with that particular phase of Silas B. ? "The day flies by . . ."

"The cafeteria food is junk," he said. "I hate vegetable soup. And the sandwich was terrible. Salmon, the bones still in it . . ."

"They've got a school magazine," I said. "A literary magazine. Anybody can submit stories and they'll print them if they're good enough."

Jules stopped walking and turned to me.

"You're a Canuck, Paul. I don't think your stories will ever be good enough for them."

"Come on, Jules," I said. "Give the place a chance."

We walked together in silence. I wanted to tell him that I had met my first Protestant that day, but dared not. A moment after Miss Walker had called the roll, checking attendance, my math book fell to the floor with a dull thud. The foot of the kid behind me tried to kick the book away but a hand shot out, grabbed his ankle and twisted it, causing a soft howl of pain. I looked up to see who had prevented the kick. That was how I met Emerson Winslow. I had never known anyone with two last names before. He smiled at me and winked, a lazy closing and opening of one eye, a wink that said: Take it easy, don't take any of this—the foot, or even life—too seriously. A lock of blond hair fell on his forehead. The sweater he wore was like no other sweater I had seen before. Beige, soft, not like wool at all but as if made of melting butterscotch. I had never seen anyone so at ease with himself, languid, casual. If a bomb exploded, I was sure Emerson Winslow would be unaffected, would simply brush himself off and walk away, untouched, amused by it all.

But I didn't mention Emerson Winslow or anything else about Silas B. to Jules as we walked through downtown Monument, past the park with all the statues, and reached the tracks and the railroad signals that served as an entrance to Frenchtown.

As we approached the corner of Fifth and Water, I spotted my uncle Adelard leaning against a mailbox, his hat tipped over his eyes, the blue bandanna around his neck. He did not wave or beckon or make any sign. But I knew he was waiting for me.

During the last days of that summer and the first days of fall, my uncle Adelard gave me instructions in the fade. Not exactly instructions, of course. He provided me with the basic information that I required, although he spoke reluctantly and I felt he was holding something back. We strolled the streets of Frenchtown and paused now and then while I asked questions or he offered information. Even now, there are places in Frenchtown that are forever connected with memories of Uncle Adelard and the things we talked about.

On the steps of St. Jean's Hall on Fourth Street, while the sound of colliding billiard balls came through the open windows:

"How did you know I was the one, Uncle Adelard?"

"The glowing, Paul. I was told by my uncle Theophile to

watch for it, a brightness around the body. He said the nephew with the fade would display the glowing to me. Just as the fader in the next generation will show it to you. One evening when you were just a baby, I was visiting your ma and pa. For a few minutes we were alone—your mother was washing dishes, your father was filling the oil jug for the stove. I looked at you in the crib and saw the skin glowing, as if light was passing through your veins. And, of course, I knew you were the one. Then the waiting began. Between the time the glowing appears and the fade manifests itself, many years may pass. For you it's happening at thirteen. With me, it was sixteen. The next generation, who knows? So you have to watch and wait, Paul."

"But suppose I don't see the glowing. Suppose I'm not there when the fader is a baby?"

"Then something will call you to the fader. I have no proof it will happen but I believe it will. Something called Theophile to me on the farm in Canada. Something called me to you this year. I was in Lincoln, Nebraska, hitchhiking across the plains, on a dusty road, everything flat, heading north. And it came to me that you were beginning to fade. How did I know? I can't tell you, but I knew. And I walked back to town, boarded a train, and headed east. Used the fade to board and then to avoid the conductors. And I got here just in time."

"What do you mean—just in time."

"Because it was beginning to work in you, Paul. Whether you know it or not. Think back now—do you remember times when unexplained things happened to you? Blackouts, maybe? Strange feelings? Fainting spells?"

I thought of the battle of Moccasin Pond and how I had stumbled and fallen while the hooded guard pursued me. The flash of pain, the cold. Most of all, the mystery of why the guard had not seen me as I lay on the beach only a few feet away from him in the bright moonlight. At the time, I had thought that he was too drunk to have noticed me. Now I realized I had faded, maybe for the first time. Later, Omer LaBatt chased me through the alleys of Frenchtown and almost caught me in Mrs. Dolbier's backyard. Mrs. Dolbier had concentrated her attack only on Omer LaBatt. No doubt I had faded from her sight. Now the memories came rapidly —a series of baffling episodes a year before when my father took me to Dr. Goldstein after I had fainted twice, once in the library while I searched for books with my cousin Jules, another time when my father found me lying on the floor in the shed, where I had apparently fallen and bruised my head. Dr. Goldstein found nothing wrong with me but had prescribed certain tonics while my mother fed me cod-liver oil in huge spoonfuls, alternating the foul, fish-tasting stuff with a concoction called Father John's Medicine, which tasted somewhat better but was thick and difficult to swallow.

I did not tell him any of these incidents. As he looked at me with sympathetic eyes, I felt that he knew what I had been going through anyway.

"Poor Paul," he said.

In the Meadow on a September evening as we sat on the identical bench where my aunt Rosanna had guided my hand to her breast, I asked him:

"What about you, Uncle Adelard?"

"What about me?" he answered, surprised, as if he could not be of the slightest interest to anyone.

"You and the fade. How's it been for you?"

"It's hard to judge by what's happened to me, Paul. In fact, I have avoided talking about my experiences because I want you to learn on your own. We are different people. What happened to me might not happen to you. You have your own life to live."

His voice held a tone of finality and I sensed that he was being purposely evasive. I pressed on, however. What did I have to lose?

"But there must be something you can tell me," I said. "How you've used the fade. If it's been good or bad. Something to guide me . . ." I thought of Mr. Dondier in the back room with Theresa Terrault and how my first adventure with the fade had left me shaken and disillusioned.

"All right," he said, sighing with resignation. "I only use the fade when it's absolutely necessary. I never use it for my own pleasure. I use it to survive. When I'm hungry on the road and have run out of money. Once, a friend of mine was in trouble and I used the fade to help him. Someday maybe I can tell you more. For now, be satisfied with this. I've told you some of the rules. I've told you all that I know about bringing on the fade and sending it away. For the rest, you have to learn by yourself, Paul. Let your instincts guide you. Your instincts are good. Use the fade in a good way. I think that's the most important thing of all."

We walked by St. Jude's Convent one evening after supper, and watched the nuns in pairs strolling the grounds in their black-and-white habits, their rosary beads in their hands.

"You know, Paul," my uncle mused, "I sometimes wonder why the fade was given to us, the Moreauxs. Modest people. Peasants in France, farmers in Canada. Me, a drifter. Maybe with you, it will be different. You belong to a generation that will be educated. Maybe you represent a new beginning. . . ."

The sun had dropped behind the church, throwing long

shadows across the convent and the nuns in prayer. They seemed to have disappeared into the shadows.

"And I sometimes wonder, Paul," he said, "what might have happened if the fade had been given to the wrong people. Evil men, unscrupulous. More than that—I often hate to think of the future, what might happen with the next generation after you, if there will be an evil fader who will use it for terrible purposes. . . ."

We fell silent then, contemplating that possibility, the awful prospect of a world dominated by a fader, using the fade to gain riches and power. Hitler in Nazi Germany—the thought of an invisible Hitler in the future was too horrible to contemplate.

"Ah, Paul," Uncle Adelard said, again sensing my feelings. "I'm sorry you have to carry the burden of the fade."

"Maybe it won't be a burden, Uncle Adelard," I said. Although I didn't believe what I was saying.

One afternoon when he waited for me across from the school, he told me that he was leaving Frenchtown and Monument.

"When?"

"In a day or two. I have to say my good-byes to the family first."

"Are you ever coming back?" I asked, afraid of the answer.

We were crossing Monument Park, walking by the statues erected to honor the men of Monument who had died in the wars.

"I'll never desert you, Paul."

He had told me so much but there was still so much that I didn't know.

"I'm afraid," I said, trying to keep the tremor from my voice. "It's scary . . ."

"I know."

"I'm not going to use the fade," I declared. "I want everything to stay the same, the way it is now."

"Do you really, Paul?"

"No," I admitted, shamefaced. I thought of my longings and my desires. The books I would write, the countries I would visit. The fame I hungered for. "But I want to do things on my own." The fade couldn't write my books for me.

"Don't make any vows, Paul," my uncle said, his voice grim.

A leap of intuition made me breathless. I almost asked: Did you make a vow because of what happened to Vincent? He had said that Vincent died because of him. I could not bring myself to ask that question, though.

Instead, I asked: "Where are you going?"

"It's a big country out there. So many places I haven't seen yet. And then old friends to see again in places where I've been. They're not family but they're consolations. . . ."

"Do you really want to go, Uncle Adelard?"

"Life is filled with things you don't want to do but have to do. And you find out in the end that it's not as bad as you thought. You accommodate yourself to the situation. Remember everything I've told you. Write it all down someday. Always be careful. Watch for the next fader. That's your mission, Paul, if there is a mission. . . ."

We didn't speak alone again. He made his rounds of the family, brief visits with lots of laughter and gentle kidding. "Next time we're going to have a good-looking woman waiting for you," my uncle Victor joked, but he turned away after he said the words, and I saw the doubting in his face.

"I hope the strike will be over soon," Uncle Adelard said.

Before he left, he hugged us all, kissed the women, shook

my hand with a firm grip. I found it hard to look into his eyes. "I'll be back, Paul," he said to me as we embraced.

A week or so later, when I drew my notebook of poems from my hiding place, I found my uncle Adelard's blue bandanna, folded neatly, freshly washed and ironed, on the closet shelf.

With my uncle Adelard gone, the events at Silas B. consumed me completely and the fade became a part of the past summer and its witchery, along with street games and garden raids and the battle of Moccasin Pond. I learned to my delight of something that had been unknown at St. Jude's Parochial School: extracurricular activities. I joined the Eugene O'Neill Drama Club and tried out for the chorus of *The Pirates of Penzance*, to be presented at Christmastime by the Silas B. Choral Group.

I submitted the story I had written about the boy and his father and the shop to *The Statue*, leaving it on Miss Walker's desk. She was the faculty adviser for the magazine. I had titled the story "Bruises in Paradise," pleased by the contrast of those two nouns linked uneasily by the plain preposition.

One afternoon Miss Walker detained me in homeroom as the bell rang, and I waited in anticipation as the classroom cleared. When we were finally alone, she looked up at me, smiled, and withdrew my manuscript from her drawer. I recognized it immediately when I saw my handwriting on the title page. I had submitted it before learning that all manuscripts had to be typed.

"This is simply not acceptable, Moreaux," she said, still smiling.

"I didn't realize it had to be typed," I said. "I'll be taking typing next semester."

"Typing doesn't really matter," she said, her smile widening, as if amused by something she did not care to share with me. "The story itself is not acceptable, Moreaux. The subject matter is not suitable for our school magazine. Neither is the writing."

Why was she smiling as she was devastating my life?

"I would suggest this," she said, voice flat and decisive. "Concentrate on your studies this year. The transition from parochial school to public school is difficult enough. You have another transition next year when you leave here and enter high school. I understand that you have tried out for the chorus in *The Pirates of Penzance*. I would suggest that you withdraw from that. Your marks come first. . . ."

The smile was frozen now. And so were those blue eyes. No softness at all in those blue eyes. Blue ice, those eyes.

I tore my eyes away from that smile and looked at the floor. Saw my shoes with the rubber soles my father had attached with liquid cement, scuff marks visible although I had polished them vigorously. I thought of what Jules had said: *You're a Canuck, Paul, and nothing you write will ever be good enough.* Despite Miss Walker's remarks, I refused to believe that Jules was right. I raised my eyes to Miss Walker. She was leafing through the manuscript, nose wrinkled now, as if an odor rose from the pages.

"I want to be a writer," I said, aware that my voice trembled. "I know I have a lot to learn—"

"Maybe you'll be a writer someday, Moreaux," she said,

looking up, "but you must have other priorities at this time in your life. Your first priority is to study. Later, there will be time to write. . . ."

Stumbling out of the classroom, running through the corridor, trying to hold back the tears that threatened to spill onto my cheeks, I tore around a second-floor corner and bumped resoundingly into someone coming the other way. My books exploded out of my hands and the pages of the manuscript flew through the air and descended like giant, soiled snowflakes to the floor.

"Hey, what's the rush?"

Emerson Winslow stood there, brushing back that blond lock of hair, wearing a green sweater, the same soft material as the beige.

"No rush," I muttered as I bent down to retrieve the spilled books and pages. He joined me, dropping to one knee. " 'Bruises in Paradise,' " he read aloud as he picked up the title page. " 'By Paul Moreaux . . .' " He glanced at me curiously. "Are you a writer, Paul?"

"I thought I was," I said. "Until Miss Walker rejected it. It's not good enough for *The Statue*."

"Do *you* think it's good enough?" he asked.

"I've got a lot to learn," I said. "Priorities."

"You didn't answer my question," he said, smiling that lazy smile.

"Okay, yes, I think it's good enough for *The Statue*." My voice sounded firm and strong. But was it good enough, after all?

Emerson Winslow shrugged, an elegant movement that reminded me of British fliers in The Great War movies who flew to their deaths with what-the-hell smiles, their white silk scarves flowing in the breeze. "That's all that counts, then," he said.

As I assembled the pages he asked, carelessly: "Goin' any-where special?" As if the answer did not matter.

"No," I said. The bleak streets of Frenchtown suddenly had no appeal for me, all those forlorn three-deckers and the shops.

"Come on," he said, walking ahead, glancing over his shoulder. I followed him. After all, he was carrying three of my books.

The house he lived in towered above the others in that North Side neighborhood, a white turreted house like those I had seen only in the movies. Birds splashed in a birdbath in the center of the lawn. In the driveway, a man in a black uniform lovingly polished a gleaming maroon sports car. As we approached, he looked up at Emerson Winslow and said: "Afternoon, sir." I had never heard someone my age called *sir* before. The man was old enough to be Emerson's grandfa-ther, with graying hair and mild blue eyes.

"Hello, Riley," Emerson said. "This is my friend, Paul Moreaux. . . ."

"That's a beautiful car," I said.

"It's a pleasure to care for," Riley said. He didn't miss a stroke as we chatted.

Inside the house, books in glass cases and chandeliers, fire-places and stately furniture polished to high gloss, a baby grand piano, floor-to-ceiling windows, like none I had ever seen in Frenchtown. Nothing in this house at all like French-town. I was overcome with the realization of my ignorance. I did not know the name of anything in this house. For in-stance, a magnificent desk of gleaming dark wood that I knew must be more than just a desk. That it must have not only a name, but a history. And the sofa of rich upholstery, yellow. No, not yellow, gold. And the carpet of exotic design beneath my feet. Almost in a panic, I thought: I don't know anything.

We ascended a curving stairway to the second floor, the railing shining so brightly that I dared not touch it and leave a fingerprint. In the second-floor hallway, the walls were the color of whipped cream. One of the doors opened and a girl stepped out. I blinked, looked away, the way actors do in movies, then looked at her again, a double take.

It was like seeing another version of Emerson Winslow but a feminine, more dazzling version, blond hair like a helmet of curls, green eyes dancing with amusement at some private joke.

"My twin sister," Emerson said. "Imagine going round a corner, Paul, and meeting yourself coming toward you. Only it's a girl."

He touched her shoulder lightly, just short of a caress.

"Page, this is Paul Moreaux . . ."

"Hi, Paul," she said, tossing my name in the air as if it were a bright balloon.

Page? Did he actually call her Page? Was *Page* a name?

I felt stupid again. Could not speak. Could not move. Felt the need to swallow but did not dare swallow because I knew it would make a terrible sound in the hallway and send me into disgrace.

"Page is the noble one of the family," Emerson said. "She's going off to boarding school. Fairfield Academy . . ."

"I'm only going so you won't have to go," she said ruefully. "Daddy says one of us has to be prepared to meet the world."

She spoke the way Emerson did, carelessly, casually, as if what she was saying wasn't really important.

"I don't have to go because I don't have any talent," Emerson said teasingly. "I'm not a whiz at anything. See what you get for being a whiz, Page?"

"A whiz," she said, dismissing the description with contempt and looking at Emerson fondly, as if she thought *he* was the whiz. How I wished she would look at me that way.

As if she could read my thoughts, she turned to me and said: "You must be something, a whiz yourself, if Emerson brought you home."

Was she teasing me? Although she was not at all like my aunt Rosanna, she had the same Rosanna quality of making me feel hot and cold at the same time, made me squirm and swallow, but all of these sensations pleasant. "Are you something, Paul?"

"Everybody's something," Emerson said, rescuing me. "Paul is a writer." He turned to me. "Page is a dancer. Ballet . . ."

Page rolled her eyes at the ceiling, looked at me, and crossed her eyes clownishly. And looked beautiful doing it.

"If she weren't my sister and I didn't love her, I would hate her," Emerson said. "She's so goddamned good at what she does. And she does everything. . . ."

"Not everything," Page Winslow said, and did an unexpected and beautiful thing. She stuck out her tongue. At him. Childish and yet perfect for that moment, just as crossing her eyes had been perfect when Emerson offered her praise. We laughed, the three of us, and our laughter floated through the hallway and I marveled that I had been called a writer by Emerson Winslow, standing with him and his sister, Page, in this magnificent house.

"Be right back," Emerson said over his shoulder as he headed down the hallway and disappeared into one of the rooms, closing the door behind him.

I was alone with Page Winslow.

I didn't know what to say. Or do.

"What do you write?" she asked.

"Stories, poems," I said, trying to control my voice, hoping it would not change keys on me.

"About what?" she asked, giving me her full attention, as if my answer mattered very much to her.

"Life," I said. "What I feel, what I see. About Frenchtown where I live." I paused, wondering if I had disclosed too much, remembering Miss Walker, wondering if I was deceiving Page Winslow. Was I really a writer or only a pretender?

She wore a white pleated skirt and a V-neck sweater of such soft pastel colors they could barely be seen: lavender, blue, pink, colors of a gentle rainbow. Her hair was more than blond, almost white, and there was a touch of blushing in her cheeks. Her breasts caused gentle roundnesses in her sweater. I didn't know where to look. Was I being a traitor to my aunt Rosanna?

I tried desperately to find something more to say while Page Winslow stood there perfectly at ease, as if waiting for the world—or me—to entertain her.

"You're still home," I said. "Does Fairfield Academy start up later?" *Start up?* I felt like a fool, a Frenchtown fool, mute, inarticulate, dumb.

"I'm leaving day after tomorrow. Emerson and I were away for a year—on the *continent*," pronouncing the last word as if quoting somebody else. "Sounds wonderful, doesn't it?" she asked wryly. "All that happened is that we fell behind in school—here I am going off to Fairfield almost fifteen—and I broke my dumb leg in Italy." She sighed and lifted her hands in resignation. "Now I'm supposed to be all fit and ready to go . . ."

"Don't you want to go?"

"I suppose I do," she said. "I'm not sure. Emerson's one of the lucky ones. He knows what he wants."

"What does he want?"

"Nothing," she said.

The sun blazed through the window, dazzling my eyes. I had never encountered people like this before, people who threw words away like toys they had tired of playing with. In Frenchtown, people spoke only to say what they meant.

"What do *you* want?" I asked.

"That's the problem," she said. "I don't know what I want. At least Emerson knows what he doesn't want. What do you want?"

"Everything," I said. "I want to write. I want to see the world. I want . . ." And dared not say it. Love. Fame. Fortune. To live in great cities and sail across oceans. To have my books in libraries.

"I envy you," she said. And again I looked for mockery in her voice. Envied me? Shy and gangling and tormented by my ignorance in this house, here in a place I did not belong, among people who were like beings from another planet, not only from the other side of town.

Emerson returned, having changed into gray slacks, sharply creased, and a crisp white shirt. At home, I changed into worn overalls and an old faded shirt after school. I knew my few moments with Page Winslow were over, done with, as she headed for the stairs. She was leaving Monument the day after tomorrow. Would I ever see her again?

"Toodle-oo," she called, pausing at the top step.

The unlikely words were perfect, the way sticking out her tongue and crossing her eyes had been perfect.

Both Emerson and I echoed, "Toodle-oo," laughing as she went on her way, sailing down the stairs, her feet barely touching the carpet.

"Did'ja ever hear of Bunny Berigan?" Emerson asked, in the emptiness of the hallway following Page's departure.

I shook my head.

"You haven't lived yet," he said.

I followed him down the hallway into his bedroom. He closed the door behind us and I was struck by the sudden sense of privacy. His own room, his own bed and bureau. A Harvard pennant, maroon with white letters, hung on the wall above his desk. ("My father's alma mater," Emerson said, shrugging.) Framed pictures on the walls, showing Emerson and Page in various stages of growing up. In bathing suits at the beach. In formal suits and dresses. At the foot of his bed, a phonograph, records stacked neatly on a shelf below. There was a record on the turntable.

A moment later, I heard for the first time the tortured beauty of Bunny Berigan's trumpet, golden notes bruised with sadness, rising and falling, and then his thin, reedy voice:

> *I've flown around the world in a plane,*
> *I've settled revolutions in Spain . . .*

Spellbound, I listened while Emerson went to the window and looked out. I bent my head to the speaker, letting the music fill my ears and my being, closing my eyes, isolating myself. Bunny Berigan swung into his solo after the vocal, the trumpet like a cry from the depths, wild and melancholy, more powerful than words, more telling than a voice. The trumpet spilled notes on the air almost haphazardly, yet I sensed that it was moving toward a climax, as if the trumpeter were building an invisible and impossible structure in the air, rising, rising, toward a pinnacle that was both triumphant and blazing with eternal loss and sadness. The trumpet staggered ever upward, reaching, reaching, and I thought of the poem by Robert Browning: *Ah, but a man's reach should exceed his grasp,/ Or what's a heaven for?* and then the high note was attained, an unbelievably impossible note that was like a breath held a moment before death comes. Then silence and the scratching of the needle on the record.

I could not speak, held by the music and wanting to hear it again, immediately, the way I wanted to call Page Winslow back again but could not, could not.

Later, we talked about books and movies and the stage plays he saw with his family in Boston. *Winterset* and *Ah, Wilderness!* "My father and mother love the theater." He exaggerated *theater*, drawing it out to several syllables, pronounced it *thee-ah-tah*, rolling his eyes.

"What does your father do?" I asked.

"Nothing," he said. Then, sighing, "Well, something, I suppose. Having to do with banks and stocks and bonds. He's off to Boston a lot. My mother does things with charities. What she calls busy-busy. . . ."

He did not ask me what my father did and I didn't volunteer the information. He turned up the volume on the record and we listened in silence. Why did I feel that keeping silent about my father's work was like another sin I needed to confess?

When the record ended, I told him that I had to leave. The bedroom was shadowed, the afternoon sun feeble as it spilled into the window. Later, I had to deliver my brother Bernard's newspaper to Mr. LeFarge.

"You'll have to come again sometime," Emerson said as we walked down the stairway and across the hallway to the front door. "I'll have Riley run you home."

"No," I said, alarmed. Arrive in Frenchtown in that

gleaming sports car with a uniformed chauffeur at the wheel? Impossible.

He walked me down the steps to the macadam driveway.

We didn't encounter Page Winslow.

"Toodle-oo" he called, laughing, as I ran across the circular driveway and waved without looking back.

"Toodle-oo," I said, but knew he didn't hear me.

No, I won't do it.

Why not?

Because.

Because why?

Because I don't want to fade. I don't want the pause and the flash of pain and the cold.

Don't you want to see her again? Enter her house, stand next to her, go to her bedroom, watch her sleeping, maybe see her undressing?

No, I don't want to do that. I don't want to do any of those things.

Yes, you do. Of course you do.

The voice was sly and insistent, the voice that had come with my knowledge of the fade, almost as if the fade had a voice of its own. Which was impossible, of course. But wasn't the fade impossible too?

C'mon Paul. Let's go. It's getting dark. You can be there, at her house, in a few minutes.

No . . .

She's leaving tomorrow. You may never see her again. Or she might not remember you next time she sees you. Might look at you blankly and say: Who's that?

Ah, but it wasn't only Page Winslow who beckoned me. It was that house, as alien as a distant planet, the style and essence of that house, the names of furnishings in that house I did not know, like visiting a museum and being ignorant of the artists who created such works of splendor. And the people in that house I had not yet seen, the father who spent his days in Boston with his stocks and bonds and the mother doing charity things while my father stalked the picket line and my mother scrubbed floors and cooked over a hot stove at home.

I knew that I did not belong in that house.

Yet, I wanted to be there.

In the darkness of evening, the house was like a giant ship tied up at a dock, shimmering even as it stood still, its windows blazing with lights. Evening dew sparkled like broken bits of glass on the lawn. Music drifted through the windows, not Bunny Berigan but symphonic music, majestic and classical, swirling violins and bursts of brass.

As I drifted across the lawn, the cold of the fade raced through my body but I ignored it, feeling light and airy, as if I could leap to the highest point of the house and stand on the topmost turret.

I went up the steps and tried the door, not surprised to find it locked. Rang the doorbell and listened to the sound of chimes inside, echoing down the hallway.

Holding a stone in my hand, I flattened myself against the house, next to the door. When it swung open, a shadow fell on the landing as Riley stepped out, peering inquisitively into the night.

I tossed the small stone into the yard, heard it bounce in the gravel, saw Riley glance toward the sound and take a step or two forward. Which was all I needed to slip into the hallway, where I shrank against the wall. After a moment or two, Riley entered the house, closed the door, and slid the bolt in place. Frowning, he walked down the hallway, his heels clicking on the tile floor. I followed, matching his footsteps to mine, my sneakers noiseless in his wake. The music grew louder as we neared a doorway to the right, near the bottom of the curved stairway.

When Riley paused at the door, a cascade of violins stopped abruptly. Riley spoke into the silence of the room: "Sorry Mr. Winslow, madam. No one at the door. Perhaps something's wrong with the bell. I'll have it looked at in the a.m."

A murmur from the room and, after a moment, the sound of music swelling again as Riley clicked his way past the staircase to the back of the house.

Walking carefully, lightly, softly, I stopped at the doorway and looked in. Two men and a woman were in the room, sitting on formal parlor chairs, the woman in a simple blue dress with a strand of pearls around her throat, her blond hair shining in the glow of a lamp beside her chair. There was no doubt that she was Emerson and Page's mother, a slightly older version of them, her hair the same almost-white color. I could not see the faces of the men. They were turned away, listening intently to what the woman was saying above the music, like figures in a painting.

I glided toward the stairs, slightly dizzy as I ascended on the thick carpet, still not accustomed to the absence of my arms and legs beneath me, as if I were trying to float, impossible, upward against a current.

Pausing at the top of the stairs, I saw that all the doors were closed, but there was a thin strip of light at the bottom of the door to Emerson's room down the hall. At the door, I stopped, glanced around, heard voices from inside. My heart accelerated as I heard the murmur of Page's voice, then her laughter, light and merry, and the faint strains of Bunny Berigan's trumpet. Pressed my ear against the door and heard the unmistakable bantering tone as Page spoke, but I couldn't make out the words.

Loneliness swept me. How I longed to be in that room with them, laughing and talking intimately, joking, a part of the loveliness and sweetness of their lives.

I pulled myself away and went to Page's door, and stepped quickly inside the room. Waited for my eyes to adjust to the darkness. Drank in the scent of her perfume, light and airy, a touch of spring, lilac maybe, or some fugitive blossom from the Meadow. After a while, I could make out her bureau against the wall to my left, the bed opposite. I took a few steps, almost tripped on a soft thick rug. Saw a small form resting on pillows on the bed and felt it with my hands. A Shirley Temple doll, which made me smile. Page Winslow, still a child, a doll on her bed.

The door opened without warning and threw a shaft of light into the room, causing me to leap with alarm, forgetting for that moment that I couldn't be seen. Page Winslow closed the door, darkness again, then she snapped on the small lamp on the bureau. Gentle, glowing light enveloped her. She was barefoot, wore a skirt and a loose-fitting sweater. A delicate gray, a whisper of color.

I stood across the room, near the closet door, hoping she would not find it necessary to go to the closet. Her loveliness ached in me. Her bedroom was all blue and white, but soft blue, gentle white. As I watched she bent down slightly to look at herself in the mirror on the bureau, raised a hand to her face, long, slender fingers, fingers that would glide beautifully over a piano keyboard. She squinted slightly into the mirror, inspected a spot of her jaw, touched it with a probing finger.

"Pimple," she said, dismay in her voice.

I could see no pimple, saw only how utterly beautiful she was.

She turned suddenly, without warning, looked directly at me. Into my eyes. I panicked—was the fade wearing off? Could she see me emerging from nothingness? Would she scream and shout my name? Accuse me of breaking into her house, spying on her in her bedroom? Was my presence in the fade doomed always to disturb people like that?

Now she turned away from me, a frown gently scrawled on her forehead. Shivering slightly, she murmured: "Spooky." And began to study her face in the mirror once more. "Ugh," she said, squinting again.

How could she doubt her beauty?

Pulling herself erect, she drew the sweater over her head, not bothering to unbutton it.

I watched, stunned, as she then dropped her skirt to the floor, where it created a gray puddle at her feet. She lifted her slip, white with lace around the edges, to her hips and raised it over her head, then tossed it carelessly on the bed.

She stood there in her brassiere and panties, both white, her skin glowing pale pink in the lamplight. She was slender and delicate in contrast to the fullness of my aunt Rosanna, and I was awed by the fact that both were so beautiful and had such a profound and similar effect on me. I dared not move, afraid that any movement on my part would make me explode into that ecstasy I reserved for my bed at night in the dark.

Without warning, she swiveled toward me again, her eyes narrowed as she glanced in my direction. Agony seized me as the cold of the fade intensified. Turning away again but still frowning, she reached for a white robe that had been folded on the bed. She draped the robe over her shoulders and performed hidden maneuvers as she took off the brassiere and slipped her panties down, tossing them both on the bed. I wanted to reach for the silken undergarments and crush them to my face. If I dared not touch her, then I could touch the things that had been closest to her.

"Hello . . ."

I heard Emerson Winslow's voice, light and playful, and saw the door swing open at the same moment. •

He stepped into the room, wearing a maroon robe, slippers on his feet, the blond hair tousled as usual. He closed the door gently behind him and stood there looking at her.

She turned at his greeting, hands at her sides, her robe slightly parted and I saw a flash of her thigh.

"Oh, Emmy," she said. "I'm going to miss you . . ."

He moved toward her, arms outstretched. She stepped into his waiting arms, resting her head on his shoulder. So much alike, the two of them, reflections embracing each other, blending together.

"I'll miss you too," he murmured into her hair.

She raised her face to his.

And they kissed. Hungrily, deeply, their mouths opening to each other. My own mouth dropped open in astonishment and I stepped back, encountered the wall behind me, tried to stifle my breath.

The kiss went on, small moaning sounds coming from them, and his hand slipped inside her robe. I closed my eyes against the sight. But, astonished, still saw them clutching each other, having forgotten that my eyelids, too, were in the fade, and could not prevent me from seeing.

I turned away, my gaze dropping to the floor as I heard her whisper: "Oh, Emmy, I love you . . ."

I heard the click of a switch and the room suddenly plunged into darkness. But the darkness did not obliterate the sounds of their lovemaking, their gasps of pleasure, as they tumbled to the bed.

I clamped my hands against my ears, sank down to the floor, crouching, my ears filled with the distant echo of a seashell's roar, but I was not at the seashore, I was in the bedroom with Emerson Winslow and his sister, Page.

After a while I removed my hands from my ears. Stillness in the room. I turned toward the bed. Emerson and Page were indistinct forms beneath the covers.

The loneliest of eternities seemed to pass as I remained crouched in the corner. At last, Emerson slipped from the bed and left the room, closing the door softly behind him. I waited until I heard Page's gentle snoring before leaving, wondering if my tears were visible on the face that could not be seen.

Later, in the shade of an elm tree down the street, after the pause and the pain, shaking and trembling from the sudden chill of the night, I remembered the time I had asked my uncle Adelard:

"If the fade is a gift, then why are you so sad all the time?"

"Did I ever say it was a gift?" he replied.

I thought a moment. "I guess not."

"What's the opposite of gift, Paul?"

"I don't know."

But now I knew. Or thought I knew.

Exhausted and limp, I stood gasping for breath on the lawn of a stranger's house on the north side of town where I did not belong but where the fade had taken me. I pondered my experiences with the fade. I had seen things I had not wanted to see, would never have wanted to see.

A dog growled nearby in the bushes, a menacing growl that I recognized instantly. I knew that kind of growl intimately, had been chased by a hundred dogs while delivering newspapers.

I didn't wait for another growl but began to run, blindly, furiously, running without looking back, as if something worse than a dog were chasing me all the way to French-town.

Omer LaBatt always had the ability to surprise me, popping up around corners or looming dangerously as I emerged from Dondier's Market or Lakier's Drug Store. Late one afternoon, as shadows gathered beside the three-deckers of Frenchtown, he surprised me again. Turning into Pee Alley, the shortcut on the way home, I encountered Omer LaBatt confronting a boy of nine or ten whom I recognized as the little brother of Artie LeGrande.

Omer's hand was outstretched, palm open, while the boy fumbled in his pocket. "Come on, hand it over," Omer commanded, unaware I had come upon the scene.

Joey LeGrande, lips trembling, drew his hand from his pocket and placed some coins in Omer's palm.

"That's my paper route money," Joey said, eyes filling with tears.

"There's only twenty cents here," Omer said in disgust, bouncing the coins in his hand. "Dig down, kid."

"It's not my money," Joey protested. "It belongs to Rudolphe Toubert. He's going to muckalize me . . ."

"That's your worry, kid," Omer said. "Get the money up."

Joey dug into his pockets again and pulled out a few more coins, dropping them one by one in Omer LaBatt's waiting palm.

Joey was sobbing now, tears coursing down his cheeks, his hair disheveled, one leg of his knickers drooping almost to his ankle. "What'll I tell Rudolphe Toubert?" he cried desperately.

"Tell him you made a donation to the missionaries," Omer said, satisfied, slipping the money into his own pocket. "Okay, kid. Down on your knees."

"No," the boy cried, his nose beginning to run.

"Down," Omer snapped.

My sudden loss of breath told me that I had begun to fade. The pause, and then the flash of pain as I saw the boy dropping to his knees with Omer LaBatt standing over him like the lord of all he surveyed. The flash of pain almost lifted me from the ground. Omer LaBatt's hand moved to his belt buckle and then to the buttons of his fly. I crouched, absorbing the cold now, the pain passing out of my body. I looked down to see that I was completely invisible, the air cold and brisk in my lungs.

I flew at Omer LaBatt. He looked up at my approach, puzzled, hearing the rush of my body toward him but unprepared for the assault as I drove my shoulder into his stomach, my head into his chest. I rejoiced at his bellow of pain when he reeled backward, grabbing at air, face twisted with pain. He sank to the ground, dazed, shaking his head in confusion, and then began to pick himself up, rising to one knee.

Joey LeGrande, eyes wide with disbelief, scrambled to his feet and backed away, staring at Omer LaBatt. I watched him run down the alley looking over his shoulder at his stricken assailant, tripping once and getting to his feet, reaching the mouth of the alley, disappearing from sight. I turned again to Omer LaBatt and paused, watching him struggle to his feet, gasping for breath. I kicked him in the groin with all the strength I possessed. In that kick was every chase through every street and alley of Frenchtown, every fear he had inflicted on me and other kids. As he clutched himself bending over, I kicked again, my shoe finding his jaw this time, and he howled in agony, dropping to the ground, moaning, flecks of foam spilling from his mouth.

Standing triumphantly above him, the sweetness of assault singing in my bones and sinews, I felt my heart beat joyously, my flesh tingle vibrantly. Never had I felt more alive, more in tune with the world.

People began to stray into the alley, peering curiously at Omer LaBatt still groveling on the ground. I wanted to shout: "I did this—Paul Moreaux did this." But instead reluctantly left the scene of my revenge, fearing the gathering crowd could hear my thudding heart.

Later, in the shed, visible again, I began to tremble as I relived my attack on Omer LaBatt. *My* attack? It seemed as if the person who had assaulted Omer LaBatt so viciously were someone other than me. I had always avoided violence and confrontations, had fled from Omer LaBatt a hundred times, knowing myself a coward, brave only in my wildest dreams. But the rescue of Joey LeGrande and the attack on Omer LaBatt were not really acts of bravery. What were they, then?

"The fade," I muttered. Nothing good had come out of my use of the fade. Would I ever forget what took place in the back room at Dondier's and in the bedroom of the Winslow house? Now, even my triumph over Omer LaBatt seemed

tainted. I had never inflicted pain on another human being
until that frenzied moment in the alley. Not only had I injured Omer LaBatt, I had enjoyed myself doing it.

My uncle Adelard had once said: "It's good that someone
like you has been given the fade, Paul. Someone kind and
gentle, not a brute."

Had I become a brute?

I tried to make myself small in the shed, knees jackknifed,
eyes closed, as if I could shut out the world and hide away.
But I knew there was no place to hide.

It wasn't until later at night, in bed, that another thought
occurred to me, and I almost cried out in the dark. In Pee
Alley that afternoon, the fade had arrived without being
summoned.

"I've got a new Bunny Berigan," Emerson Winslow said.

"That's good."

"Want to come hear it? This afternoon?"

He had detained me after the bell rang, and Miss Walker
had dismissed classes for the day, the other students headed
for freedom, creating the usual daily traffic jam at the door. I
had avoided him for three days. When I didn't answer, he
asked:

"Are you going to continue writing stories?"

"I don't know," I said, arranging my books in a pile on the
desk. "Sometime, maybe. Not now." Picked up my books
and turned away, still not looking at him. "Hey, look, I've
got to go. See you around sometime." Hoping he didn't hear
the tremor in my voice.

"Oh," he said.

I had never heard such an *oh*. An elegant syllable that
seemed to go on forever, echoing in the classroom like a soft

chime, the room quiet now after the scampering departure of the students. The word continued to echo in my mind, imbued with a meaning beyond its brevity. Such a finality in the word. As I regarded Emerson Winslow standing in the splash of light from the window, that smile on his face, the slightly quizzical look in his eye, I knew I was saying good-bye to him and that shining house on the North Side and that I had lost Page Winslow forever. But then, she had never been mine, only Emerson's.

Never had the streets of Frenchtown been as barren and bleak, the three-deckers plain and ugly, the trees stark, bereft of leaves as November brought biting winds and pelting rain.

The strike showed no sign of ending: at the supper table one night, my father announced that the negotiations had broken down.

"There's a rumor the company's bringing in scabs."

Yvonne made a face. "Scabs?"

"It's somebody the owners hire to cross the picket lines and work in the shop. Strikebreakers. Usually men from out of town."

"It could mean fighting, right, Dad?" Armand asked, excited. "Uncle Victor says we can't let scabs cross the lines. If they do, they'll take your jobs and the strike will fail. . . ."

"I'm glad we've got an expert in the house," my father said sarcastically. "It saves me a lot of talking. . . ."

Armand concentrated on his food and so did the rest of the family. I looked up once and saw my father and mother exchange troubled glances. If it was difficult for me to accept my father as a striker carrying a picket sign, it was impossible for me to picture him in a fight.

* * *

I wrote no more stories that year. Paid attention in class, did my homework faithfully, passed all my tests, and made the Second Honor Roll for the first semester. I stopped going to meetings of the Eugene O'Neill Drama Club and nobody seemed to miss me. I was not chosen for the chorus of *The Pirates of Penzance*.

So the days and evenings of that autumn passed. School and the library. Books in which to escape the loneliness. During the first snow of November, I brought my father a thermos of hot soup as he stalked the picket lines, cheeks rouged with cold, hands enclosed in the woolen gloves my mother knitted.

"When will it end, Dad?" I asked, stamping my feet against the cold.

He shivered as he slurped the steaming soup while I stood there watching him, in my own cold and loneliness.

The scabs are here.

These words spread quickly through Frenchtown on that frozen afternoon in December the way Paul Revere's cry must have echoed from Boston to Lexington almost two centuries before. I felt, in fact, like a twentieth-century Paul Revere as I raced through Frenchtown bursting with the news. Lexington and Concord lay only twenty miles to the east of Monument and our U.S. history class at Silas B. had visited the "rude bridge that arched the flood" as a project in October. Streaking homeward that December day, I felt like a part of history in the making, eager to report what I had seen.

Three dump trucks had been waiting at the traffic lights at Main and Mechanic. The trucks were old and sagging and decrepit. Their astonishing cargo was men. Men who huddled together in the backs of the trucks exposed to the raw afternoon, caps pulled down over their eyes against the cold, bulky in their heavy jackets and mackinaws. The trucks belched blue exhaust, their engines idling while waiting for the light to change. I felt a wave of pity for the men. They looked old and battered and used up, like the trucks. How far had they come and how far were they going? Searching for clues, I saw Maine license plates on one of the trucks, the legend METRO SAND & GRAVEL, BANGOR, ME. on the door of another.

Two men stood beside me waiting for the yellow pedestrian light. They wore black overcoats with narrow velvet collars. I glanced at their white shirts and thin ties. Bankers, I thought, playing my old game of guessing the occupations of strangers.

"I see the importees have arrived," one of the men said. His face was not familiar but the voice might have been the voice of Emerson Winslow's father.

"Bound to happen sooner or later," the other answered, in a clipped Yankee twang.

Importees. Which I transferred immediately into *scabs*.

The light turned yellow, the truck engines gasped and groaned in anticipation of the green light, and I dashed across the street, leaving the bankers behind, almost knocking over a woman pushing a baby carriage, in my eagerness to spread the news to Frenchtown.

But I had forgotten about Frenchtown's unique communication network. News of a fire at one of the shops, for instance, always reached the homes of the workers even before the whistles sounded or the fire trucks, with sirens howling, blazed down Mechanic Street. Now as I turned from Mechanic Street into the heart of Frenchtown, I felt excitement in the air. Men had gathered in front of the stores, women called to each other from piazza to piazza, store owners stood in their doorways, and everyone seemed to be talking at once.

Bounding up the stairs to our tenement, I encountered Armand, who had just filled the oil jug for the kitchen stove from the big barrel in the shed.

"Did you hear the news?" Armand asked as I paused to catch my breath. "The scabs are here."

"I know," I said. "I saw them downtown."

Armand's jaw dropped open in astonishment. "Come on inside. Dad and some of the men are there," he said.

In the warmth of the kitchen, I told my story in rapid sentences, my tongue running as fast as my legs had carried me home. I felt like an actor performing on a stage with all eyes on me.

"Maine license plates," my father said when my performance was finished. He shook his head and fell silent.

"Canucks," Mr. Lagniard declared, voice sharp with hatred. "Potato workers." He was a huge man with a gargantuan thirst, although he seldom missed a day's work. "Then what they said about Toubert is true. . . ."

I sensed that my moment in the spotlight was over and sank down beside Armand on the floor. "Are they talking about Rudolphe Toubert?" I whispered to him.

He beckoned me into the bedroom and I followed, reluctantly leaving the scene of my triumph. As we sat on the edge of the bed, Armand said: "They say Rudolphe Toubert arranged for the scabs to come here. The factory owners went to him to supply the scabs and Rudolphe Toubert was only too glad to do it. They say he got so much money per head. Of all the double-crossers . . ."

"He's worse than Hector Monard," I said, astounded at Rudolphe Toubert's treachery.

"They're both traitors. One is as bad as the other."

The voice of the men in the kitchen reached us in low murmurs.

"What happens now?" I asked Armand.

"We wait," he said. "The workers meet with the owners tomorrow night. A final meeting to straighten out the situation. Everybody hopes that the scabs won't have to be used. . . ."

"But why bring them here all the way from Maine?"

"A show of force," Armand explained. "The owners want to show that they mean business. It's like holding a gun to our heads. Ready to be used if the meeting fails."

At the supper table that night, my father said: "Let me tell you about the scabs." And we all fell quiet.

"They're people like us. Men like me and all the other workers. Times are bad in Maine too. Maybe worse, because farm workers have to depend on the weather as well as work conditions. Us, we don't have to worry about the weather, at least. When the strike is settled, we'll have our jobs. Rain or shine."

"Would you go to Maine as a scab?" Armand asked.

"You can't judge another man until you lace on his shoes," my father said.

"But you'd never become a scab, would you?" Armand insisted.

"These are hard times, Armand," my father replied, his voice surprisingly tender. "Nobody's a bad guy. We're all trying to earn a living and support our families. . . ."

The meeting began on Thursday evening at 7:00 P.M. and continued throughout the night and into the following morning when the negotiators adjourned for three hours and then resumed their talks at noontime.

The meeting gave rise to optimism in Frenchtown. For weeks, the strikers had walked up and down in front of the shop without results. Although the arrival of the scabs was threatening, the meeting was the first sign that the owners were willing to sit down and talk with the workers. Thus, despite the presence of the scabs in Monument, enthusiasm filled the air as the meeting began.

The weather seemed an omen of good things about to happen. The December temperatures rose above normal and sunshine melted the early frosts and dissipated the remains of the first snowfalls. The frozen ground softened and in some places turned to mud—to a boy in Frenchtown, mud signified spring and now a kind of false spring seemed to have arrived.

As families joined the workers in the shopyard while the talks went on, a carnival atmosphere prevailed. The fires were lit in the barrels not so much for protection from the cold but as symbols of hope and devotion, much as candles burned in St. Jude's Church like prayers made visible.

My mother bundled up my baby sister, Rose, and took Yvonne and Yvette to the shop yard, where Bernard and I kept watch with the others. Armand hung around the platform near the shop entrance with the strikers. As the favorite of my uncle Victor, who was inside as one of the negotiators, Armand was treated with a measure of respect by the workers. He made himself useful running errands, carrying messages, and had already adopted the mannerisms of the workers, laughing quickly at the jokes, knowing when to sit still and be silent.

A hush fell on the crowd and all eyes were drawn to the platform as the door opened and my uncle Victor stepped out, followed by two or three others. No one moved, even the babies were quiet.

My uncle Victor raised his arms.

"We're taking a break," he said.

A moan of disappointment from the crowd.

"Go home," he called, raising his voice. "The talks will go on all night. You'll need your rest for what's coming if we fail."

His words cast a pall over the yard, obliterating the pleasant atmosphere that had prevailed earlier.

My mother gestured to me, and I rounded up Bernard. When I told Armand it was time to go home, my father said: "That's all right, Paul. He can stay. . . ." Armand beamed.

Most of the workers remained in the yard, in small groups huddled together as the night turned cold, the flames in the barrels flickering low. A sharp wind nipped at our cheeks as we made our way homeward. I envied Armand, who had stayed behind. He belonged to something, at least. Had a sense of his destiny, even though that destiny was nothing I wanted.

The talks entered their second day. At school, I flunked a test: Math, my worst subject. In my homeroom I found that Emerson Winslow had changed his seat. He no longer sat beside me. That chair and desk was now occupied by a red-haired boy with a noisy sniffle and a runny nose. Glancing around surreptitiously, I saw that Emerson Winslow had taken a place near the window, five rows away. The red-haired boy, whose name I did not know and did not care to find out, wiped his nose with the sleeve of his plaid shirt.

When I got home from school, my mother said that the talks were still going on. My father had returned to take a bath and gulp a quick snack and then had gone back to the vigil.

* * *

A noise, a whisper of sound, woke me, and I opened my eyes to the darkness of the bedroom, the sleep instantly gone from my body. The bedsprings creaked as I raised myself to look past Bernard, who always slept curled up like a snail. I saw Armand's dim figure beside the bed, hastily drawing on his clothes.

Propping myself up on an elbow, I whispered: "What's going on?"

He pressed a finger against his lips as he shrugged into a sweater. Then circled the bed, on tiptoe, in a half crouch.

"I'm going to the shop," he said on his knees beside me. "I heard the talk earlier. The scabs, they're going to try to get into the shop just before the sun comes up."

"I'm going with you," I said, although I hated to leave that warm, safe bed.

"Hurry up," he urged. "It's almost five o'clock. . . ."

We stumbled out of the house and down the stairs into the strange stillness of early morning, the sky eggshell white on the horizon and dark above.

When we reached the shop, we took up a vigil at the far side of the yard, crouched behind low piles of lumber, our eyes riveted on the clusters of men in the yard. Spotlights had been erected by the shop owners at the start of the strike and they caught the men in their stark, merciless light, casting their skin in a pale yellow glow. They paced the yard sullenly, heads down, puffs of steam issuing from their mouths. I searched for my father and did not see him. Two policemen patrolled the sidewalk, guns in their holsters and billy clubs dangling from their belts.

"Do you really think there'll be a fight?" I asked Armand.

"Of course," he said. "There's no way around it. Look close. See the bulges in their jackets? Those are weapons."

"Weapons?" The word ugly as I spoke it.

"Oh, not guns," Armand reassured me. "Billy clubs, like the cops use."

I spotted my father in the crowd, arms at his sides, looking vulnerable and defenseless. I would have bet a million dollars that he carried no billy club in his mackinaw.

The policemen chatted with the strikers occasionally, their voices carrying across the yard to us. Then everyone turned to the street as a car pulled up, the motor purring softly as it came to a stop. Rudolphe Toubert's gray Packard like a jungle beast breathing heavily in the night. Exhaust curled out of its tailpipe. The car moved off into the night.

"Bastard," Armand muttered.

A moment later, he said: "Listen."

I lifted my head, cocking my ear, heard the murmur of the men, the hiss of flames in the barrels. Listened more closely and then heard, yes, something beyond these sounds, almost out of reach but more distinct even as I strained to hear. The faint rumble and coughing of old trucks moving in the night, the grinding of engines, growing louder by the moment.

The policemen came instantly alert, hands on their hips, legs spread apart. Several strikers slipped their hands inside their jackets and I knew they were gripping the clubs hidden next to their bodies. I searched for my father, saw his face as a blur until he became lost in the crowd.

Then silence, so sudden that it was itself a sound in the air, everyone caught by surprise, the men in the yard motionless, the cops as still as the statues in Monument Park.

"Have they gone away?" I whispered to Armand, the question a wish more than a question. They had not come all this way from Maine only to turn back within shouting distance of the shop.

"They're gonna sneak up on us," Armand said. *Us.* His spirit out there in the yard with the workers.

I sat back, waiting, remembered the last time I had spied like this, when the men of Monument had charged into the hooded Klansmen at Moccasin Pond. But that clash had been a battle of good and evil, an attack on people who set fire to churches and wanted to rid the world of Catholics and Negroes and Jews. The fight that was imminent now was different, a sad kind of fight, workers against workers, men like my own father who must fight men like himself who had probably left their own wives and children behind in Maine.

When I looked up again, the scabs appeared, like grim ghosts lumbering out of the half darkness, marchers in a disorderly parade, seven or eight abreast, unseen columns behind them. They crossed the street, out of step, one man stumbling, their faces unknowable in the dark, as if their features had not been formed.

The strikers formed a line of defense at the mouth of the yard while the two policemen stationed themselves on the sidewalk.

"Halt," one of the cops called. "Don't come any closer."

But the scabs kept coming, their steps heavy on the pavement. Now that they were in the periphery of the spotlights, I could see them clearly, their faces gleaming blue and grizzly in the harsh glare.

The fighting erupted without warning. One moment, the men faced each other in grim silence, hesitant, tentative, massive in their stillness. Then, the lines broke and they rushed at each other as if a signal had sounded that only they could hear. They clashed and grappled each other awkwardly, amateurs at combat, performers in a grotesque ballet.

The silence of the fight was eerie, not like the battle of

Moccasin Pond, which had been loud and furious with screams and yells and horns blowing and automobiles being pounded like giant drums. In the shopyard as daylight began to invade the darkness, the sounds of their brawling were muted and subdued except for sudden gasps and groans and muffled cries, as if the participants had pledged themselves to a battle that would not disturb the rest of the world.

Armand leapt to his feet, impatient, bobbing and weaving as he screamed: "Give 'em hell. Kill the bastards . . ." And he ran off to join the fighters.

"Come back, Armand," I screamed. "Come back."

But he disappeared into the battle.

I looked for the cops. Surely they'd spot Armand and pull him from the skirmish. The policemen, however, were rushing around ineffectually, trying to drag or pull men from each other, tugging at jackets, dodging blows, imploring the men to *stop, stop, give up, somebody's going to get hurt . . .*

As the fighting continued, the white light of morning overcame the yellow glow of the spotlights. I tried to spot my father and Armand and realized that I could not tell the strikers from the scabs as they swarmed and struggled. They were all strangers.

Suddenly, the weapons appeared, the way magicians plucked rabbits and scarves from hats or hidden places. These were not stage props but clubs and hammers and sawed-off bats. I saw the first blood splash from the cheek of Rubberman Robillard. And at the same time, a knife blade glinted lethally in the morning light.

I finally spotted my father, who was tugging at a giant of a man holding someone in a headlock, the knees of his victim buckling, his body sagging. Unable to make the giant loosen his grip, my father leapt on his back, looking ridiculous for a moment, as if he were playing a parody of piggyback. The giant loosened his hold—his victim fell in a heap to the ground—and swiveled around, trying to shake my father loose. My father held on for dear life, his knees scissoring the giant's waist. Turning furiously now, the giant shook himself free of my father and sent him hurtling into the crowd as if he were a ball aimed at pins in a bowling alley.

I saw the flash of the knife again.

A moment later my father staggered from the crowd, clutching his chest, blood cascading through his fingers. His face was lifted to the sky in the awful anguish of pain, his knees wobbling. He did not cry or scream but seemed to have gathered the pain within himself. As I watched, stricken, paralyzed, he looked down to see the blood on his hands, dark, spreading, spurting now the way water bursts from a spring.

"No," I cried.

A small space appeared around my father as men fell away, realizing what had happened. My father halted in his tracks, face bone-white in the morning light, eyes wide with disbelief. He began to fall slowly, by degrees, one part of his body following another, legs buckling beneath him, knees sagging, the upper part of his body pitching forward. He finally crumpled completely to the ground, his hands reaching into emptiness, his head striking the gravel.

As I began to run toward him, I heard the wail of sirens and the roaring of engines in the distance and then saw crowds arriving, running toward the scene and my father there on the ground, surrounded by a forest of legs. I could see him no longer, my eyes blinded by tears.

The next few minutes were a blur. Cops arriving in black cruisers, sirens screaming. A stretcher appeared, not a real stretcher but poles and a blanket improvised to serve as a stretcher. My father was carried to a pickup truck, policemen and workers clearing a place for him in the rear, tossing equipment to the ground.

Where was Armand?

An arm went around my shoulder and I drew away and looked up into the eyes of Rubberman Robillard. He held a bloody handkerchief to his cheek. His eyes were filled with tears and I knew they were tears for my father and not his own wound.

Armand appeared at my side, white-faced, in a state of shock. "We've got to tell Ma," he said. "We've got to tell her."

I tore myself away. "You tell her," I cried, from the depths of my pain and sorrow.

And I ran.

Always ran when something bad happened.

Ran the streets, chased and chasing.

And now I ran again.

Behind the garage, I invited the fade. Prayed for it. *Do not fail me this time.* And I was not failed. I was caught breathless in the pause and then withstood the flash of pain. As the cold swept me, my breath came back, the pain disappeared and I was free. I looked down and did not see my body. Held my hands before me and did not see them.

I walked around the corner of the garage. Saw the sleek Packard. Squinted through the window. Rudolphe Toubert was inside, holding the black telephone receiver to his ear, the small moustache dainty above his lip. I studied him, watched his lips moving, his eyes darting here and there around his office.

I walked to the front of the garage. Paused, glanced to my right then my left, shivered with the cold of the fade, but ignored the cold, offered it up for my father, who must have arrived at the hospital by now, who also might be dead by now.

I opened the door, careful with the knob. Closed it quickly as a wave of cold accompanied me into the room. Rudolphe Toubert glanced up, phone still at his ear, puzzled as he arranged some sheets of paper that the air had disturbed.

"Wait a minute," he said into the receiver. He lowered the phone and glanced through me. Said into the mouthpiece again, "Funny, I could swear the door opened and somebody came in. But nothing . . ."

I advanced a step or two as he continued speaking: "Two thousand dollars, I don't think that's unreasonable . . ."

The office had not changed from the days of my delivery routes. His desk at the center, covered with papers and ledgers. Counters to his left where the newspapers were stacked and arranged in bundles for the delivery boys. The odor of newspaper ink in the air. As I drew closer I smelled Rudolphe Toubert's cologne, sweet and cloying. His long fingers gripped the telephone, the nails polished and buffered. His eyes were slits as he listened.

"Yes, somebody has to get hurt," he said into the phone. "Somebody always gets hurt. That's the way the ball bounces. But two thousand is the price. Cash on delivery."

What was he delivering? Another wounded person like my father to the hospital?

He hung up. He patted his moustache, smiling, seemed pleased with himself. His white shirt was crisp, the collars pointed. A red tie spotted with small white flowers. A blue handkerchief spilling out of his lapel pocket. Striped red-and-white shirt and red suspenders.

He shuffled papers on his desk. Glanced up suspiciously, eyes almost meeting mine. The smile gone now.

I had become accustomed to how people reacted to the fade and I smiled maliciously.

Frowning, perplexed, he glanced around the office cautiously, eyes sweeping the place slowly, searching the far corners, peering into the shadows.

A touch of fear in his eyes?

He reached for the telephone, lifted the receiver to his ear, spoke into the mouthpiece. "Operator," he said, "get me 3648-R."

Waited, phone to his ear, tapping his finger on the desk, whistling tunelessly, forehead damp with perspiration. He loosened his collar.

I did not move closer, remained six or seven feet in front of his desk.

"Herve," he said into the phone. "I want you to come over." Listened, shaking his head. "I don't care what time it is." Listened again. "Tell me, Herve, who's more important —your wife or me?" Smiling without warmth or joy. "The hell with her." A pause, then: "Get your ass over here." The words crackling with command.

With Herve Boissoneau, his right-hand man, on the way, I had to act quickly. Knew what I had to do. But how? I glanced around the office, moved to the counter, saw in my peripheral vision Rudolphe Toubert still at the desk, still whistling a tune that wasn't a song, the way I hummed a small tune of terror whenever I walked by St. Jude's Cemetery.

Rudolphe Toubert had turned to his right, almost as if he had followed my progress. Perhaps I had been careless. His moustache glistened with moisture and he pulled the gaudy handkerchief from his lapel and dabbed at his forehead.

I looked at him, hating him.

I thought of my aunt Rosanna in his bed. The paper

routes, Bernard and all the other kids at his mercy. The men beaten up in alleys. The scabs he had brought to French-town, turning workers into fighters, men into monsters. I thought of my father, wounded and bleeding, and maybe dead by now.

Turning away from him, I searched the counter and among lengths of rope and old newspapers found the weapon I needed, the long knife used to cut the ropes that held the bundles of newspaper together.

I picked it up.

When I turned into Sixth Street, I saw the crowd gathered in front of our three-decker, huddled together in that weary attitude of prolonged waiting. They allowed me room to pass among them, looking at me with big eyes, the look people reserve for accident victims. I saw Pete in the crowd, arms folded across his chest. He raised his hand in a salute, a brief gesture of sympathy.

My uncle Victor stood at the bottom of the outside stairs, his cigar unlit in his mouth, a dab of brown juice dripping from the corner of his lips. Armand sat on the banister, head down, disconsolate.

"My father," I said, trying to control my voice.

"He's at the hospital," my uncle Victor said. "They're operating. They sent us home. Dr. Goldstein said he'd let us know when it's over."

Armand leapt from the banister and confronted me. "Where have you been?"

I shrugged, could not find words to answer, could not answer even if I found the words.

My mother called from the piazza upstairs. "Come up, Paul, come up. You must be freezing . . ."

I was suddenly aware of the cold, and my teeth began to

chatter. Frost covered the terrain and glimmered white on the windows. I had never known the sun to be cold before. Looking closely at Uncle Victor, I saw the weariness in his face, lines raking his cheeks, his eyes dull and lusterless.

"Did the scabs win, Uncle Victor?" I asked.

"Nobody wins a fight like that," he answered.

"We gave them hell," Armand said, fierce and fiery, eyes blazing. "The police rode them out of town, put them in their trucks, and sent them on their way. Except for the ones in the hospital. They won't come back, right, Uncle Victor?"

"Right," Uncle Victor said, placing his arm around Armand's shoulder. His voice lacked Armand's fire and pride.

"How about the strike?" I asked, still shivering, still numbed by what had happened in Rudolphe Toubert's office, and amazed that I should be standing here asking my uncle questions about the strike.

"It goes on," Uncle Victor said. "But it will be settled. We'll win a little and lose a little. But what we win will be more important than what we lose. . . ."

I ascended the steps to my mother's waiting arms, let myself be folded in them. I shivered with chills. She felt my forehead. "You have a fever, Paul," she said, and led me into the bedroom. She brought me aspirin and hot cocoa and watched me sip from the cup. Her face looked shattered, her eyes glazed, as if she had been struck blind, was doing everything—walking, talking, tending to my needs—by memory.

"I hope Pa will be all right," I whispered as her lips brushed my cheek.

"We've got to be strong, Paul," she said. "No matter what happens. Pray, Paul, and be strong . . ."

I fell into a deep, dreamless sleep, plunging into fathomless depths, into the heart of a bottomless darkness, obliterated, becoming a zero, a cipher.

I woke to the sound of laughter and merriment and clinking glasses and muffled shouts of gladness. Rubbing my eyes, I crept to the doorway, gazed out at the kitchen, saw my mother radiant at the table, my brothers and sisters at their places, my uncle Victor at the door.

She saw me standing there.

"Your father, Paul," she cried, eyes luminous, cheeks flushed with happiness and joy. "He survived. Dr. Goldstein just left. He's going to be fine. . . ."

"Good," I said, my voice hollow.

I thought of Rudolphe Toubert and the knife and the peculiar sound that passed his lips as the knife penetrated his flesh and found its mark. I turned away so that no one would see me trembling.

Three weeks later, Bernard died.

In his sleep.

Cold and forever remote when we tried to wake him on the last day of that doomed year.

SUSAN

Let me introduce myself.

My name is Susan Roget and I am sitting at the typewriter here in Meredith Martin's ninth-floor apartment in Peter Cooper Village, New York, New York, and if I look out the window, I can see the East River where a tugboat is pulling a huge tanker through the choppy waters. It's a sparkling day in July—Saturday, July 9, to be exact—and I am haunted by something, by those final words in the manuscript I've just read for, like, the tenth time. *Cold and forever remote when we tried to wake him on the last day of that doomed year.*

Shit.

This isn't the way I want to begin. What I want to do is keep things plain and simple and direct. Professor Waronski in Creative Writing 209 says that the best way is to plunge in, make a beginning, any beginning at all, as long as you start. Most of all, he said, be yourself.

Oh, I'm myself, all right. That's what got me into this predicament. I shouldn't have read the manuscript in the first place, had no business finding it the way I did. Then I wouldn't have known about the boy Paul and the fade and all the rest of it.

Okay, I guess I *have* made a beginning.

Next, I suppose I should explain how I arrived in Manhattan, a thousand miles from Farley, Iowa, by way of Boston University, houseguest of a famous literary agent.

Pure nerve, that's how, plus a willingness to take risks. Professor Waronski says that a writer must take risks, defy the odds, be a bit obsessed and a little mad. So I gathered up my nerve (which didn't require much effort because I am not exactly a shrinking violet) and took the risk of sending Meredith Martin a letter.

In the letter, I explained that:

1. I burn with desire to be a writer, have always wanted to be a writer, would rather write than eat or drink, which is only a slight exaggeration.

2. I will be starting my junior year at B.U. in the fall, majoring in communications, which is actually a major in writing.

Then I dropped my bomb:

3. I am a cousin of one of her most famous clients—the author of *Bruises in Paradise* and all those other wonderful novels. (Distant cousin, yes, but still related.)

Then the payoff.

4. Would it be possible for me to work as a summer intern in her agency? Salary would not be a problem because I did not require any. (My father's guilt since his divorce from my mother has been so tremendous that he has overwhelmed me with gifts and affection and promised to subsidize me if I was successful in my pursuit of an internship with Meredith Martin.)

My final risk: including my telephone number at the dorm, in the event she wanted to call me. Which my roommate, Dorrie Feingold, said was not only nerve but chutzpah.

Lo and behold, Meredith Martin *did* call. And, perhaps out of curiosity, invited me to New York. We hit it off. I learned that she is accustomed to Manhattan visitors, constantly entertains her many nieces and nephews from the Midwest— Meredith was once a small-town librarian in Kansas—and has a room in her apartment reserved for vacationing guests. Not only did she hire me—at minimum salary with maximum duties—but she invited me to move into her apartment. She would not even let me thank her.

"I owe Paul much more than that," she said.

What does she owe him?

I did not ask. I don't have *that* much nerve.

So here I am in Manhattan, in Meredith's apartment and in my third week of employment at Broome & Company, opening mail, typing contracts, answering the telephone, and finding it all very exciting, to say nothing of the razzle-dazzle of the city itself in this gorgeous summer of 1988.

A bit more background before I go on:

It is one of the tragedies of my life that I never met my famous cousin, the novelist. (I have always referred to him that way—after all, he is famous, and he was my cousin.) He died in 1967 at the age of forty-two. I was not even born then. I am not exaggerating when I say that he has been the most important influence in my life. I have gorged myself on his novels and short stories, can recite long sections of them by heart. Have written countless theme papers about his work during high school and my first two years at B.U. Have tracked down various articles and reviews he wrote for small and obscure magazines.

The reason why I chose to go to Boston University is its proximity to Monument, where he lived all his life. I have walked the streets he walked, knelt in prayer in St. Jude's Church, lingered in front of the apartment house across from the church where he lived on the top floor, as if I expected his ghost to wander out of the place and greet me with a smile. (I wonder if he ever did smile—my grandfather said he was a serious, sensitive person who always seemed a bit sad and wistful.) My grandfather, of course, is my direct link with my famous relative. They were first cousins, grew up together, graduated in the same class from Monument High School. Whenever I visit Monument, I go directly to my grandfather's office at police headquarters. He answers my questions, patiently, painstakingly, and sometimes drives me around Frenchtown, pointing out sights and scenes that turned up only slightly disguised in the novels and stories.

Time now for true confessions:

I must admit I am often haunted by the possibility that I am not truly a writer, that perhaps I have been led astray by the fact that the blood of a famous writer flows through my veins. Does blood guarantee that I am really a writer? When the words don't flow or when they seem flat and stale on the page, I am racked—and wrecked—by doubts. That's my dilemma, the baggage I carry with me all the time.

One of the reasons—if *not* the major reason—I sought a position with Meredith Martin was the hope that I might show her some of my work so she could answer that terrible question: Who am I? A writer or only a pretender?

Another confession. Major. And why I sit here agonizing as I write this: I am a terrible snoop. And I eavesdrop shamelessly. I do not open other people's mail or listen in on extension telephones. But I *do* poke my nose in other people's business. I aspire to be a writer, after all. I have to find out about people. What they do and why they do what they do. So. I admit that I was snooping the day—exactly a week ago —when I discovered the manuscript in one of Meredith's closets. I wasn't searching the apartment for dark and dirty secrets. (In fact, I ignored the packets of letters in her mahogany secretary.) I simply wanted to get to know her better. What kind of cologne she prefers. Her choice of personal stationery. Stuff like that.

Meredith is very neat and organized. (A woman comes in twice a week to tidy up, but there is very little to tidy up.) If there is any clutter in the apartment, it comes in the form of boxes. Royal blue boxes, measuring eight and a half by eleven inches, labeled BROOME & COMPANY, and they can be found everywhere. In stacks, in piles, in columns. They contain, of course, the manuscripts Meredith must read every day of her life, in almost every waking hour.

In my quest for knowledge about Meredith, I pulled out drawers and opened closets, was impressed by the labels on everything from luggage to dresses—Vuitton, Halston, Laura Ashley. Meredith is crazy about hats. Big hats, wide-brimmed, floppy. ("I was born in the wrong century," she says.) One closet contains nothing but shelf after shelf of hats.

It was in this closet that I made the discovery. On the top shelf, tucked away in a corner. A box. The kind of box that usually contains a ream of typewriter paper. Frayed and well worn, buckling at the corners, unlike the official Broome & Company boxes. I stood on tiptoe and carefully took it down. Although Meredith had allowed me as an intern to read some of the manuscripts in the Broome boxes, I hesitated now. Should I open this anonymous box? Shit, why not?

I removed the cover and stood breathless as I read the brief note on the yellowed first page.

> By the time you read this, dear Meredith, I will be dead, probably for many years. (See what faith I have in you— gambling that you will outlive me by that long a time?) Make of this what you will. My thanks for everything.
>
> Paul

Stunned, I sank to the floor. After a while, I began to read, swiftly, with no pauses, from the opening paragraph when the photograph was taken in Canada to those last sad words that told of Bernard's death.

Time passed. I didn't know how long. I wished fervently that I smoked or drank or did drugs. Because I needed desperately to do *something*. I made my way to the living room unaware of my passage through the rooms. I gobbled up a few Godiva chocolates without tasting them and felt slightly sickish.

My God. I had stumbled across a posthumous unpublished manuscript by one of the country's most famous writers, secretly kept here by his agent. And now I was part of the secret.

That's what you get for snooping, Susan baby. Maybe this will cure you of that rotten habit.

My conscience talking.

The big problem: What do I do now?

As it turned out, I did not have to do anything. Meredith came into the apartment that evening, windblown, tossed her wide-brimmed straw hat on the table in the foyer, looked at me, looked away, looked again, and said: "You found it, didn't you?"

I began to stammer apologies, didn't know what to do with my hands or legs.

"Please, Susan, no apologies," Meredith said. "Maybe I wanted you to find it. I could have tucked it away in a better, less accessible place. Down at the office in the big old safe there. Let me soak awhile—I'm beat—and then we'll talk."

Later, sitting across from each other, the box with the manuscript on the coffee table, Meredith said: "Paul told me once that a writer is allowed one major coincidence in a novel. Maybe that applies in real life too. Anyway, my coincidence is this—the day I received your letter asking about the internship was the day I was brought Paul's manuscript. . . ."

"Where did it come from? Where has it been all these years?" I asked.

"It was sent to me by an attorney in Monument. Lionel Duschenes, an old-timer. He said that Paul personally delivered the manuscript to him a few weeks before his death back in 1967 with instructions to hold it until 1988 and then deliver it to me." She leaned back, closing her eyes. "Poor Paul. Never seemed happy. Always haunted by—something. I had a special place in my heart for him. *Bruises in Paradise*, his first novel, was also the first novel I sold as an agent. Both of us starting out together, me, the shy young thing from Kansas and Paul, the shy writer from New England. . . ."

She opened her eyes, they glistened—tears?

"Why are you so troubled, Meredith?" I asked.

"The manuscript troubles me, Susan. I can't get it out of my mind. Is it . . ." She paused, the question left unasked. "You've read it. Tell me what you think."

"Well, first of all, it's only a fragment. Incomplete. But I was very moved by it . . ."

Meredith was as still as the crystal paperweight, shaped like a fawn, on the table next to the manuscript.

Warming up now, because I am a ham when I get the spotlight, I said: "What also struck me is that, for the first time in his writing, Paul used real names of people. Okay, first names only. *Moreaux* instead of the real family name, Roget . . ."

"Some real names, though," Meredith amended. "Silas B. Thornton Junior High is a real name. Monument is also real. . . ."

"Right," I agreed. "You can also recognize people. Like my grandfather, his cousin Jules. Gramps has told me a lot about Paul. About when they were kids together. And the manuscript sounds exactly the way Gramps described those days . . ."

"What else?" Meredith asked.

"Well, it certainly resembles his novels and short stories. He always used Frenchtown as his background. Some critics accused him of being an autobiographical novelist, but he really wasn't. I mean, he employed his familiar surroundings, the Franco-American scene, but his plots were fiction. For instance, *Bruises in Paradise*. It's a story of a father-son relationship in the Depression years . . ." I realized that I had been quoting myself, reciting verbatim from a paper I wrote for Professor Waronski last semester. "The father worked in a shop and the son wanted to be an artist, dreamed of roaming the world. The climax of the novel was a fire that claimed the life of the father. As a tribute to him, the son gave up his dream of traveling the globe and took his father's place in the shop. In real life, Paul's father died in his own bed at the ripe old age of seventy-six. And Paul became a writer and never worked a day of his life in the shop. This was his usual method of placing a fictional story against a very real background."

"Right, Susan," Meredith said. "That was his pattern throughout all his books—*Come Home, Come Home* and *Dialogue at Midnight*. The same Frenchtown background but the characters—he disguised them all. Why? Because Frenchtown is a small place, everybody knows everybody, would recognize real people . . . But now he's naming names, actual streets. It's as if—"

A slow dawning on my part as I listened to her speak, watched as she frowned, cleared her throat, positioned the paperweight exactly in the center of the table.

"As if what?"

"This sounds crazy, I know, but—as if he were writing an autobiography. The details check out. Paul was thirteen years old in 1938 and so is the fictional character—whose name also happens to be Paul. During the years I was his agent, I visited Monument several times because Paul would never come to New York. Even when *Dialogue at Midnight* won the Coover. The Coover is even greater than the Pulitzer—it's not awarded every year, only when a deserving novel comes along. But Paul would not attend the banquet to receive the award, something other writers would kill for. He wrote a speech that he asked me to deliver. He also avoided publication parties—Harbor House is famous for the fancy bashes they throw when their important writers publish. Paul skipped them. He always threw a party in Monument but invited no one from the publishing world, except me. So, I got to know him and his family. Your grandfather Jules. His mother and father. His brother Armand, and his twin sisters, especially his youngest sister, Rose, whom he obviously adored. They are all there in the manuscript, Susan. The entire family, exactly as he described them to me when he talked about his childhood."

I said nothing, waited for her to go on, knew there was more to come.

"What also puzzles me is this—why did he ask that lawyer to hold the manuscript until 1988? So that people who are recognizable in the story might not be alive?"

"But most of them *are* alive, Meredith. My grandfather, his brother Armand, his sisters . . ."

"The old folks aren't. His mother and father. Most of his aunts and uncles are dead—those who aren't are very old now. Perhaps Paul wanted that time span to protect them. He probably figured that his contemporaries, like your grandfather, would not be hurt or upset by the story. . . ."

"Why should anybody be upset?" I asked. "They weren't upset by his other novels."

"This isn't like his other novels. . . ."

What she was hinting at was preposterous, of course. And yet—

I felt the color draining from my cheeks. At the same time wondered if a person could actually *feel* color draining from her cheeks. Ridiculous.

"What is it?" Meredith asked.

"Nothing." But it was something, something my grandfather had told me during one of my visits to Monument. But I did not want to talk about that now. Not yet.

"Meredith, what are you planning to do with the manuscript? Is it publishable? It seems like only part of a novel. . . ."

"Oh, it's publishable, all right. Not as a novel, naturally, but as part of a collection of Paul's writings." Her tone was now businesslike, untroubled, the agent speaking. "Harbor House has been talking for some time about bringing out a collection of Paul's essays, reviews, some of the short stories that have not been published in book form before. This manuscript would fit right in. Imagine, an unpublished work by Paul Roget. Could be the centerpiece. But—"

"Why are you so doubtful?"

She sighed, hugely, sank back onto the sofa, no longer the agent. "Did Paul mean it to be published?"

"He arranged to have it sent to you, didn't he? You are his agent—your business is getting stuff published."

"I know, I know . . ." She picked up the manuscript. "But I realize how troubled his later years were. He stopped writing, secluded himself. And then this manuscript appears out of nowhere. A puzzling manuscript. I wondered whether I should be the person to make a decision about it. Whether someone in Paul's family should be involved. Someone who could give me an objective opinion. So, I went to your grandfather . . ."

"Gramps? But he was Paul's cousin, grew up with him. How could he be more objective?"

"He's a detective. An investigator. His job is finding facts, the truth. So, I went to Monument, two weeks ago. Took the manuscript with me. Asked him to read it, to give me an opinion. What kind of opinion, he wanted to know. I said— but wait, Susan. You can read what he said."

On the way to her desk, she spoke over her shoulder: "As I suspected, your grandfather is a very methodical man. He sent me a report." She pulled open a drawer and withdrew an ordinary white envelope. Paused as she pondered the envelope, and then brought it across the room. Handed it to me.

"Read it," Meredith said. "Then we'll talk. . . ."

As I opened the envelope I realized that not once during our conversation had Meredith and I mentioned the fade.

DATE: 7/3/88
TO: Ms. Meredith E. Martin
FROM: Lt Jules J. Roget
SUBJECT: Untitled Manuscript of Paul Roget

What follows is my report on the manuscript you presented to me in my office on 6/30/88.

When you sat across from me that day, I could see that you were obviously troubled by the manuscript. Since I am not a literary critic, I deduced that your concern had to do with facts and figures you wished me to check out or even the possibility of libelous statements. Paul always stuck close to the truth in his books and stories, and often it took someone familiar with the scene to show where reality ended and fiction began.

I must admit that it was a shock to "hear" Paul's voice again so many years after his death. More than once, I had to discontinue reading as emotions overcame me. Despite the sadness, I was pleased that you brought me the manuscript, Meredith. Because of your frequent visits to Monument and Frenchtown through the years and your long devotion to Paul and his career, my family and I feel that you are one of us.

To return to the business at hand:

During the course of reading the manuscript, I realized that you had not been asking me to check facts and figures, after all. I know now the nature of the question that you wanted to ask but hesitated to put into words.

Let me answer the question:

This narrative is not autobiographical.

I will present evidence in this report to support my conclusion that what Paul has written is completely fiction.

Let us first consider invisibility.

The fade—as Paul called it—is impossible to accept as fact. Any rational person has to reject it as being fantasy of the wildest kind. Paul always dealt with realism in his novels and never showed any tendency toward science fiction or fantasy. However, he was addicted to the movies like so many of us who were members of the double-feature generation of the thirties and forties. A great many of those movies, particularly the serials of those days, dealt with the fantastic. For instance: the Buck Rogers and Flash Gordon serials, which dealt with adventures in space. More than that, there was a film that was impossible to forget, which had a definite impact on viewers, both young and old, of that era. The film—*The Invisible Man* starring Claude Rains. It's possible, I believe, that Paul received the idea for the fade from the movie and waited several years before using the idea in order to find his own approach to the subject.

Aside from all this, I think no one can doubt that invisibility, whether it's called the fade or by any other name, is impossible to achieve.

The fade, all by itself, proves that the narrative is fiction.

This is such an obvious conclusion, however, that I feel that you were searching for other evidence or even searching for something that doesn't exist.

To fulfill what I feel is my responsibility, I will indicate other instances to support my belief that this work is fiction.

The photograph, for instance.

We must deal immediately with the photograph because it is the centerpiece of the story, without which Paul might not have embarked on the narrative at all.

The photograph was certainly real and actually existed. I speak in the past tense because it has evidently been either lost or destroyed. I have spent a good deal of time trying to track down the photograph since reading the narrative and have questioned my aunt Olivine and uncle Edgar about the picture. (They are my only surviving aunt and uncle.) In her old age (she is now eighty-seven) Aunt Olivine speaks constantly of Canada and the small farm on which she grew up. She recalls very clearly the day the photograph was taken because she was heartsick at the thought of leaving Canada and coming to the States. She recalls that Adelard was not in the picture but dismissed his absence as another of his pranks (he was always a pest, she said). She then began to talk about the day she was confirmed in the small church in St. Jacques and it was impossible for me to bring her back to the subject of the picture. When I asked again about Adelard, her eyes glazed over and she soon fell asleep.

My uncle Edgar also has very specific memories of the photograph. Although in his late seventies, he works us a handyman around St. Jude's Church doing odd jobs. He says that his father —Paul's grandfather and mine—would never discuss the photograph because he had thought Adelard's absence from the picture on the eve of starting a new life in a new country was a bad omen. Uncle Edgar is a very practical man. He does not believe in omens. He has always believed that Adelard tricked the photographer by ducking out of sight at the crucial moment.

Uncle Edgar did not know what had become of the picture. He also did not know what had happened to the photo album itself. He said that when his parents died (within five weeks of each other in 1965), their sons and daughters, Edgar included, each took pictures of particular personal value to them from the album. Uncle Edgar selected a photograph of his sisters posing on the front lawn of the family home on Eighth Street. He never saw the album or the other pictures again.

I also questioned Paul's brother Armand and his twin sisters about the photograph, all on separate occasions. (His youngest sister, Rose, died of a brain tumor in 1978.) Armand and Yvette said they had been aware of the picture and remembered glancing at it now and then with a measure of curiosity but no more than that. Yvonne told me that she had never actually seen the photograph and only dimly remembered hearing it discussed. In my conversations with them, I brought up the subject of Paul's idiosyncrasies—his refusal to have his picture taken or to drive a car—hoping to find other clues to his behavior that might lend credence to the events in the manuscript. The answers were negative.

Fearing that I was taking a terrible risk, I asked each of them, "Did Paul ever disappear from sight?" I learned that there was no risk, really, because none of them took the question literally. Armand's reply was typical: "Oh, he dropped out of sight now and then but always came back to Frenchtown."

I have withheld my own comment on the photograph until I had reported on the reactions of others. Yes, I remember it well, but I don't remember, as Paul claims on page two of his manuscript, that I first told him of its mystery and swore him to se-

crecy. I have underlined those words to emphasize their impor-
tance as an instance where I am directly involved in the
manuscript and where my own memory does not support what
Paul has written. I cite this as vital evidence that Paul embarked
on a work of fiction when he began to write about the photograph and the fade. I heard the same stories Paul heard but did
not pay much attention to them. My uncle Adelard was such a
vagabond character in my life that he hardly existed for me.

So much for the photograph. I admit that it remains an
enigma and that its existence, with or without explanation, was
enough to inspire someone with Paul's sense of drama to make
an imaginative leap from the impossible to the possible. After
all, his trade has always been the writing of fiction. He once told
me that his entire literary career was the answer to a very simple
question: "What if?"

Let me now turn to the characters and the setting of the narrative. It is obvious that Paul again is demonstrating his talent for
taking real people in a real place and transforming them into
fictional characters in an artificial setting. He seizes the truth
and molds it to the design he has in mind. His characters, particularly those in this fragment, appear to be real when seen from a
distance but they are much different when viewed close up.

Aunt Rosanna, for instance.

Aunt Rosanna was not the person in real life that Paul created
on the page. I have a vivid picture of her and I also heard my
parents discussing her at length through the years. If he loved
her—and this, of course, is possible—I saw no inkling of his
passion, no hints at all. I don't wish to disparage her looks or her
character but she was not exactly the beauty or the sweet victim
that Paul made her out to be. She was pretty, yes, but in the
common everyday manner of any healthy young woman. She
was plump, if anything, and liked garish clothing—her favorite
color seemed to be orange—and always wore high heels, as Paul
indicated. Her hair was her best feature (I remember my mother
saying) and she had a flair for hairdressing. Other people's hair,
that is. Her own hair always looked frowsy and windblown. She
was a person of good nature, however, an easy mark for a loan

and would not hurt a fly, my mother said. But she had bad luck with men.

As far as her relationship with Rudolphe Toubert is concerned, there was no doubt among members of the family that he was the father of her child. (It was not the well-kept secret Paul made it out to be.) But I don't think anyone believed that Rudolphe seduced an innocent girl. There is no reason to suppose that Rosanna was even a virgin when she took up with him.

Rosanna was one of the few students actually expelled from St. Jude's Parochial School. In the seventh grade when she was thirteen years old, she was caught by Mr. LeFarge in the boys' basement (the nuns' name for toilet) doing a striptease while six or seven boys cheered her on, tossing coins at her feet. Mr. LeFarge, who believed in live and let live—probably because he spent most of his time at the cemetery among the dead—did not report the incident to the nuns or the priests (the boys themselves spread the word), but Rosanna was discovered later that year by Mother Superior in one of the broom closets off the second-floor corridor. She was with two boys, performing an act that Mother Superior could not bring herself to describe, although she let it be known that it was certainly a mortal sin worthy of damnation to hell.

It's entirely possible that Paul had a crush on his aunt and that she excited him physically. Rosanna could have easily become the object of an adolescent's fantasy. My own memories of her cease at an early age. Despite her talent for hairdressing, I do not recall that she ever opened a shop of her own, in either Canada or the United States. She seldom returned to Frenchtown and I have no distinct memories of her visits. She was never a topic in my parents' house. No one in the family knows whether she is dead or alive.

I have been frank in my remarks about Rosanna and I hope it does not seem as if I have spoken ill of her. I think it is important, however, to show how Paul idealized his aunt in the narrative and I make mention of this to support my belief that his narrative is fiction and that he was making use of his standard approach to his writing; that is, taking actual people and places and coloring them with his own brushstrokes, rendering them finally as figures of his imagination.

Regarding Rudolphe Toubert:

While hardly a paragon of virtue—as our police records indicate—he was not the vicious person Paul depicts in the narrative. He was less than heroic and often strayed beyond the law. He cheated on his wife, which Paul reports, and carried on affairs with women only a stone's throw from his home. Yet, his wife, who deserves sympathy because of the illness that confined her to a wheelchair, was not the most likable person in Frenchtown and not the easiest woman to live with. (Her illness today would probably be considered psychosomatic.) She was sharptongued and never had a kind word for anyone even before she became a prisoner of her wheelchair. This does not excuse Rudolphe Toubert's extramarital affairs, of course, but it does help explain his promiscuous ways.

It is true that Rudolphe Toubert served the people—however, illegally—of Frenchtown in the Depression era. It must be remembered that French Canadians were still considered poor immigrants in those days and were not highly regarded by bankers and business leaders. Rudolphe gave people hope through his various lotteries. (*Sold* them hope is a more accurate way of putting it, as Paul's father said in the narrative.) But Rudolphe Toubert never welshed, always paid off the winners, and regularly lent large amounts of money to the people of Frenchtown without collateral, asking people to simply pay off the debt at interest rates that, while high, were not prohibitive.

In the matter of Rudolphe Toubert's cruelty, it is a fact that he arranged for the man Paul called Jean Paul Rodier to be taught a lesson for refusing to pay his debt. Without punishment, his entire system would break down. However, Rudolphe Toubert ordered his goons to merely shake Jean Paul up a bit, give him a slap or two. But the goons got carried away with their assignment. Jean Paul was among the most disliked persons in Frenchtown, had a big mouth, was known to beat up his wife, who weighed no more than ninety pounds, and did not pay his debts. Few people mourned the assault on Jean Paul Rodier.

I realized that all of this makes me sound as if I'm apologizing

for Rudolphe Toubert just as I realize that I have painted an
unflattering portrait of our Aunt Rosanna. But my purposes are
different from Paul's. He was writing fiction and I am trying to
devote myself to fact. I also believe that I am in a better position
than Paul was to know the facts and to recognize them as such.

I once had a conversation with Paul—after the publication of
his second novel, *Come Home, Come Home*— in which we talked
about the old family celebrations, particularly New Year's Day,
which the French Canadians call the *Jour de l'An*. The family
always gathered at my grandfather's house, and there was much
food and drink and singing of old songs. It was, in a way, a
bigger celebration than Christmas.

At any rate, Paul and I began to reminisce about the celebrations of our childhood and one *Jour de l'An* in particular, during
which he and I stole away in the barn to smoke some forbidden
cigarettes and accidentally set fire to the hay. We had to scramble
to extinguish the flames and were fortunate to do so before they
spread. I will never forget the panicky whinnying of my grandfather's old horse, Richard. The horse sounded almost human in
its terror of the smoke and flames.

Paul fell into silence after we had discussed the incident.
"That really happened, didn't it?" he finally asked.

"Of course it happened," I replied. "Why? Don't you remember?"

"Yes, yes," he said. "But you know, Jules, I have fictionalized
so much of what happened in those days that sometimes, reread-
ing my books and thinking of the past, I'm not sure what's real
and what isn't."

That's one of the reasons why we cannot trust Paul to write
factually. His imagination, which was one of his great gifts, not
only ran wild but enabled him to take the ordinary events and
people of his life and make them larger than life. The father in
Bruises in Paradise was a memorable character whom critics com-
pared to the fisherman in Hemingway's *Old Man and the Sea*,
while my uncle, Paul's father, on whom the character was based,
was an ordinary man, a good man, but hardly the tragic figure
Paul created out of his art and craft.

I was once told by the chief of police here that I had little or no imagination. I took the remark as criticism until he told me that he was, in fact, giving me high praise. He said that my strength as a detective was my ability to see the facts as simply facts, to be always logical in my investigations. He said I was seldom thrown off the track or went off on a wild-goose chase because I was able to separate clues from false leads or red herrings. I think these same qualities allow me to judge Paul's manuscript accurately. I am also justified in making the observations about Frenchtown and the events Paul writes about not only because I have been a lifelong resident but because of my position as a police officer. A great amount of information comes in and out of police headquarters in a small city, information that concerns the past as well as the present. We have a complete file, for instance, on Rudolphe Toubert, including the fact that he received citations from the city for his activities on behalf of the youth of Frenchtown. Paul takes a dim view of Rudolphe Toubert's monopoly of the newspaper routes in the story. While Rudolphe Toubert may have enjoyed his power over the youngsters, he also gave hundreds of Frenchtown boys their first opportunity to earn money during the hard days of the Depression. He provided them with protection (the paper boys in the other sections of town were often beaten up or intimidated by older boys and a timid one like Bernard, for instance, would not have survived the rough-and-tumble world of downtown Monument). Paul also fails to note the annual Christmas parties Rudolphe Toubert held for the boys and the gifts each of them received. I believe that for dramatic purposes in his novel Paul needed a villain and Rudolphe Toubert served ideally in that role.

That leads us to Rudolphe Toubert's death. We still carry his death here in our files as an unsolved murder.

His body was found in his office on December 19, 1938, with a number of stab wounds. That same night, one of Rudolphe Toubert's employees, Herve Boisseneau, left town (was observed by a reliable witness boarding the B&M train for Boston). Rudolphe Toubert's safe had been rifled (Boisseneau knew the combination). Herve Boisseneau was never seen again and the murder weapon was never found. Rudolphe Toubert and Herve Boisseneau had been engaged in a fierce argument the day before the killing. Boisseneau was a huge man, capable of overpowering Rudolphe Toubert and inflicting the fatal wounds.

It is important to note that in the narrative Paul does not actually describe Rudolphe Toubert's murder. Why this omission when he did not hesitate to describe so many other scenes in detail?

The events of that tragic night are matters of fact. Paul's father was wounded in the skirmish and rushed to the Monument Hospital. Although he lost a great amount of blood, his wound was not considered critical and he made a complete recovery. At no time was his life in danger, according to police reports still available here in the files. Paul obviously exaggerated his father's injury to provide a climax for the events of that night. It is also tragic that his brother Bernard died three weeks later, suddenly and without apparent cause, according to Paul's narrative. In reality, an autopsy was performed and revealed his brother suffered from a congenital heart defect of which his family was unaware. As so often happened in those days, Paul's brother was considered "delicate" and this was given as the reason for his lack of vigorous appetite and low energy level.

As to the sudden death of our uncle Vincent years before— which Paul attempts to link with the fade and Bernard's death— I am using the resources of my own memory as well as my interrogation of Uncle Edgar to corroborate the fact that Vincent was besieged by illness from the day of his birth, seldom went out of doors to play, and was a grade behind other children his age because he missed so much school. His death, which naturally plunged the family into sadness, was not entirely unexpected.

It amazes me that Paul took so many disparate events and forged them into a narrative that smacks of reality until one inspects each incident and character separately and sees how Paul distorted them for fictional purposes.

One further note on the now famous strike at the Monument Comb Shop. Paul describes the strike in very simple terms without going into any details of a complex situation. An important omission is the complete absence of Howard Haynes, owner of the comb shop. Howard Haynes dealt directly with the strikers and his office at the factory was the scene of the negotiations. He passed through the picket lines every day and was booed soundly on occasion. He was never the object of violence, because Howard Haynes had always been a fair employer. The time of the unions had arrived, however, and industry was in an era of change. Men like Howard Haynes soon parted from the scene.

Why did Paul not mention Howard Haynes at all or deal with the strike issues? I believe there is a simple answer. He ignored Howard Haynes because he wanted to focus on Rudolphe Toubert as the villain of his manuscript. This is only my theory, of course, but I am convinced that there is merit in it.

I must deal now with my own relationship with my cousin Paul, although I have only a minor role in this narrative. Nevertheless, I was surprised to find that my character was so bitter about Silas B. Thornton Junior High School when I remember my one year there and my subsequent years at Monument High School as among the happiest of my life. It is true, of course, that I was apprehensive about Silas B. Most of the students who arrived there in the ninth grade from parochial schools were latecomers—the public school system in those days operated on a three-year junior high system (7th, 8th, and 9th grades)—and we all felt lost and abandoned in our first contacts with public school teachers and students. Most of us adjusted quickly. It is possible, however, that I warned Paul about his writing and my fear that his work would not be accepted because he was a Canuck. This rings true. However (and again I emphasize), I do not remember making the statement. Isn't this what Paul has always done—made use of a real emotion for fictional purposes?

Let me point out that Paul disguised only slightly the identity of the teacher who rejected his story. That story, very much revised, later was included in the Baker collection of best short stories of the year (1949) and eventually became the first chapter and gave the title to Paul's first novel. (In his introduction to his later short-story collection, Paul paid tribute to this teacher for her honesty and candor.)

Paul and I were not close for the remainder of our year at Silas B. and did not become close again until our senior year in high school when Paul was chosen as Class Poet and I was chosen as

Most Friendly in a poll of our classmates for the school year-book. Two Frenchtown boys given praise and homage by their classmates, a kind of landmark for our time! In celebration, Paul and I sneaked into our grandfather's cellar and toasted our triumph with his homemade elderberry wine and pledged our undying loyalty to each other just before we both vomited onto the dirt-covered floor. Paul went on to be more than a high school poet, of course, while I eventually joined the Monument Police Force.

Along with 90 percent of my class, I was drafted into the World War II army in July of 1942, only five weeks after receiving my high school diploma and a few months after the Japanese bombed Pearl Harbor. Paul was rejected because of a perforated eardrum, a minor affliction that caused many military rejections on the basis that no one with an ear defect could withstand the booming sounds of battle.

Paul was shattered by his designation as a 4-F and actually wept tears one night as we sat on the back porch at his house. It is difficult for people today to appreciate the wild patriotism of those years and how young men (and women) were eager to serve their country even at the risk of dying.

Many from Monument died during the war, either in battle or in war-related accidents. Their names are inscribed in bronze letters on the World War II Memorial in Monument Park, across from headquarters, a statue I see whenever I look out my window here in the office. Among the names on that Monument is that of Omer Batisse, whom Paul identified as Omer LaBatt in his narrative. Omer lost his life on Iwo Jima in one of the bloodiest battles of the South Pacific, a member of a Marine detachment that assaulted the island on the second day of fighting. Although he died a hero, I remember him as a big stupid hulk of a boy (this does not mean he could not die a hero, of course) who hung around the streets and picked up money doing odd jobs (probably strong-arm stuff) for Rudolphe Toubert. Thus, it's entirely possible that he bullied and chased Paul through the streets and alleys of Frenchtown, although Paul gave no indication of those happenings to anyone as I recall. As to the boy Omer accosted in the alley, I have been unable to verify any part of this incident. Since it involves the use of the fade, I take it as fabrication.

I must now address the topic of sex in the narrative, particularly as it applies to the store owner Paul named Mr. Dondier and also the twins he identifies as Emerson and Page Winslow. To Paul's credit, he used completely fictitious names for these characters and I am inclined to regard them as altogether fictional, although they are based loosely on actual people. I have little firsthand knowledge of the real twins he portrayed in the narrative, but I knew very well the man who might have been Mr. Dondier and I am frankly stunned at Paul's revelation and feel very strongly that he invented the entire episode. That store owner (it was not a meat market, incidentally) was above suspicion. The girl is nobody whom I can identify. If the fade is fiction—can it be anything else?—isn't it logical to accept everything connected with the fade, instances of spying, in particular, as fiction?

This same logic applies to the characters Paul named Emerson and Page Winslow. The act of incest Paul describes is shocking to me, although he was not explicit in his details and he has dealt with more explicit sexual scenes in his earlier books.

Page Winslow (to use Paul's pseudonym for her) stands out vividly in my memory because of one moment in my life. I saw her coming out of the Monument Ladies' Apparel store one winter afternoon in brilliant sunlight, her hands hidden in a fur muff, a long brown fur coat enclosing her body. She stepped out of the store and through the snow and slush and into a waiting automobile like a princess passing through her subjects. She was probably the most beautiful girl I had ever seen and I felt my jaw dropping as I stood dazzled on the sidewalk watching her passage.

Her brother, known as Emerson Winslow in the narrative, remained in our class at school until his junior year. I knew him slightly, enough to greet him with a casual hello as we passed. He always looked—the word we would use these days is *cool*. Never ruffled. He did not move in any clique but could have been the leader of his own clique if he chose to. The scene Paul wrote in which the brother and sister made love was all the more

shocking to me because of what happened in the future. The girl
Paul called Page Winslow died at the age of sixteen in a boating
accident off the coast of Maine. Later that year, Emerson, who
was a junior, left Monument High School. There were reports
that he enrolled in an exclusive prep school in northern Ver-
mont. Someone later said that he became a conscientious objec-
tor during World War II and served as a medical aide in a hospital in England. I know this much to be certain: The boy Paul
named Emerson Winslow is now a contemplative monk in a
Roman Catholic monastery in the foothills of the Smoky Mountains in Tennessee.

It is now 2:43 A.M. by the digital clock on my desk and my back
aches and my eyes are on fire.

A moment ago I read over what I have written thus far and,
frankly, do not like the way I sound on paper. The police reports
I write are impersonal and there is a specific vocabulary available for your use with certain words serving as crutches—*perpe-
trator, warrant, incarcerate, unlawful possession,* etc. In writing this
report, it was necessary for me to develop an instant and completely new vocabulary. I have tried to be objective, as if giving
testimony in court, where the only impression I have to make is
one of honesty and competence. Have I accomplished this at the
cost of sounding less humane and compassionate than I really
am?

Thus, this report provides no clue to the high regard I have
always had for Paul, how proud I and his family have been, our
concern for the happiness that always seemed to elude him.
He never married, never knew the bliss of wife and children. He
never took advantage of his fame, never traveled to foreign
places (he turned down dozens of speaking engagements and
invitations to visit places like the great cities of Europe). He
avoided interviews, did not allow his picture to be taken,
devoted himself completely to his writing, and to his family—his
parents, brothers and sisters, cousins, nephews and nieces.
He was loyal to old friends. I have not mentioned Pete Lagniard
and how, as a silent partner, Paul set Pete up in a printing business. (Pete, who was perhaps the only character in the narrative

portrayed with utter truth and no fictional touches, died of a heart attack in 1973 while attending a Red Sox baseball game in Fenway Park.) Paul seldom left Monument or Frenchtown, always lived alone, gave most of his money away (he supported his parents). His only pleasures aside from his writing (if writing was a pleasure for him) seemed to derive from his nephews and nieces, whom he obviously adored and who visited him often, making his apartment their headquarters in Frenchtown.

My fingers stumble as I finish this report and sadness holds me in its grip. Am I sad because reading the manuscript has brought back the memory of days long gone that could have been happier for all of us? Writing about Paul and his narrative has been like looking into a mirror as I typed. A trick mirror, maybe, like the kind found in carnivals and amusement parks. The tricky mirror of memory—making it difficult to separate the real from the unreal.

I believe what I have written is the truth, however. I am convinced that I have sifted fact from fantasy, fiction from reality. *Thus, what Paul has written in the manuscript is fiction. Without any doubt or conjecture. To believe otherwise is to believe in the impossible.*

My grandfather, Detective Jules Roget, does not look like a detective, and he does not look like a grandfather, either. I think of detectives as tough-talking private eyes in the movies and I think of grandfathers as kindly old men with potbellies, silver hair, and spectacles perched on red noses. My grandfather Roget is not like either of those. His voice is soft, almost a murmur. He has only touches of gray in his iron-black hair. He is tall and slim, without the slightest hint of a paunch.

He also does not resemble the person who wrote the report on the manuscript. That is, obviously, the side of him I have never seen—the police detective whom suspects face under questioning. Yet I was grateful for that relentless logic, that impersonal parade of evidence he marched past my eyes in the report.

Paul's narrative of life in Frenchtown fifty years ago had enchanted me. I delighted in the autobiographical overtones simply because I have devoured every piece of material about him and here was new, exciting stuff. The people in the story—from his parents to his uncle Victor to his best friend, Pete, and even the brief appearance of my grandfather—held me in thrall. I never for a moment considered that the narrative was more than just that—the fragment of a novel, fiction. In fact, as I read the manuscript I realized that Paul had been reaching into new territory, the realm of fantasy. I grieved for all the lost possibilities because this probably was the last thing he had written.

However, confronted by Meredith's reaction to the story, her doubts, her veiled hints, her troubled countenance, I had allowed myself to regard the manuscript as possibly, just possibly, autobiographical. *What if* . . . Paul Roget's own question coming back to haunt me.

Having finished my grandfather's report, I slumped with relief on the sofa. The fade, of course, had to be fiction. To think otherwise was to confront the impossible, as Gramps, that most rational of men, had pointed out. *That way madness lies*— Shakespeare, whom Professor Waronski quotes incessantly.

"Finished?" Meredith asked a few moments later, peeking around the corner of the bedroom doorway. She had sequestered herself with a Broome manuscript while I read the report.

Hugging the report to my chest, I nodded.

"Impressed?" she asked as she sat beside me on the sofa.

"Very," I said. "It was like a dash of cold water, Meredith. Just what I needed."

"I agree," Meredith said. "When I first read it, I clutched it just as you're doing. Like holding on to a lifesaver."

When I first read it . . . Shit—would the doubts begin once more?

She evidently saw my face change—did color drain from my cheeks again or did I just register surprise? She said: "Please bear with me, Susan, okay? Let me play the devil's advocate for a little while. . . ."

Again I nodded, not trusting my voice this time.

"You see, Susan, what your grandfather writes in his report isn't entirely contrary to my interpretation of the manuscript if we put the fade aside for a moment." This was the first time she had mentioned the word. "Can we?"

"Let's," I said, still stingy with words.

"Okay, then, invisibility aside, I am certain that Paul was writing the truth. About his family, his aunt Rosanna, his friend Pete, the whole bit. You see, your grandfather continually betrays himself in that report. For instance, he saw his aunt Rosanna one way, Paul saw her another way. But he does not deny her existence. In fact, he doesn't deny the existence of any of the people in the manuscript. He only denies the way Paul portrayed them. And who can say whether your grandfather is right and Paul is wrong? The point is that the characters in the manuscript were clearly recognizable to him. And this is not true of Paul's other work, except for the father and son in *Bruises* and even then the resemblances to Paul and his father were superficial. In none of his other novels or stories were the characters recognized as real people. But in this manuscript, everybody is. The first names are real names."

I got up and went to the window and looked out at the night, the lights winking distantly across the river, the water pebbled like a certain kind of black leather. Lights flashed in the air as a helicopter whirled its way through the sky. I sensed that Meredith was waiting for me to say something.

"But where does all this lead us, Meredith?" I asked, turning back to her.

"It leads us to the fact that Paul Roget has written his most realistic, autobiographical novel yet. And if he wrote it that way, then he wanted us to believe what happened in the novel. And we must believe all of it or none of it."

"I have a theory," I said, not certain whether I *did* have a theory at all. "Maybe Paul had to create a real world so that the reader would be *forced* to believe the fantasy. But that doesn't mean the fantasy was real." A dart of pain appeared above my left eye, like an old enemy, asserting itself when I've pulled an all-nighter before a big exam or have written long past the arrival of fatigue.

Meredith joined me at the window, our shoulders brushing. "I never tire of this view," she said. "It's always changing, never the same."

The intimacy of the night and the moment gave me courage. "Why are you so adamant, Meredith?" I asked. "Why do you insist that Paul was writing the truth?" Plunging on, I said: "Do you realize what the truth would mean? That the fade was real? That Paul had the ability to render himself invisible? That he killed a man fifty years ago in Monument?" I almost shuddered saying these words.

"I know, I know," she murmured wearily, regretfully, leaning her forehead against the windowpane, her eyes closed. "It's crazy, but . . ."

I waited, hoping she would say: You're right, your grandfather is right, let's call it a day, let's put out the lights and go to sleep. Weariness enveloped my own body and that vulnerable spot above my eye pulsed with a brighter pain.

Meredith turned to me abruptly, clasping her hands together. "One more thing, Susan." Voice brisk again. "Please?" Without waiting for a reply, she asked: "Remember Paul's refusal to be photographed and, in the manuscript, Adelard's warning about photographs?"

"Yes," I said, reluctantly, trying to disguise my impatience.

"I have something to tell you about photographs," she said, "and then we'll call it quits. I won't even ask you to comment."

I said nothing, waiting for her to go on, knowing that my protests would be useless. Besides, I was a guest in her apartment and she had been kind to me from the moment we met.

"I told you about the Coover, how Paul refused to come to Manhattan, didn't I? There was an epilogue to that particular episode. Paul was suddenly vaulted into more prominence than ever before. People were curious about this man who sidestepped publicity, whose photo had never appeared anywhere. As might have been expected, there were people who were determined to photograph him. A hotshot photographer with a reputation for tracking down the most elusive of subjects got an assignment from *Lit Times* to shoot Paul Roget. *Lit Times* was a trendy literary magazine that loved gossip, inside news, exclusives. It failed after a few years but it was powerful and influential in its heyday.

"*Lit Times* dispatched the hotshot to Monument. All hush-hush. She was a friend of mine, Virginia Blakely, my roommate at Kansas State, but didn't confide in me, anticipating that I would have tipped off Paul, which I would have done. It took her a week but she managed to track him down and took three quick shots of him, at a distance, as he came out of his apartment building and got into a car—"

"Photographs? Of Paul?" Excitement sent my voice an octave above normal.

She smiled wryly, held up her hands. "Hold off, Susan. Let me finish. Virginia brought them to me after *Lit Times* rejected them. Let me show you why they rejected them. . . ."

She went to the secretary again and opened that same drawer and this time withdrew a manila envelope. I literally held my breath, my heart behaving erratically, the headache almost forgotten. Even an obscure, rejected, out-of-focus photo of Paul Roget would be a discovery of major proportions to the world. And priceless to me.

I left the window as Meredith placed the envelope on the coffee table, and removed three eight-by-ten photographs, black and white, grainy, stark, like newspaper photos. They showed the front end of an automobile, the front steps of a building, a curtained window in the background. The focal point was the blurred figure of a man caught in midstride as he moved toward the car.

But wait.

As my eyes scanned the photographs I saw that the figure in the first photo had grown fainter in the second photograph and was not in the third photo at all, having disappeared into the car when the third picture was snapped.

"Notice anything special?" Meredith asked.

"Of course," I replied impatiently, disappointed at having come so close to seeing a photo of Paul Roget and then not seeing him. "It's all blurred. That hotshot photographer goofed up."

"Look again," Meredith said. "Closely. See how sharp the pictures are? The car, the front steps, that lace curtain? Fine details, remarkable, really, for a high-speed telephoto lens."

I looked up, wary again, knowing I was being led to places I did not want to go.

"The fact is, Susan, that Virginia didn't goof up. Neither

did her camera. Everything in the photos is clear, and sharp, except Paul. The figure of Paul isn't really blurred or out of focus. He's like a ghost image, a figure that was either about to materialize or vanish altogether in the first two pictures. And he's entirely gone in the third photo. . . ."

"He's in the car," I said, keeping my voice level and reasonable.

"Is he?" Meredith asked. "Or has he faded? Started fading in the first photo and was completely invisible in the last?"

Sleep was elusive that night. Traffic sounds, the swishing of tires on the pavement nine floors below—had it begun to rain?—reached my ears and the grandmother clock in the living room chimed at quarterly intervals and tolled the hours, like notes of doom in the quiet apartment. No dramatics, Susan, I muttered as I tossed and turned on the bed, punching the pillow, tugging at the sheet, and then lying still, unmoving, hoping to invite sleep that way. Thank God my headache was gone.

I must have slept occasionally because I suddenly plunged into dreams, vague and insubstantial, faces swimming in mist and rain. One of the faces was my grandfather's and I emerged from sleep, saw by the digital clock that it was three forty-five. I thought of what my grandfather had told me about Paul and the public library in Monument and why I had not mentioned it to Meredith, but the thought was too much to manage as I drifted off again, this time into a deeper, encompassing sleep. When I woke up, morning light filtered into the room through dripping windows, a foghorn sending its mournful call up from the river.

The digital clock announced nine forty-two—the alarm had not gone off at nine.

Padding down the hallway, I passed Meredith's bedroom,

glanced in, saw the bed unoccupied and unmade. Listened for sounds of the shower at the bathroom door. Peeked in, not there. She was not in the kitchen or the living room. At the window, I looked out at a gray morning, the waters of the river like chips of slate, the high-rises shimmering in the rain and mists.

Meredith and I usually went to midmorning mass at St. Pat's on Sunday, busing it back and forth, picking up the *Times* and croissants on the way back. She had evidently gone off without me today. Was she angry? Or merely avoiding me? Had those final words of hers last night suddenly sounded unreal and impossible this morning—to her as they did to me?—and sent her running out of the apartment?

On the coffee table I found a neatly stacked pile of manuscript pages, a note on top of them.

Dearest Susan:

So sorry—I did not play fair with you last night. Haven't played fair since the beginning. Attached is the remainder of Paul's manuscript, which I did not show you or Jules. Maybe it will explain all—maybe nothing. Anyway, forgive me. See you later today.

Meredith

Almost dreamlike, my hand moving in slow motion, I lifted the note and looked down at the first page of the manuscript.

I am writing now of Frenchtown in the late spring of 1963 when I lived in . . .

I glanced away, rubbed my eyes, lowered myself on the sofa, drew the stack of pages toward me, and began to read those first words again.

PAUL

I am writing now of Frenchtown in the late spring of 1963 when I lived in a three-room tenement on Mechanic Street, on the top floor of a three-decker across from St. Jude's Church. The tenement was adequate for my needs: a kitchen where I prepared simple meals or heated up my mother's casseroles on the old gas stove; the bedroom where I slept fitfully in the small hours of the night; and the front room where I wrote, directly opposite the huge stained-glass window portraying St. Jude. From the outside, I saw only the leaded outlines of his figure, like a giant paint-by-number portrait.

There was a small porch where I sat sometimes in the evening, aware of Frenchtown all around me. The house is still there and so is the church, and so is Frenchtown, although it isn't French anymore and was never a town to begin with. That first generation of French Canadians who gave the area its name have either died or live out their days in housing projects with terrible names like Sunset Park or Last Horizon. Most of their sons and daughters have left

Frenchtown, although some remain in Monument in homes constructed during the boom years after World War II. As the Canucks moved out of Frenchtown, others moved in. First the blacks, who swarmed the streets and quickened the tempo of life, bringing jazz and blues from the ghettos of Boston and New York City and Chicago. The Puerto Ricans came next, mingling with the blacks and sometimes fighting with them, both races finally accommodating each other in a tentative and uneasy peace. Now the Puerto Ricans outnumber the blacks and the Canucks, and fill the air with spicy smells, the acrid odor of celluloid only a dim memory.

The shop whistles no longer blast through the air of Frenchtown. The old button shop ceased operation years ago, the building torn down to make room for a low-income housing development. The shirt factory closed its doors soon after World War II, windows boarded up, clapboards peeling like old skin while the city debated its future in an urban-renewal program that never happened. The Monument Comb Shop has a new identity and is now Monument Plastics, part of a conglomerate with headquarters in New York State. All kinds of toys, combs, flowerpots, footstools, boxes emerge from molding machines that operate twenty-four hours a day. My brother Armand is in charge of personnel and community relations, positions that were unknown during the Depression. He still lives in Frenchtown, in a ranch-style home, with a swimming pool in the backyard, one of the new streets laid out on the site of the old municipal dump. He is married to the former Sheila Orsini, who was employed as a secretary in the office of the shop. At the time of which I write they had three sons: Kevin, who was thirteen, Dennis, eleven, and Michael, nine, and a daughter, Debbie, who was six.

Armand was a comfort to my father in his old age, although they argued constantly.

My father was contemptuous of plastic. "Fake stuff," he called it.

"But safer than celluloid," Armand countered.

"Safe but cheap. A celluloid comb, now. We still have some in the house. They never wear out."

"But they can catch fire," Armand pointed out.

My father snorted and lapsed into silence.

"What's the matter with us, Paul?" Armand asked me later. "I always get under his skin. Why do we always argue? I try to be a good son. Christ, I followed his footsteps into the shop. . . ."

"Age, time," I said. "That's what he's mad about. Not you or me or anybody."

My father sat on the piazza bundled against the chill, the thin sunlight not warm enough to bake his bones. I sat with him several times a week after my stint at the typewriter. He always rose to embrace me when I arrived, his cheek dry and smooth next to mine, like old paper that might crumble at a touch. His troubles began when he was struck by a car on Spruce Street and thrown into the gutter. His injuries hastened the aging process, the way an early frost kills flowers still in bloom, and he was forced to retire early from the shop. I think he loved his days at the shop despite the hard years.

Although I visited him regularly and lived only a few streets away, he was unhappy because I refused to move in with him and my mother. "A waste of money," he said, "throwing it away on rent. And food—isn't your mother's cooking good enough for you anymore?"

"I eat more of her food than ever before," I told him. My mother pressed casseroles and pies and cakes and cookies on me when I visited or brought them to me when she dropped in to see me, which she did every day or so.

"He's a writer," my mother called in my defense from inside the house. "He needs to be alone when he writes. He doesn't need an old hen like me or an old rooster like you bothering him. . . ."

My sisters the twins, Yvonne and Yvette, were regular visitors to my parents' home, although Yvette lived in Gardner, a few miles away, and Yvonne in Worcester, a forty-five minute drive. They spent most of their visits in the kitchen with my mother and were affectionate with my father in an absentminded kind of way, maternal toward him, as if they were mothers instead of daughters. It had been my mother's fancy to dress them identically when they were young. Yvette and Yvonne dressed differently when they grew up— Yvette tended toward tailored clothing in subdued colors, Yvonne loved flouncy dresses and bright hues and high heels. Sometimes when the light caught her in a certain way, she reminded me of Rosanna, and my heart ached. When Yvette and Yvonne visited, the house was filled with laughter and small talk. The talk was of babies and recipes and hair styles and sales and it was all jolly and happy and light. They each had three children, two sons and a daughter each as if the pattern of their dual identity remained intact despite the changes the years had brought. Yvonne's children were Brian who was eleven, Donna, ten, and Timothy, who had just turned eight. Yvette's children were Richard, ten, Laura, nine and Bernard, six.

This leaves Rose, the youngest, and the brilliant, beautiful one of the family. A graduate of Medallion, a small Catholic women's college on the Fenway in Boston, she obtained her law degree at Boston University and became a practicing attorney with her husband, Harry Barringer, in Albany, specializing in corporate law. Her husband is Jewish, intellectual, intense about politics—he once ran unsuccessfully for the Democratic nomination for state representative—a liberal whose passion doesn't match the corporate image he projects. Rose converted to Judaism during their courtship and was married in Temple Emanuel in Albany. Harry was born in Albany and they continue to live there. I sometimes wondered if my father cried about Rose when the tears streamed down his cheeks on the piazza for no apparent reason and whether Rose was a claw in my mother's heart as she did her housework. My father and mother never discussed Rose's conversion. They went to mass every Sunday. They never missed Holy Days of Obligation and went to confession on the first Saturday of each month, although I cannot imagine what sins they confessed.

I did not go to confession anymore and did not attend mass. They did not question me about religion just as they did not question Rose. Sometimes, in the evening, I slipped into St. Jude's and offered prayers in the shadows. Sister Angela once said that one of the great sins was despairing of being saved. I prayed for my mother and father and everyone in the family, and for my aunt Rosanna wherever she might be, hoping that my unconfessed sins did not taint the prayers.

The family always gathered for holidays and although Rose had become Jewish, she observed the Catholic celebrations. She and Harry were lavish with gifts at Christmastime and never missed an Easter Sunday dinner. My mother stopped baking her Easter ham and served turkey instead with all the fixings. The first time I inhaled the aroma of turkey and stuffing in the kitchen on Easter morning, I threw my arms around my mother and kissed her firmly on the cheek and she shooed me away, the way she used to shoo us off to bed when I was a kid. My mother also stopped asking Rose when she would have children.

Ah, the children.

I have mentioned the children only in passing and yet they concerned me more than anyone or anything else. They often visited me at my apartment, especially Armand's sons and daughters, who lived in Frenchtown and dropped in frequently, after school and on weekends. Yvette's and Yvonne's children usually found their way to my tenement when their mothers visited Frenchtown and never failed to spend part of their summer vacations here, Armand's swimming pool being a major attraction.

I had business going with the kids. My nieces performed household duties, sweeping the floors and drying dishes and dusting the furniture. My nephews ran errands, picked up groceries (mostly cakes and cookies and doughnuts and candy, which they later consumed) and mailed my letters and manuscripts at the post office. I insisted on paying them. I tried to anticipate their interests, stocked my shelves with books and games they might enjoy at certain ages. I had a complete collection of Elvis Presley records that Armand's older sons, Kevin and Dennis, played incessantly.

I felt like a traitor sometimes, as if I were using the children for my own purposes. But it also went beyond just that. I wasn't married, had no children of my own, and except when the writing was going well, the words dancing and singing on the page, the apartment was a lonesome place. An old couple, the Contoirs, lived downstairs, but I was only aware of their presence when they turned up the volume on their television set. When my nephews and nieces arrived, they brought color and sound and riot to my home. They invaded the place and took over operations. The girls experimented at the stove and concocted all kinds of dishes from cookbooks I picked up at secondhand bookstores. We went for long walks, although I avoided St. Jude's Cemetery and could not take them to the Meadow because that immensity of grass and trees was now a shopping mall and the Moosock River had been diverted and no longer ran red or green on certain days of the week.

As I spent time with the children I studied them closely, always searching. I did this carefully, surreptitiously, casually, but searching all the same. I had kept them under constant observation since their births.

I learned to love them. I ached at Debbie's painful shyness and the way she hung behind when the others were whooping it up. I was inordinately proud when Michael won first prize in the history fair at school for his masterful depiction of the battle of Gettysburg, complete with miniature soldiers and cannon he carved himself throughout an entire winter. Laura was so beautiful and fragile that I wanted to be a knight in shining armor for her, to protect her from all the thugs and wise guys she would inevitably encounter.

There was an echo of Rosanna in the new generation. Just as my sister Yvonne had a touch of Rosanna in her wild colors and easy ways with people so did Donna retain for me souvenirs of Rosanna. There are old photographs of Rosanna as a child that look exactly like Donna at that age except that Donna's features are more delicate, as if the blood that flowed through the Moreaux veins had become more refined as new babies were born. I sometimes found my vision blurred with tears when I looked at Donna.

No one ever knew of Rosanna and how much I loved her. A futile love because she had disappeared from my life and the life of the family. She did not write letters anymore or send postcards, and did not show up for holidays. As time went on, my longing for her dwindled and lost its intensity.

Except for certain moments, when Donna entered a room or I caught a glimpse of a woman on the street who reminded me of her—a touch of Rosanna in her walk or windblown hair—and the old anguish would return.

I searched the children incessantly for clues, signals, but never found any evidence.

Kevin came down with a rash one summer day. He was sturdy like his father, broad-shouldered, with hands that in earlier times would have been ideal for working in the shops. The rash developed after a walk we took across the streets of Frenchtown, out toward Moccasin Pond. The band of us picking blueberries. The rash spread out across his arms and his chest, small puckerings of the flesh and a kind of radiance providing a sheen to his skin. I stared at the radiance, heart pounding. Was this a sign of the fade? I perused his flesh the way I would a specimen in a laboratory, trying to be objective but not able to deny the churning in my blood, the pulse leaping at my temples. The rash turned out to be an allergic reaction, according to the doctor's report. Yet I had known all along that Kevin was not the fader I had been searching for. None of the children was.

How did I know?

I didn't know *how* I knew. But I knew. My uncle Adelard had said that something in the blood drew him back to Frenchtown when I was ready for the fade, a beckoning he could not deny. And in that third-floor tenement that spring, that same beckoning came to me. I woke up sometimes in the night, as if answering a distant call, a voice raised in supplication in the darkness. Other times, a restlessness kept me awake into the far reaches of the night, haunted by something just out of sight, beyond my grasp, like a memory I could not recall. Lying in bed, tossing and turning, unable to induce the sweetness of sleep, the knowledge flowered in me that the next fader, the fader of the new generation, was already walking the streets and inhabiting the world. Where? I did not know. But knew he was present somewhere on the planet.

My sister Rose knocked at my door one afternoon. I was surprised to find her standing in the hallway with her suitcase. Seeing my frown, she said: "Can you use a visitor for a day or two? I can sleep on the couch. . . ."

She looked weary and defeated, as she entered the kitchen. "I needed to get away," she said, "and realized I had no place to go except here, Frenchtown. But I didn't want to bother Ma and Pa, or cause them worry. I stayed in a motel last night. Couldn't take that again. So thought maybe I could stay with you for a couple of days."

"What's mine is yours," I said. "I'll take the couch, though —I hardly sleep anyway."

I didn't ask her any questions. She seemed at a point of desperation. Touching her shoulder lightly, I kissed her on the cheek. She raised her hand and caressed my own cheek. "Good old Paul," she said. "Always dependable."

My baby sister, fully grown, a wife now, but still my baby sister. Troubled, overweight—"I have a tendency to eat and eat when things go wrong and I've been a glutton lately," she said as she collapsed on the couch.

She took a long bath, changed into slacks and a loose navy blue sweater. "I'm famished," she announced, "starved for something outrageous. Like pizza with everything on it . . ."

A pizza parlor occupied what used to be Lakier's Drug Store and I picked up the fanciest pizza possible, which Rose and I devoured with great gulps of beer. "Eating well is the best revenge," Rose said.

Finally, while I sat on the floor, legs jackknifed, and Rose slouched on the couch, chewing on the last vestige of pizza, she began to talk.

"The problem," she said, "is children. It's very simple and uncomplicated and not so simple and complicated. I want them and Harry doesn't." She sighed, wiped a dab of tomato sauce from her cheek, looked down at me, frowning, face dark. "I more than want children, Paul, I *have* to have them. I'm not asking for a houseful. One, to begin with. But he won't listen to that. He doesn't want to bring children into this terrible world, he says. Crap, I say. We battle. We argue. I try to seduce him. He grows cold. It's ruined our sex life. Hell, it's ruined our life, period."

"Maybe time will change him," I said. "A yearning for immortality. The true immortality, Rose: a child to carry your blood, your genes into the future . . . Maybe he'll eventually see that. . . ."

"Don't bet on it," she said. "When you live with someone all this time, you come to know them. I know Harry. That's what's so disheartening, so defeating. He does not change."

Forlornly, she brushed a strand of hair back from her forehead. A frown on her forehead, the graffiti of sorrow.

"In all other things he is kind and considerate and loving and caring. And listen, I'm not perfect. I keep gaining weight. I have a temper. I'm far from the perfect wife and roommate. . . ."

"You're perfect in my book," I said.

"No, I'm not," she said, a poignant acceptance in her voice that made me sad. "In fact, this thing about children is kind of ironic. Pathetic, maybe, and ironic too."

A leap of my heart for some reason, something in her words putting me on alert.

The floor throbbed beneath me as the old couple downstairs turned on their television, full volume as usual, a drummer banging out a beat now and then. Canned laughter found its way through the thin floor.

I had a sense of déjà vu, as if we had had this conversation before, in these exact positions, she on the couch and me on the floor. I almost knew what she would say next but not quite, not quite.

"Remember when I was at Medallion? The summer between my sophomore and junior years? The summer I didn't come home? Went to Maine as a junior counselor at a summer camp for girls? Remember?"

"Yes," I said, "but only vaguely." That was the summer I began to write *Bruises in Paradise,* and the real world of Frenchtown and family receded.

"You probably don't remember that I didn't come home at all that spring. Made it for Easter, otherwise Ma and Pa would have thrown fits. But not after that. And Easter was early that year. . . ."

I said nothing, looking away from her, studying the faded flowered wallpaper, waiting for her to speak and somehow knowing what she was going to say.

"Anyway, I was pregnant. It was crazy." Her voice had a touch of awe and it was as if she were speaking of someone else, not herself. "One time, the first time and my precious virginity which I had battled to save was gone. Just like that. How I had protected that virginity. Fought with guys, cajoled them, almost took up judo at one time. The battle of the hands of all those guys, at dances, at mixers. But quick cheap feels are one thing. I could cope with them. What I couldn't fight was this gorgeous hunk from Boston College. I've never gone for the handsome, virile, the-world-is-mine type. But I did with this guy. Swept me off my feet. I was on a merry-go-round. He was a basketball star. Six three, I mean, I came up to his nipples . . ."

She looked directly at me: "Does this offend you, Paul? Disillusion you about your little sister? Will you love me less now?"

"Don't be ridiculous," I said.

"But you look so . . . so sad."

"Sad because I didn't realize at the time what was happening to you. It scares me sometimes to think how the family is so close and yet so far apart. All the secrets we have from each other." And my own dark secret.

"Well, the amazing thing, Paul, is that I *kept* it a secret. All these years. Nobody knew. Nobody knows even now. Nobody at home, here in Frenchtown, anyway. Nobody except my two best friends at school. I'd have been lost without them. . . ."

"How about the guy?"

"He never knew. I never told him. By the time I was sure —three months gone—he was off on another chase. And me? I was glad he was gone. Nothing like five or six weeks of vomiting every morning in the john of a dorm to send romance out the window. . . ."

"What did you do?" I asked. And knew the answer.

"I might have been pregnant but that didn't mean I wasn't still a good Catholic girl," she said. "I knew I had to have the baby. Oh, we'd heard stories about backroom abortions in South Boston. Horror stories. But it could be done for a price. I didn't consider abortion for a minute. Take the life of a child and a child growing inside me? Impossible. For me, anyway. . . ."

"So you had the baby," I said.

The fader. Here in this world, all the time, somewhere.

"It wasn't easy," she said, blowing air out of the corner of her mouth, a little girl suddenly. "Arrangements had to be made. My roommate, a girl named Hettie, and my best friend, Annie, at college, I don't know what I'd have done without them. And a nun. Sister Anunciata. A sweetheart. Not the type to preach, to lift eyebrows, to be shocked at anything. But tough. Small, built like a fire hydrant. No nonsense. She took care of everything, even took care of me. . . ."

The endless, unceasing repetitions. The tides of life and living. I thought of Rosanna and her journey to Canada and the baby born dead in a small parish. And now another time and place. And a baby brought into the world. My fader.

"So I went to Maine that summer but not to the camp and not as a counselor. Stayed at the convent of the Sisters of Mercy, a contemplative order. Sent cards home.

"I gained so much weight, it was unbelievable. I don't think I've ever lost all of it. Maybe still carry some of it around, the weight, like penance. The baby was born at the end of August. A week early, thank God. I was back in school in September, after a short visit home. Ironic—Ma and Pa thought I looked terrific. They always measured health by weight, anyway. Fat babies were the thing in those days. And there I was, a fat and healthy daughter."

It was difficult for me not to ask the question that had formed in my mind from the beginning of her story, but I remained silent, waiting, telling myself to be patient.

"So I have to have a baby, Paul. I lost one already. . . ."

"Lost?" Had her baby failed to survive? Died in a room somewhere in a convent in Maine?

"Lost to *me*, Paul. . . ."

"Did the baby live?"

"Yes, although I never saw it. *Him*. Terrible to call him *it*. I've never spoken of this to anyone before, not even to Hettie and Annie. Anyway, things were never the same at Medallion when I returned. Hettie fell in love with a boy from Hah-vahd and we seldom saw each other after that. We took different roommates the next year. Annie was an art major and spent her junior year in Florence."

We were silent for a while.

"So there's the terrible secret." She raised her face to the ceiling, stretched her arms above her head, sighed magnificently. "I feel free," she said. "For the first time in years. I've never told anyone this before, Paul. It's like confession. Like a hundred-dollar session with a therapist. Suddenly, I feel good. Still overweight but lighter, as if I'd dropped fifty pounds." Looking at me now, troubled and tender. "Thanks, Paul. I hated to burden you with this, but thanks."

In the middle of the night, I lay awake, unable to sleep, thinking of that son of hers—how old? twelve, thirteen now? —knowing somehow that he was calling to me, beckoning to me. I heard footsteps whispering across the kitchen linoleum and saw her ample figure in the white flannel nightgown at the doorway. She came to me, knelt by the bed, and I saw in the dim light of the moon spilling into the room, the tear-stained cheeks, heard her sobs. "I gave him up, Paul, gave him away. The only child I'll probably ever have." I drew her to me, placed my arms around her shoulders, absorbed her muffled sobs as she dug her face into my chest.

"My poor lost boy," she murmured inconsolably.

"Maybe he's not lost," I said, my voice tentative.

"What do you mean?"

"Your son, he's out there somewhere in the world." Hated myself for going on but went on anyway: "Do you have any idea where he is? Maybe you could trace him, find him, see him?"

I felt her stiffen as she withdrew from me. "I haven't allowed myself to think that, Paul. I gave up all that when I gave him up."

"How old would he be, now? Twelve? Thirteen?"

"Thirteen, this coming August. August twenty-first. I wonder if he's short or tall. His father was tall, a basketball star. Good-looking, too. I hope he's tall like his father, not short and dumpy like me. . . ."

"You're not dumpy. . . ."

She smiled, wanly. Cheeks still stained with tears.

"Good old Paul." Then, brushing back her hair: "No. I could never look him up. Gave my word. Wouldn't know where to look anyway."

"He was born in Maine. Where did you say in Maine?"

"He was born in the hospital in Bangor. But the convent was on the outskirts of a small town called Ramsey. A spooky old stone building that rambled all over the place. Part of the convent was sealed off for the contemplative nuns. They never left that section of the convent except for daily mass and vespers in the evening. Sister Anunciata and a few others did the chores, cooked and cleaned."

Ramsey. The order of the Sisters of Mercy. Could she provide more information?

"God, they were good to me," Rose continued. "Wonderful Sister Anunciata with her blue eyes brimming over with cheer and hope. She was my buddy. Don't worry, she told me the day I· left, we have found a good home for him."

She rose to her feet, tears gone. "Thank you for the good shoulder to cry on."

She kissed me on the cheek as she encircled me with her arms. At the doorway, she paused in the semidarkness, the white nightgown flowing dimly around her, and waved good night.

Later, lying on the old couch, unable as usual to summon the sweet oblivion of sleep, excited by the knowledge that the fader existed and was perhaps even now waiting for my arrival, I felt the signals of the fade's arrival, the taking away of the breath that meant the pause. I tried to fight it off, girding myself uselessly for the flash of pain because I had never solved the problem of holding off the fade. As I lost the battle again this time, I was grateful at least that Rose was sleeping in the next room and had not seen my body becoming nothing before her eyes.

There is this about the fade:
Its ever-changing nature, the many faces it presents.

At first, the fade was controllable and I held the power to summon or dismiss it. After a while, it began to manifest itself without invitation and without warning.

Once at a dinner party at Andre's Restaurant celebrating Armand's fortieth birthday, I felt the imminence of the fade as we raised our glasses in a champagne toast. I put the glass down immediately and excused myself. I made my way without delay to the men's room, rushing among the tables, absorbing the flash of pain. Inside, I caught a glimpse of myself in the mirror above one of the sinks and saw my body disintegrating. Engulfed by the cold, I rushed into one of the stalls, slammed the door shut and slipped the bolt into place. Even as I did so, I did not see the hand that secured the bolt. Heart beating furiously, flesh damp with perspiration on flesh I could not see, I marveled at my narrow escape. Throughout my life, my biggest fear had been the manifestation of the fade in the presence of others.

I dreaded illness, feared the possibility of a disease or a

condition that would call for surgery or a stay in the hospital during which I would have no control over the fade and no place to hide. My tenement became my hiding place. For three weeks one year, when pain tore at my intestines, I isolated myself at home, curled up in bed, gritting my teeth when the pain accelerated, fearing a burst appendix or internal hemorrhaging. I kept a chart of my rising temperature, 102, 103. Chills accompanying the fever, the pain sometimes fugitive in my stomach, sometimes fierce. Looked at myself in the mirror in the bedroom and said over and over again: I will not go to the hospital, I will not go to the hospital. Finally the symptoms grew less intense, the pain a distant echo of its former self, my temperature receding, returning to normal. Afterward, I remained always on guard, bundled up well in winter to avoid chills, drank fruit juices every day, watched my weight, strolled the streets as exercise, careful not to eat too much or drink too much.

The fade exhibited other variations as the years passed. It began to diminish me. In the aftermath of the experience, I was left limp with exhaustion, without appetite, listless, with no direction or ambition. This lassitude sometimes remained for days, a week or two. I found it impossible to sit at the typewriter and I remained in bed or on the couch for days at a time, trying finally to set down words with pen and paper. This never worked for me. My best writing always comes when I am at the typewriter, at the old L. C. Smith, the keys clattering beneath my fingers, trying to capture in type the swift words leaping from my mind.

The last time my uncle Adelard returned to Frenchtown —the autumn before he died—I was appalled to see the toll that the years and the fade had taken. He had lost weight alarmingly, the flesh of his face taut over his cheekbones, eyes sunk deep into their sockets. "Every time the fade comes," he said, "it takes more out of me. No flash of pain these days, nothing like that. But it's killing me by inches, Paul, eating away at me."

I realized as I stared at my uncle that I was looking at my own future.

During that last visit we didn't walk the streets of French-town but sat on my porch in the cool evenings, wearing bulky sweaters, drinking beer, silent for long intervals but companionable in our silences. I pointed out how ironic it was that the fade had made him wander to far places while it had kept me here in Frenchtown.

"Why have you stayed here, Paul?" he asked.

Wasn't it obvious? "Because here, in Frenchtown, Uncle, I have some control over the unpredictability of the fade. I feel safe here. If the fade happens unexpectedly—and it comes that way more and more—I am never far from home." Yet there was more. "In a way, the fade has made me the writer I am. I always wanted to roam the world, envied you and your wanderings. But I discovered that I didn't have to leave Frenchtown to write. I had dreamed of fame and fortune, crowds cheering me on my arrival in great cities, beautiful women throwing themselves at me. But I learned that the beauty comes from the writing itself and that fame has nothing to do with cheering crowds and being chased by women." I paused then:

"And you, Uncle, did you find out there what I found here?"

"It was different for me, Paul, because the fade itself was different in my case. There were things . . ."

Across the street in St. Jude's Church the choir was rehearsing as it always did on certain nights of the week, faint voices raised in song.

"What things?" I asked, my voice hushed, sensing that at long last he perhaps was ready to speak in some detail about the fade.

"These days, the fade wears me out. In the old days, the fade made me crazy. Took command of my body, my senses. Made me want to do things that were opposite to my nature. Gave me wild desires. Made me feel as if I could do anything. More than that: I *wanted* to do things.

"Sometimes I gave in. Stole, broke into stores, a warehouse once. Always in the dark, at night. Break a window and into the store I went. Or went in earlier and remained there after the owner locked up and left. Saw where he hid the money, unless he took it to a night deposit at the bank. I learned the tricks of hiding money after a while. They put the money in cigar boxes or behind bottles on a shelf, never in a drawer. One night I robbed ten stores, in a town in Ohio. Broke into them in a frenzy, crazy. In my room later, I counted up the money. Almost twelve hundred dollars, in small bills. Counted the money, laughing while the glow of the fade was still with me but the next morning, like a hangover, I looked at the money in panic. And gave it away. Mailed some back to a few of the stores. The sin, Paul, is that I *wanted* that money, wanted to go on a big spree. But could not. Had to give it back. Maybe that is the real curse of the fade. That I couldn't use it for pleasure."

I said nothing, amazed at last that he was speaking so frankly and afraid he might stop if I made a comment.

"And women. It was the same with women, worse, I guess. I have never been a lady's man—awkward with them, shy. I was nothing particular to look at. The fade never helped. It was only good for spying on them, or standing close for a moment before they felt me there. One night, in this rooming house in North Dakota, I wandered the corridors after one o'clock, burning for a woman. The fade made me burn, set me on fire. I found a door unlocked, had seen the woman who occupied the room. Young, beautiful. I slipped into her room, saw her sleeping, in a nightgown, no blankets, a warm night. I stood by her bed. Moved closer. Lifted my hand, gentle, gentle, easy, touched her shoulder. She moaned, stirred in her sleep, her body moving, which made me burn more. I caressed her. Know what I mean, Paul? *Caressed* her. Her eyes flew open, I pulled back my hand. She screamed. I have never heard such a scream, such terror in a voice. Screamed and screamed again. She stared at me. Not at me but at the space where I stood. She *sensed* me there, knew something was there and this made it more horrible for her. Everybody came running, knocks at the door, lights went on, and I was almost trampled, had to fall back against a wall. She did not stop screaming for a long time and then cried, could not be consoled, and I had to remain there, looking at her. I heard her say: Something touched me. *Something* touched me. On my knees, in a corner of the room, I saw what I had become. A something, a monster. This is what the fade made me. A monster."

But I already knew that.

And knew that I, too, was a monster.

During all those years we shared the fade, during all of my uncle's comings and goings in my life, we spoke only once of my uncle Vincent, who was his brother, and my brother Bernard, who was his nephew. The conversation took place during the time of Bernard's wake.

My uncle had appeared without advance notice, as usual, as if emerging from the fade, on the steps of my grandfather's house, the second evening of Bernard's wake. In those days, the wakes went on for three days and three nights, around the clock, at the home of the deceased, the house never empty or silent, coffee always bubbling on the stove, the smell of food mingling with the sweet-sick scent of flowers. Bernard's coffin was placed in the parlor, all the curtains drawn. A bouquet of white carnations hung by the front door announcing the death in our family.

I could not bear to look at Bernard in the coffin, his beauty waxen now and unreal, his First Communion rosary in his pale clasped hands. Yet I was drawn again and again to his coffin, knelt to pray even though the words were empty and meaningless.

My mother turned out to be the strong one in the family, bustling about the rooms, presiding at the stove, greeting my aunts and the neighborhood women who brought steaming dishes and platters of sandwiches and pastries into the house. My father was mute with grief, standing wordlessly near the coffin for long periods, his eyes like shattered marbles.

My brother and sisters went through the terrible rituals of bereavement, eyes downcast, speaking in monosyllables, stunned with the sudden fact of death in the midst of our days and evenings. While all this time within me was the flowering knowledge that told me I was to blame for Bernard's death.

Let me now put into words what I have not been able to do during the long, aching passage of the years.

I killed Rudolphe Toubert.

Held the knife that entered his body. And stabbed him again and again.

The scene is as vivid in my mind at this moment as it was a lifetime ago.

* * *

I stood with the knife in my hand and Rudolphe Toubert
saw it.

But what did he really see?

A knife suspended in the air. A miracle, magic, and, of
course, utterly impossible.

Forgetting that I was in the fade, I had picked up the knife
from the counter and turned to face him. Found him facing
me, and immediately realized my mistake. My uncle Adelard
had warned me that once I was in the fade, any object that I
touched or picked up or moved would give the game away,
would appear to be moving by itself.

I pondered my next move. I knew that it was necessary for
me to inflict injury on him as revenge for what he did to my
father and the workers, to my aunt Rosanna, to Bernard and
hundreds of Frenchtown boys, myself included. Did I want
to kill him? Can I truly answer that after all these years?
Maybe there was murder in my heart, but is the wish father
to the act?

At any rate, he saw the knife.

I looked at it, too, floating in the air, above the counter,
held in my right hand but the hand unseen.

Rudolphe Toubert stared. More than stared. His eyes almost popped out of his head. At the same time, he began to
rise from the chair, his two hands flat on the desk, pushing
himself up, his eyes riveted to the knife.

Then he looked away, shook his head vigorously, eyes on
the door, leaning against the desk. He raised one hand and
rubbed his eyes and I knew it was imperative that I move
quickly, to hide the knife so that when he looked back it
would be gone and he would consign what he had seen a
moment before to a fancy of light or his own mind playing
tricks on him.

But I was not quick enough.

He peeked at me, his hands covering his face but one eye visible between two spread fingers, and the eye pinned itself on that knife.

"Jesus," he said, his mouth still gaping. He came around to the front of the desk, as if hypnotized by the knife.

I laughed.

Not exactly a laugh but a giggle, a giggle of delight and triumph, enjoying not only the sight of Rudolphe Toubert sweating with fear but knowing also that my laugh, my chuckle, would hurl him into further horrors.

His eyes left the knife and lifted to the source of that chuckle and he began to babble incoherently, his body twitching, his mouth working to bring forth sounds—a scream for help, perhaps, or for sanity—and then his babbling ceased. He could not speak. He stood mute and paralyzed.

That was when he did the unexpected, catching me off guard and unaware. As if propelled by a catapult, he shot across the floor, legs springing him forward, hands extended, eyes wild and frenzied. Caught by surprise, I stood rooted to the spot, hands extended, the knife still pointing toward him as he came. He reached out as if to bat the knife away but ran into it and into me at the same time, knocking me backward. I held on to the knife and saw it enter his chest, spilling blood immediately on the striped shirt. He looked down, staring in disbelief, placed his hand on his chest and watched his hand being covered with blood. Like my father an hour before.

Raising his head, he let out a scream. "No . . ." The word echoing stridently in the garage.

He began to fall. As he fell he reached out, and his hands brushed my legs, clutching for support, and I pulled away.

As I did so, I stabbed at him with the knife, sinking the blade into his back as he fell to his knees. Stabbed him again and again. For my father, for the strikers, for Bernard, for Rosanna. For me.

He sank to the floor in a puddle of blood.

The story of Rudolphe Toubert's murder filled the pages of the *Monument Times* for three days. Pictures of the office where his body was found, an inset showing his face, his bow tie, his thin moustache.

On the second day, there was a blurred photo of Herve Boisseneau, evidently taken by a box camera, as he stood on the steps of the three-decker on Seventh Street.

The headline over his picture said:

MURDER SUSPECT SOUGHT

In smaller print below:

Weapon Missing

The murder took the spotlight away from the settlement of the strike, although the *Times* ran a story at the bottom of page one reporting that "management and employees have reached an agreement on disputes that had occasioned a near five-month walkout that halted operations at the shop."

Armand threw the paper down on the kitchen table, snorting: "They can't come right out and say the shop lost and the workers won."

My father explained: "It's not as simple as that, Armand. We've got a long way to go. Some experts are coming from Washington to arrange for an election. The workers have to vote for a union if they want one. Maybe, they'll vote against it. . . ."

Fire in Armand's eyes as he answered: "Never in a million years, Dad. Uncle Victor says—"

"I know, Armand, I know," my father said, and Armand saw that he had been joking. My father had not joked for a long time. "Listen, Armand, I've been thinking it over. If you want to quit school and work in the shop, okay. Go ahead. The times are different now. Maybe we need young guys like you to see that things will change."

Armand whooped with delight, leaping from his chair, clasping his hands above his head, like Joe Louis being crowned champion of the world. I saw a shadow cross my father's face and vowed that I would graduate from high school and bring home a diploma to hang on the wall in the parlor.

The church.

Once again, I knelt in a pew in a shadowed area, watching the penitents come and go. Once again, I felt a need to confess, to unburden myself, to whisper to the priest the sin I had committed. Murdered, broken the fifth commandment. My earlier sins seemed paltry now—touching my aunt's breast reduced to a venial sin by comparison. If I had found it difficult to confess small sins, how could I utter words to describe an act of murder? I shuddered, anticipating the reaction of the priest. I had been taught in school that the seal of the confessional could not be violated, that the priest must listen in silence and remain silent. Kneeling there, as candle flame leapt against the dim walls, I knew that my act went beyond whispering words in the ear of a priest. I had offended God. Who had made the world and made me.

Forgive me, dear Jesus.

And waited for a sign.

The penitents came and went, the candles flickered, the sun slanted through the window that depicted the end of the world.

No sign—should I have expected one?

After a while, I left the church.

A headline in the *Times*:

LEADS DWINDLING

IN MURDER CASE;

SEARCH FRUITLESS

> The search for Herve Boisseneau and the knife allegedly used in the three-week-old murder of Rudolphe Toubert has reached a virtual dead end, police announced today . . .

I put down the newspaper after reading the story, feeling neither relief nor dread.

I told myself: If Herve Boisseneau is ever found, I will give myself up.

I thought of Sidney Carton in *A Tale of Two Cities* we were studying at Silas B. "It is a far, far better thing that I do, than I have ever done."

But I did not feel noble like Sidney Carton.

Did not feel anything at all.

I cut the newspaper story out of the *Times* with my mother's scissors and placed it carefully folded with the poems and stories I kept on the closet shelf along with my uncle's blue bandanna.

* * *

A house in which no one sleeps is a haunted house. You wake up in the middle of the night and hear muffled voices and soft footsteps and even if you strain your ears and hear nothing, you know that the house is not still, people are in the rooms, standing watch.

The men always kept the all-night vigil at wakes, letting the women sleep. The women carried most of the burden of the wake, providing food and drink and comforts hour after hour, tending to the children and keeping the household going. Certain things never stop even with death. Washing and ironing and preparing the meals, soothing an unhappy child, making beds. When the night hours came, the women went home, except for my aunt Olivine, who remained behind to help my mother until they both collapsed in bed in exhaustion. My aunt Rosanna was not present at the wake. It had been impossible to notify her of Bernard's death. No one knew her address. She had not sent any postcards or letters since her departure a few months before.

"She was going to open a beauty shop in Montreal," I told my father when he reported that no one knew how to get in touch with her.

My father's lips twisted in contempt. "Rosanna run a business? What a pipe dream. She's probably waiting on tables somewhere."

In my bed, as I listened to the vague comings and goings of the all-night vigil, the voices gave me no rest.

You killed him.

A heart attack. Bernard died of a heart attack.

Eight-year-olds don't have heart attacks.

It's rare. But it happens. Dr. Goldstein said so.

Dr. Goldstein can be wrong. Dr. Goldstein is not God.

Bernard was always delicate.

Not delicate enough to die.

Please, leave me alone.

Why should you be left alone when you are to blame?

The argument went on during the small, still hours of the night, the voice inside me with its accusations, and I recoiled in horror because the voice was me: I was the voice.

During the day, I went through the motions of mourning, knelt before the coffin, murmuring prayers, avoiding after a while looking at Bernard as he lay stiff and unmoving. By the evening of the second day, I made myself look at him. His flesh had begun to alter, no longer pale now but darkening. His features also seemed to grow thicker, lips, nostrils. He was changing before our eyes but nobody said anything, nobody made comment. Perhaps they did not notice. Perhaps Bernard was changing only for me. I fled the room, the cloying flowers, the suffocating closeness.

My uncle Adelard found me in the shed.

He sat himself down on an old kitchen chair that my father had thrown out because the legs were wobbly. He looked at me with such sadness—the old sadness I knew so well—that my anger deserted me, and left me empty.

I had schemed in the first few hours to approach my uncle and confess what had happened. He would have the answers for me. But now I hesitated.

"When Uncle Vincent died . . ." I began.

"Yes . . . I know how you feel, Paul. He was my brother, the way Bernard is yours . . ."

"In the cemetery that day," I said, gathering my nerve, "you said that Vincent died because of you . . ." I almost added: because of the fade. But did not.

"I blamed myself for a long time, Paul," he said. "Still do, maybe. But learned to live with it . . ."

"Why did you blame yourself?"

"Because I did nothing to help him. He was in a lot of pain but kept it to himself. He told only me. Pledged me to secrecy. In the night, he'd wake up and I'd hold him. Don't tell Papa, he'd say. And I didn't. I should have told our papa. I used the fade to help him. . . ."

"How did the fade help?"

"I used the fade to slip into Lakier's. Found medicine there. I had heard that a medicine called paregoric had dope in it. To ease pain. Found the paregoric and brought it to him. He slept.

"The thing is, Paul, I did not think he was sick enough to die. I thought he was only sick and in pain and wanted me to help him. Wanted me to help him keep his condition a secret from everyone else. If that is what made him happy, then I was glad to do it. I used the fade to bring him toys. Went out at night and broke into the stores, brought him things. Did all I could. Loved him, kept his secrets, used the fade to help his pain. But he died anyway. In fact, he might have lived if I had not interfered. Or if I had told my parents what he was going through." Tears gathered in his eyes. "But I did not expect him to die."

I touched his arm in sympathy and knew that I could not confide in him after all. The circumstances of Vincent's death were different from Bernard's. My uncle Adelard had not killed anyone. Vincent's death was not an act of revenge.

I left him and knelt before the coffin, not praying, looking at the poor frail thing that had been my brother.

I'm sorry, Bernard, I'm sorry.

But knew that words were not enough.

Bernard was buried on a wind-howling morning, the cold biting at our cheeks as we stood under a faded green canopy that was no protection at all. We huddled together, shivering and shuddering, looking at the gray metal coffin held by straps above the hole beneath it. I averted my eyes and saw Mr. LeFarge at a distance, standing near the fence, leaning stolidly on his shovel, as if this were a summer afternoon.

The words of Father Belander were tossed on the air and blown away by the wind, French and Latin phrases dissipating on the air. Booming thunderclaps accompanied the wind, out of season, as if heaven itself protested Bernard's death and burial. Armand and I clung together, arms around each other, sniffing, tears frozen on our cheeks.

Snow began to fall, whirling madly as the procession made its way home in borrowed cars and a black limousine supplied by Tessier's Funeral Home. The car I rode in belonged to Mr. Lakier and it had a plush interior, everything maroon, and a smell peculiar to my senses: the smell of newness.

"A blizzard," someone yelled as we hurried out of the cars and up the steps to our tenement.

Everyone settled in the kitchen and parlor, my mother and aunts bustling about preparing food and the men in small groups, drinking whiskey in quick gulps.

After a while, I slipped into the bedroom and closed the door softly behind me, did not look at the bed where Bernard had slept between Armand and me. I went to the window. The panes were white with frost. I tried to wipe the frost away with my sleeve but failed to clear even a small spot.

I tried to cry but could not.

It came to me that hell would not be fire and smoke after all but arctic, everything white and frigid. Hell would be not anger but indifference.

With numbed fingers I unfastened the latch and raised the window, and was immediately buffeted by the swirling wind and snow. The sting of the cold stabbed my eyes, seared my cheeks.

Thinking of Bernard sealed in the coffin, buried in the earth, still and silent until he became dust—my little brother, dust—I placed my hands on the windowsill, my face remaining exposed to the cold and the snow and the wind.

"Bastard," I yelled, but did not know whom I was calling a bastard.

"I will never fade again," I vowed, not knowing whether I spoke aloud or not.

"The hell with the fade," I cried, repudiating this thing that had entered my life like something evil. "I make this promise. I will never use the fade again. Kill me if I do. . . ."

I waited. For what? I did not know. But waited all the same.

A small noise reached my ears. Barely a noise, a rattle of metal hitting wood. Looking down, I saw the old tin can that Pete Lagniard and I used to send messages up and down to each other from the first floor to the second.

I picked it up, remembering the hot, lush summertime when Pete and I had ghosted through the night on our way to Moccasin Pond. How innocent I had been. As I tilted the can a bit of snow spilled out, and I saw something inside, a piece of paper, flattened and folded. My fingers were so numbed that it was difficult to pull the paper out. I unfolded it eagerly because it was precious suddenly, a souvenir of the summer, an old message left by Pete before the strike and the violence and all the bad things that had happened. Before the fade.

I opened the folded note and saw the scrawled words, twisting like tiny snakes on the paper.

Hello, Paul.
The handwriting was unmistakably Bernard's.

Pete and I had often been discouraged in our use of the pulley system for communication because our brothers and sisters, aware of what we were doing—it was hard to keep the system a secret—played tricks on us. We found everything from dead mice to disgusting pieces of garbage in the can. I knew that Armand had been the one to leave the mice, while Pete swore that his brother, Herbie, had donated the garbage. We stopped using the system for a while, resuming it after a few weeks went by. My sisters used to leave notes in the can reminding me to take out the rubbish or that it was my turn to wipe the dishes, a chore I hated. Bernard left me a note occasionally, usually a crazy riddle or just a greeting. He never signed them but I always recognized his handwriting.

I stared at the note, the paper brittle, the penciled lines stark and distinct on the whiteness of the paper.

Hello, Paul.

As if he had spoken to me.

I knew that I would never use the fade again, no matter how long I lived. I did not want others to die because of me.

On Sunday, I went to mass with my mother and father. The time for communion arrived. I joined them in the aisle, knelt at the communion rail, my hands folded under the white linen cloth. Raised my head to the priest, opened my mouth, allowed the wafer to be placed on my tongue. Trudged back to my seat, the wafer melting on my tongue. I was careful not to let it touch my teeth. I swallowed the wafer, telling myself: Think of it as a wafer, not communion, not the Body of Christ.

Kneeling, I waited for thunder and lightning, for the walls of the church to crumble, the pillars to tumble against each other. But nothing happened.

That was the worst thing of all.

The nothingness. The emptiness that never would be filled in all the years to come.

Twenty-five years later, I lay in my bed in the third-floor tenement across from St. Jude's Church, in the fade, in the middle of the night, my sister sleeping nearby in the bedroom, innocent of my condition.

I had never broken the vow I had made the day Bernard was buried and refused to consider what nightmares would be unleashed if I invited the fade. The fade had invited itself, however, depleting me, coming again and again, and I was helpless to prevent its assault.

In the safety of the darkness I endured the fade one more time, putting off the moment when I would force it away, postponing for a little while whatever symptoms would appear—the pause, the pain, the cold.

That night, however, there was almost bliss in the way the fade possessed me. I thought of that other fader out there, that unknown nephew who would carry the fade to another generation, whom I had been helpless to assist until tonight.

Rose had given me the clues I needed.

I would find him.

Warn him, protect him.

I would try to do for that poor fader what my uncle Adelard had never been able to do for me.

OZZIE

The nuns took him in, fed him, nursed his colds and fevers, treated his wounds and gave him their tender loving care. Thank Christ for the nuns, although he hated the convent itself. Hated the rest of the world too. Hated himself as well, especially the parts of himself he could do nothing about, the headaches and the sniveling. Never could get rid of it, the running nose, ever since the Pa who was not his Pa had knocked him on the nose and sent him reeling across the room. Then, seeing the blood and the warped bone, hit him again and again in the same spot. Ever since, Ozzie's nose had run incessantly and fierce pains sometimes raged in his head above his eyes and shot down to his cheekbones.

"Stop the sniveling," commanded his Pa who was not his Pa, but a fake and a fraud, then hit him again. "And stop the crying." When he was a little kid, he would cry when the old fraud struck him and the crying sent the fraud into a frenzy and he would hit Ozzie again, yelling at him to *stop the crying, damn you.* He tried to explain that he was crying *because* he was being hit and it was impossible to stop unless the hitting stopped but he could not get the words out because the blows were relentless. Finally, after a long while, he learned to stop crying. Or did something dry up inside him, in the place where tears formed? He could not stop the sniveling, but, by Christ, he could stop the crying. And that's what he did. He did not cry anymore, no matter what happened.

His mother was the reason he went to live with the nuns. Poor Ma, that he loved so much. He remembered her as the smell of bottles. The smell, really, that came *out* of the bottles, which he learned later was the booze. Gulping the booze behind the door, out of sight, when she thought nobody was looking. It took him a long time to realize she was hiding the sips and the gulps, until finally she hid them no longer and drank the stuff down hungrily like it was food and she was starving. And when the fraud came home, he would hit her for the drinking and hide the bottles and later break them, smashing them into the sink and smashing her too.

At night, Ozzie tried to block his ears against the noises he heard in the bedroom. The strange noise of the bedsprings, yes, but more than that, the cries of his Ma and sometimes the moaning and then her muffled screams and the grunting of the old man like a wild animal. Ozzie could not bear to hear the sounds and he would block his ears and dig himself deep into the bed and the blankets.

Finally, one night, her cheek purple with bruises and her jaw scarlet and swollen, she crawled to Ozzie's bed and whispered frantically to him that she had to leave, kissing him good-bye and hugging him and telling him that she would come and get him soon but she never did. "Try to stay out of his way," she said. She went to live in that terrible house on Bowker Street where the whores lived, although she was never a whore. And she died before she could come and rescue him. When the old fraud discovered she was gone, he gave Ozzie one of the worst beatings of all, and then the old faker tore the house apart, smashed chairs against the wall and slammed dishes to the floor, before he finally fell asleep in a heap on the kitchen floor, where Ozzie found him in the morning.

Your Pa is poor and your Ma is a whore.

That was the refrain he heard in school after his Ma went to live on Bowker Street. That's why he hated the kids, especially Bull Zimmer, who chased him every day and caught him sometimes and rubbed Ozzie's nose in the dirt or squashed it on the sidewalk while the other kids laughed. By this time he had learned something else besides not crying. He had learned to endure. *Endure,* a word from school. Looked it up. So he endured. Did not cry. Suffered the blows. Refused the help of Sister Anunciata, angry at her that time she chased Bull Zimmer away after Bull Zimmer had followed him to the convent throwing rocks and hitting Ozzie on the back of the head with one.

Later in the convent, Sister Anunciata bathed his wound, and ran a cool hand across his brow. She smelled of old medicine on the shelf too long. She was old herself, brown spots on the backs of her hands, face wrinkled like a crumpled paper bag. That's all he ever saw of her, the face and the hands, the rest of her enclosed in the black and white. He felt her hand cool on his forehead and almost, almost, yielded to it, almost but not quite, holding back.

"Summer's coming, Ozzie," she whispered. "And you won't have to go to school for a while. You can work here in the convent."

School was the old brick building downtown where his teacher, Miss Ball, in the eighth grade, was as hard as her name and gave him the freeze, pretended he wasn't there,

never called on him to recite, which was as bad in its way as
Bull Zimmer hitting him after classes were done. When she
looked him straight in the eye one time, he saw something
worse than hate. Saw nothing in her eyes. As if he did not
exist, did not matter.

"Poor Ozzie," Sister Anunciata said.

And he pulled away from her but in a gentle way, because
she was his only friend. But he still did not want her pity,
wanted nobody's pity.

"But I don't pity you, poor Ozzie," she said. "Pity is placing myself above you."

"What is it then?" he said, puzzled.

"Compassion," Sister Anunciata said. "Compassion, boy.
And love. What Our Lord feels for us all, although I am not
setting myself up as the Lord."

Always so modest, the nuns, so proper, whispering in the
convent, so fearful of being more than they seemed.

"Mea culpa," Sister Anunciata said, kneeling by his bed.
"Mea culpa . . ."

He looked at her suspiciously, did not trust anyone speaking in another language. "What's that mean?" he asked, eyes
narrow, fearing she was playing a trick on him.

"Nothing for you to concern yourself about," she said.

But the words lingered in his ears.

"Let us pray together," she said.

He prayed for his Ma, nobody else, not even himself.

Poor Ma, who was not really his Ma, but loved him and he
loved her. He knew that he was adopted, that the Ma of his
blood had given him away. Often, when he was little, Ozzie
got confused by them all. His real Ma and Pa, the blood ones,
were gone forever, of course. And good riddance. He would
never know their names or where they came from or where
they went to. Which was fine and dandy with him. He hated

them both, as much as you could hate anyone you'd never known. They had abandoned him, left him behind. Gave him away, for Christ's sake. What kind of people gave their baby away?

He was lucky the nuns found the Ma who brought him up even if her blood was different from his. She was small and sweet and told him stories and sang him songs in her soft lilt of a voice, songs about Ireland across the sea and green fields and the little people and the house where she was born. She crooned to him about the Pa that he could not remember, the one she had loved, and how happy they were when they took Ozzie home for the first time. That was his second Pa, not the fake and fraud and not the Pa of his blood, whoever *he* was. This second Pa, the one his Ma loved, was tall and handsome and could make miracles on paper, she said. He could draw a few lines and, lo, there would be a rabbit or a fawn or one of the little people. He was too good to go on living, she said. Too beautiful for this world. He had laughter on his lips and Christmas in his eyes. And it was Christmas when he died. People should not die at Christmastime but his good Pa did, a freak accident, they said, killed by falling wires in the fierce winter storm as he came home with presents for Ozzie in his arms. All night long they cried, Ozzie and his Ma, until Ozzie fell asleep as cold dawn touched the windows.

His Ma took sick after the good Pa died. She was frail to begin with, a whisper of a girl, hardly a woman at all. And that was when old man Slater came along. Not really old, maybe, but not young anymore. A woodworker when he worked, the smell of sawdust surrounding him, and it seemed he even had sawdust in his eyes, his pupils dark with specks in them like sawdust. He gave Ozzie his last name and made it legal and proper, Oscar Slater. Your name is Slater and be proud of it, the new Pa told him. And Ozzie tried to be proud until this Pa began to give him slappings and cuffs behind the ears and finally found his nose. What happened to turn the new Pa into a monster like that? Ozzie didn't know and would never find out. In fact, he could not, after a while, remember when this fraud of a Pa was *not* a monster, beating up on him and his Ma.

And then she died. In that house on Bowker Street.

She lay white and brief in the coffin and Ozzie knelt there in the night, the candles burning low, and he made an attempt to cry, wanted to cry, *needed* to cry for his mother, to weep for the terrible thing her life had been and he could not, could not cry. And hated the fraud of a Pa even more now, hated him worse than ever because the fraud had taken away his ability to cry, had forced him to stop crying and now he could not summon tears for his Ma, could not honor her with his tears. Sniveling instead, his nose leaking as he leaned his aching head against the coffin, he vowed his revenge.

I will kill you someday, you fraud and fake, Ozzie vowed, would kill him not only for the blows to the nose and the other beatings but most of all for what he did to Ma, for driving her finally out of the house to the terrible tenement on Bowker Street, the house the kids hooted at and pointed fingers at and threw stones against. *Your Pa is poor and your Ma is a whore.* Yes, he would kill the others too. One by one. Starting with the Bull and Miss Ball. Then, Dennis O'Shea with his orange hair and sharp tongue who made up the songs and chants. Clever Dennis O'Shea, who loved to trip kids walking up the aisle and then putting on his innocent face. The girls were no better. Fiona Finley, who walked in clouds of perfume, in her fancy dresses and shoes with heels and nylon stockings and who wrinkled her nose when he

came near her as if she smelled something bad. And Alice
Robillard, who invited everybody in the class to her birthday
party, everybody except Ozzie, that is.

Living in the convent spared him the experience of the
town. Where he always had to avoid people's eyes, duck
down alleys, take shortcuts. He was ugly, of course, and
mean. Kicked cats, chased dogs before they chased him.
Swore at people who saw him as the son of a brute, with a
terrible nose and a mother they said was a whore when she
wasn't. He got back at them by spitting at them, stealing
from them, sneaking stuff out of stores. After a while they
wouldn't let him go into the stores unless he showed them
his money first. Kelcey's Grocery and Dempsey's Drug Store
and the five-and-ten banished him from their places forever.
Before that, Kelcey hired him to sweep up and stock the
shelves but always yelling at him to stop his sniveling. "It's
not appetizing to the customers," Kelcey said. That did it.
I'll show you appetizing, he thought as he sneaked nine Baby
Ruths, his favorite candy bar, into his jacket. Which was a
foolish thing to do, of course, but the only way he could take
his revenge at the moment, stealing from Kelcey and taking
something that was good to eat. But the Baby Ruths bulged
in his jacket and Kelcey grabbed him by the collar and the
candy bars spilled to the floor in front of the customers—
Calafano the barber and Mrs. Spritzer with her stuck-up airs
because her husband was a selectman—and he stood there in
his humiliation, caught and sniveling. Vowing revenge.

His only friend in town was old man Pinder, who drank
too much and reeled down the sidewalk, bumping into
things and falling down. Old man Pinder was the oldest person he knew. He kept busy doing odd jobs for the store owners, taking out the rubbish, sweeping sidewalks, sleeping

sometimes in the alley in the back of the five-and-ten if he was too drunk or weary to make it home.

Home was the cellar of the rooming house where the whores lived, where his mother lived after she left the tenement, although she wasn't a whore. "Your mother, lad, was a real lady," the old man told him one time. "She drank like a fish but she was a lady through and through." Sometimes, late at night, before he went to live with the nuns in the convent and didn't want to risk going home and meeting the wrath of the fake and the fraud who was not his Pa, he would sleep next to old man Pinder in the alley, back to back, drawing a bit of warmth from him. The old man always wore several sweaters and jackets and at least two overcoats and he would drape one of the coats around Ozzie's shoulders and they would sleep cozy in the chill of the night until they awakened at dawn as Reap, the cop, kicked their feet while stray dogs barked at them. He and the old man would struggle up and away from the alley, all aches and shivers.

One night when he stole into town from the convent, he saw the old man, bleary-eyed from drink, leaning against a parking meter. "You're better off out there with the nuns," the old man said, shaking with the drink and the cold, smelling terrible.

So he settled in the ways of the convent, sleeping on the cot in the small room no bigger than a closet off the kitchen. The nuns fed him their food from the table, plain stuff, tasteless, but he swallowed it to fill the emptiness in his stomach. He performed chores for them, scrubbed floors and walls. Sister Anunciata sang songs as she did her own chores and he liked the sound of her voice, although it wavered and cracked sometimes, making him chuckle. No one beat him up in the convent. He felt safe here away from school.

After his Ma died, the kids did not sing about her anymore but started in on his nose. His curse of a nose. His nose with the pimples and the broken veins under the skin so that it looked like a battered and bruised strawberry. When the unholy choir at school stopped chanting about his mother, they started on the nose. *Faucet nose, faucet nose, always leaking like a hose.* Dennis O'Shea and more of his clever words. But by that time he was expert at pretending he did not hear the voices. And the Bull had finally gotten tired of beating him up and let him alone, did not chase him anymore. He bided his time. Waiting.

Waiting for what?

He did not know.

But he knew that he was waiting for *something* to happen. Something incredible. Lying in his cot at night, he felt it in his bones, in his soul if he had a soul which Sister Anunciata insisted he had although he doubted it. Anyways, he knew deep inside of him that something was coming, something was about to happen.

Patient, marking time, enduring, he made up his lists. Just before falling to sleep at night, he made lists of those who would be the targets of his revenge when whatever he was waiting for came. That vicious fraud of a Pa was at the top of his list and then Bull Zimmer and the other kids at school, Dennis O'Shea and Alice Robillard. And something special for Miss Ball, who would finally know that he existed, all right. He entertained himself with images of blood and broken bones and screams of agony as he closed his eyes.

He smiled as he drifted off to sleep, waiting for that incredible thing to happen.

And, finally, it did.

He killed the old fraud first, of course, hammering the head of the Pa who was not his Pa and would certainly never be after that hammering was done with. Made like he was driving a spike home, hitting him square in the middle of the forehead again and again.

He killed the old fraud as he lay sleeping in the tenement where the three of them, his Ma and the fake who called himself his pa, had lived all those years. He'd heard that the fraud was back in town, back from where he didn't know and didn't care. First time the faker had shown his face in town since Ma had died. The return of the fraud and the faker had coincided with the incredible thing that had happened. Like an omen. What he had been waiting for all that time.

He had no name for it, the incredible thing. How could you name a thing like that? But then it did not require a name. It would require a name only if you spoke of it aloud. And he would never do that. Would never speak to anyone about it. How could he possibly speak about it?

*   *   *

It.

How it came.

Finally, after all his waiting.

He had awakened in the night, which was unusual because he always slept clear through until morning, without dreams, sleep being merely a blank period in his life, and he always woke up quickly at first light of day. That night, however, he had bolted from sleep in the middle of the night, in darkness.

His body felt strange, funny, light, chilled, a different kind of cold, an inside cold, as if a block of ice had melted in his stomach and was spreading through his body. He had a dim memory of pain quickly come and gone.

He snapped on the small lamp next to his bed.

And saw what he did not see.

He knew his arm had reached out to snap on the light. He also knew that his fingers had gripped the switch to turn it on. But as the light filled the room, making his eyes blink, he did not see his arm or his hand or his fingers. Crazy. He knew they were there, could *feel* them there, wiggled them, snapped two of them together and heard the sound of the snap. But he could not see his fingers.

He closed his eyes, lay back, reached out and turned off the light, listening to the small click of the switch. Lay in the dark, enduring the nightmare as he had endured so many things. He heard once that the real nightmare was the kind where you dreamed you were awake in your bed, in your room, lights on, believing it was real. And that's when the monsters came through the windows or the door.

Shivering, he reached out again and snapped on the light. Held his hand up but couldn't see his hand. Could see the room, the floor, the windows and the white curtain, the chair against the wall, but could not see himself. Threw back the covers with the hand he could not see, saw that the rest of him was not there either. His old faded pajamas that the nuns made him wear were gone too.

Disappeared.

Waved his arms and legs, thrashed around in the bed, saw the way the thin mattress sagged under his weight. Swung his legs over the side of the cot and sat up. At least, he *figured* he was sitting up, could only feel his feet kissing the cold boards of the floor. Shivered again with the cold but didn't mind the cold, really.

Panic filled him then. How do I get my body back? Was he doomed to stay this way forever?

Suddenly, he pressed forward, as if in answer to a force pulling him that way, like he was leaning against an invisible wall, the wall unseen, as his body was unseen. A sudden surge and the cold left him in a whoosh, his breath taken away, a sweep of pain and then he was back again, pain gone as fast as it came, his body, himself, visible again, hands and arms back, legs back, pajamas back, pajamas moist and clinging. He padded across the cold floor and looked in the mirror, saw that terrible strawberry of a nose, the small eyes, the pointed chin. He was here, all right. Never thought he would be glad to see that face again.

He waited in the room for a minute, now that the blood had stopped and the Pa who would never again be his Pa was still, more than still, had become a thing rather than a man. He waited, listened, straining his ears, heard nothing in the night. Looked at the bloody hammer dancing in the air, held by his gone right hand, the rest of him gone too.

"For you, Ma," he whispered, wiping the hammer with

the bedsheet. Then he tossed the hammer on the bed next to the legs of the thing who had been such a fraud and a fake.

The first one.

Smiled in the dark, smiled a smile no one could see, would never see. A smile filled with—what? Sweetness. More than that. Triumph, victory. It was the first time in his life as he swung the hammer and felt bone give under the blow, the first time he had known the power of revenge, the sweetness of giving back.

He wanted to linger here a while longer but dared not. He had been gone from the convent for almost an hour and must return again unseen, must slip through the corridors and the kitchen without making a noise, without making a sound because there was always someone awake there, all hours, and Sister Anunciata sometimes looked in on him.

"Good-bye, you bastard of a Pa that was never my Pa," he said, looking at the bed again, letting the chuckle come out of him.

And then made off into the night.

As he cruised through the town, still gone, still disappeared, he laughed as he saw the damage.

Felt pride in the damage he saw. *Nice, nice.*

His creation, all of it.

They had boarded up the window of Kelcey's Grocery and he was waiting for Kelcey to replace it and then he would break it again as he had a week ago. That same night, he had also savaged the tires of three cars parked on Main Street, slashing with a butcher knife he had taken from the convent kitchen, getting a laugh out of that, a nun's knife doing damage that way. That first trip into town had been an experiment, to see what it was like to visit the place when he couldn't be seen.

The real test had been going to town in broad daylight
when people were up and about, stores open, the cop Reap
on the beat. By then he had practiced disappearing and coming back in the room at the convent. He had learned that
practice *does* make perfect. He had made himself come and
go, go and come, enduring that moment with no breath at
all, then the brief stab of pain until he could do it all as easy
as snapping his fingers. He never minded the cold. He had
set off for downtown one day and made himself gone, unseen
in the old alley. Then he ambled into Main Street, dodging
between the people, heading for Kelcey's. The window still
boarded up. Entered the store and walked down the aisles.
Old Kelcey at the cash register, looking bossy as ever. He
knocked over a display of canned corn chowder that had
been all nice and neat in a pyramid the way Kelcey liked
things done. Kelcey heard the racket and came running, put
on the brakes when he saw the cans capsized and tumbling
all over the floor. And while Kelcey was on his knees picking
up the cans, Ozzie tipped over the island holding all the
boxed cakes and other pastries in the next aisle. Bang, down
they went, and he heard Kelcey call out: "What the
hell . . ." Ozzie had to press his lips together to contain the
laugh, the chuckle that threatened to escape. As Kelcey
charged over to the spot where the island lay upended, surrounded by the spilled pastries, old John Stanton came in the
door. He found a bewildered Kelcey standing there with
hands on hips, looking at the damage, his face all puzzled.
And there was Ozzie, not five feet away.

"What's going on, Kelcey?" Mr. Stanton asked. He was a
retired fireman. Ozzie did not hate him as he hated other
people. When Ozzie was just a tot, Mr. Stanton had let him
sit on the seat of the big hook-and-ladder, lifted him high and
put him there and told him to ring the big silver bell. Ozzie

rang it, pulling the cord, he was maybe six or seven years old at the time. Mr. Stanton wore red suspenders over his blue shirt that day in the fire station and Ozzie's dream was to grow up and become a fireman like Mr. Stanton and wear red suspenders. Fat chance of that, though. As Mr. Stanton joined Kelcey looking at the boxes strewn all over the floor, Ozzie felt a rage gathering in him. Why a rage? He was having such a good time wrecking Kelcey's store a minute ago, having to suppress a chuckle. And now the rage was stirring in him, like a storm, and the rage was directed at Mr. Stanton. *Hit him.* But Mr. Stanton was a nice old guy, who had once treated Ozzie with kindness. *Yes, but.* . . .

Next thing Ozzie knew, he was approaching Mr. Stanton and the old fireman looked up at the same moment, looked directly at Ozzie as if he could actually see him but couldn't, of course, his eyes opening up wide and his mouth opening too. And that's when Ozzie hit him. Didn't want to hit him, really, had no desire to hit him at all but struck him all the same. A short, swift blow to the back of the neck, at the base of the old fireman's skull, using his hand like an ax. And the old fireman bellowed with pain, fell forward and dropped to his knees among the topsy-turvy pastry boxes, one hand flattened on a box and sinking into a cake with pink frosting.

"What's the matter, John?" Kelcey asked, bending over the old fireman while Mr. Stanton moaned and groaned, on all fours now.

Ozzie's stomach churned. Vomit gathered in his stomach and rose to his throat. His veins grew hot, boiling as the blood shot through his body. Gotta get out of here, he thought. It was not fun anymore. He made for the door, left the men there in their befuddlement. He had not really wanted to hit the old fireman who had done him a kindness once. Why did he hit him, then? He had had no choice. And, truth to tell, the blow to the old guy's neck had been terrific. It was terrific to hit out like that and know that you are the boss, in charge, and no one to see you do it. And it was terrific to start wrecking the store. He would have to return someday and do it again, do a complete job, bring the whole goddamned store down around Kelcey's shoulders and bury Kelcey in the debris that he would cause.

Anyways. That was kid stuff.

More important things were ahead.

The cops came to the convent and questioned him.

Did not question him at first but expressed their—condolences, they called it. But it was all a mockery, of course. Everybody knew that the old fraud had abused Ozzie and his mother. Beaten them both. Neighbors on more than one occasion had summoned the cops to the house and they led the old fraud off to the jail. But he never reached court because the cops said that his Ma would have to make an official complaint, swear out a warrant, and she would never do a thing like that because the fraud would come home sooner or later and beat them both up worse than ever if she did.

"Where were you the night your Pa was killed?" Police Sergeant McAllister asked in his soft voice, his blue eyes mild. He didn't wear a uniform. He wore a green plaid jacket. He spoke like a teacher or a priest.

"Right here in the convent," Ozzie spoke up, and only a moment later realized that the cops had not come here merely to say they were sorry his Pa was dead, after all.

Sister Anunciata piped up, her voice shrill and angry, the voice she used on kids like Bull Zimmer and the wise guys. "He was here the entire night." Eyes blazing like small fires.

"Now, now, Sister, these are just questions we have to ask," Officer McAllister replied in his mild, unhurried way.

"And answers we have to obtain. For the record." He scratched his graying hair. "Now, Mr. Slater was murdered sometime between nine and eleven in the evening. With his own hammer that was always kept in the shed. So we have to question the whereabouts of anyone who knew about the hammer and who might have been around his place. Maybe the somebody who was around there that night might have seen something to help us." Then looking at Ozzie: "See what I mean?"

"I was in here all night," he said, wondering whether he ought to put this quiet-talking but quite dangerous policeman on his list.

"Mister, this place is never empty or still," Sister Anunciata said. "Ozzie is a good boy. He is in our charge. We know when he comes and goes. That night, he was here the entire time. Even if he tried to sneak out—which our Ozzie would never do—one of us would have seen him. You may take my word. . . ."

"And I do, Sister," the officer said, tipping his head toward her. "The word of a Sister of Mercy is good enough for the police. . . ."

But Sister Anunciata was still on fire with anger.

"And I don't like the implication of a boy his age doing a thing like that to his own father. . . ."

"Ah, but you see, Sister, it was not his own father." And turning to Ozzie: "Was he now?"

"He was a fake and fraud," Ozzie said, saying the words out loud and pleased to be saying them, the words he had said to himself so many thousands of times. "My mother married him because she needed a roof over her head. She didn't love him. Nobody could love him. He was a mean man." His sniveling strawberry nose was proof of that, and they all knew it. "And I can't say that I'm sorry he's dead.

But I didn't do it." It was easy to lie when you were in the right.

"No one's accusing you, Ozzie," Sister Anunciata said, her rosary beads in her hands.

Close call, Ozzie thought later. Better lie low for a while. Bide his time, wait, he was patient at waiting.

Kelcey's was still his favorite target and he stole in the store on occasion and knocked down a display or two. Heard the stories circulating in the town that Kelcey's store was haunted. Visited the store every few days and didn't see many people in the place now. Who wanted to trade in a place that might be haunted? He picked up the conversations as he sauntered along the streets, pausing to eavesdrop, listening to the talk. But he didn't linger long, afraid an urge might come upon him.

More and more when he was gone, unseen, disappeared, the urges came to him, nudging him, tugging at him, first faintly, hardly noticeable, and then stronger as time went on. He fought against the urges because they interrupted him, prevented him from doing what he had planned to do.

One day, the voice grew out of the urges. He'd stopped by the alley as usual, drawn himself into a corner to become unseen, planning to frolic a bit in the town. He came out of the alley, feeling his oats, standing in the sun, proud of having disappeared, proud that no one could see him. He spotted a young woman across the street pushing a baby carriage, a long black pigtail down her back. She paused, bent over, and glanced into the carriage, to see if the baby was fine. He wondered if his mother had pushed him in a carriage like that. Couldn't remember even seeing a carriage around the tenement. Felt sad watching them. The urge told him to cross the street and—he turned away from the thought, the urge—do something to them. Strike them down. Who? Both of them. Make them hurt. But I don't want to do that.

Ah, yes, you do. It's better than fooling around Kelcey's.

But I want to have fun with Kelcey today.

The woman is more important than Kelcey. So is the baby. Hurt them. Hurt them both.

I don't even know that woman. I don't even know that baby.

You don't have to know them to hurt them.

The voice began to plague him after that. Crazy conversations. Conversations that really weren't conversations at all. Sometimes it seemed like there was somebody else inside of him or as if there were two sides of him, as if he were split in half like an apple.

Shut up, he sometimes told that voice, that other side of him. And sometimes that other side of him shut up. Sometimes didn't. When that happened, he came out of the unseen to get away from the voice. Like that day across the street from the woman and the baby carriage. He stepped back into the alley and found his corner and pressed himself into appearing. That got rid of the voice.

Then, heading back to the convent, Ozzie did something he hated to do. Gave himself away to sadness. He did not allow this to happen very often. But sometimes, first thing in the morning or, like now, when he was alone on the road back from town to the convent, sniveling, a lonesomeness came to him and he wished he were still a little baby and his mother rocked him and sang to him. He wished, too, for someone to talk to, someone to tell about the incredible thing that had happened. Could he tell Sister Anunciata? Maybe he could, maybe he couldn't. Sister Anunciata often came in his room at night and ran her hand across his brow, murmuring *Poor Ozzie boy*. He always turned away, then felt more lonesome than ever.

Then a bad thing happened.

He was spotted by old man Pinder in the alley as he underwent the change from seen to unseen. The discovery occurred on a Saturday afternoon when Ozzie had sauntered downtown to have more fun at the expense of Kelcey. He basked in the power of what he had done to Kelcey, but he was disappointed too. His biggest disappointment in his unseen state was his inability to steal from the store because anything he might take—money from the register or the groceries themselves—would be visible, would seem to float in the air and create all kinds of disturbance. One night, he broke into two other stores on Main Street, first into Dempsey's Drug Store and another time into the Ramsey Diner. Broke small windows in the night, crawled through, was dismayed with the small amount of cash he found in the registers—a total of $23.55 from both places. After that, he bided his time about the stealing, waiting for the day when he would pull off a real big robbery—like at the Ramsey Savings Bank, when the Brink's truck picked up thousands of dollars in big burlap bags. He would have to figure a way to get the bags from the scene and stash them away somewhere, but knew he could do it. It would be a carefully planned robbery like in the movies with enough loot to get him out of this town and on his way in the world. But now he waited and indulged in small invasions of the town and sweet torments to the likes of that appetizing Kelcey. It was one of these times downtown that he stepped into the alley behind the five-and-ten that the old man spotted him. Ozzie had believed himself alone and he faced the wall, leaning against it, to give slight support to the pressing he had to do to change from here to gone. He turned around, satisfied at

disappearing, and heard a noise to his right, like a small animal scrabbling away. Whirled and saw the old man heading
lickety-split out of the alley, glancing over his shoulder at the
place where Ozzie had disappeared, his eyes bulging in disbelief.

Ozzie stood there indecisively, yet knew what he must do.
Kill the old man before he told anybody. Silence him forever. He ran quickly to the mouth of the alley, saw the old
man weaving his way along the wooden sidewalk, shaking
his head as he walked toward the diner. Where, Ozzie knew,
he would try to beg a drink. Harmless old buzzard, probably
thought he'd been seeing things, a vision from the booze or
his hangover or both. Ozzie let him go. Wait and see. Who
would believe the old codger anyways if he told them he'd
seen Ozzie Slater disappear from sight in the alley? He remembered how the old man gave him his coat when they
slept together on cold nights and assured him that his
mother was a real lady, a fine figure of a woman. Let him go,
for now.

Then another bad thing happened.

The urge, stronger than ever.

The urge took possession of him when he reached the corner of Main and Cotton, across from the library, and saw the
library woman coming down the steps. She was beautiful.
Small and dainty, took quick small steps like a little girl trying to catch up to someone who had left her behind. He
sneaked into the library now and then to glance through the
magazines but mostly to keep warm on cold days or dry on
rainy ones. She never told him to leave the library, always
greeted him in her musical voice. He knew that someday if
he married, he would search for someone like her.

Now she clicked off down the sidewalk, head high, walking quick as always, wearing pink. The sight of her cheered him up. He sighed as he watched the loveliness of her moving through the summer morning.

Then, the sly voice within him:

You know what you should do to her.

What?

You know.

No, I don't.

Yes, you do.

You tell me.

Hurt her.

No.

You're only saying no. You mean yes, don't you? You want to do it, don't you?

Shut up, he cried, shut up.

And began running. Away from the librarian and away from Main Street toward the convent and safety, away from the voice that he couldn't really run away from. The voice was with him, inside him.

He did not run far. Down to the corner of Spruce and Pine and paused. Drew in a deep breath.

The voice: *Go back.*

And he went. Back to Main, rushing, feet flying over the concrete, unseen and free to run, nobody to observe his flight as he stayed on the street, away from the wooden sidewalk where his footsteps would be heard.

She was passing Kelcey's now and then Dempsey's. She crossed over to the Ramsey Diner and turned left on Spring. His mind leapt ahead, trying to figure out her destination and what secret places were located on her way, where he could seize her and drag her out of sight.

She clicked along on those high heels, looking neither right nor left, her tan legs glistening in the sun, her black hair bouncing softly in the same rhythm as her body. His mind raced ahead. If she continued straight out this way, past Blossom and Summer, she would pass directly in front of the old Barnard place, all gone now and the cellar hole covered with brush. Perfect for what he would do to her. His hands tingled with anticipation, squeezing open and shut, the way they would squeeze her, squeeze that lovely slender neck, squeeze and squeeze until—

She stopped walking, coming to a quick halt right in the middle of the sidewalk. Didn't turn right or left but stopped in her tracks. Like a mannequin in a store window. Trapped in one spot.

Had he grown careless? Had she heard his footsteps? Or did she feel his presence, the way some people did?

She began to walk again, hurrying, legs flashing in the sun like scissors, almost running in her haste, and he ran, too, but carefully, running on his tiptoes, careful not to make any noise, had to be careful.

She stopped again. Only fifteen feet or so in front of him. He stopped too. She turned and looked his way, looked straight at him. As if she could see, although she couldn't. Fear in the look too.

That was when the dog attacked.

The dog did not bark or even growl. Ozzie never heard the dog approaching, but was suddenly almost knocked down when it bounded into him, teeth bared, long yellow teeth.

Then he heard a low and deadly growl. But the dog, a German shepherd, was thoroughly confused after that first assault, drew back, growling still but a whine in the growl. Ozzie recovered, held his ground.

"Nice doggie," Ozzie whispered, voice low and confidential.

The dog froze at the sound of the voice, then lifted its

pointed nose, whined a bit, and Ozzie chuckled, thinking
what the dog would be thinking, seeing nobody there, but
feeling someone there and hearing a voice from out of the
nothing.

Ozzie made ready to kick the dog, this intruder into his
pursuit of the librarian, but he held back when he glanced
up to see the librarian almost running up the flagstone walk
leading to a red-brick house, a sleek and shining car in the
driveway. She disappeared inside.

"Shit," he said.

And blamed the dog.

The dog lingered nearby, not a threat to him now, puzzled, head tilted.

Ozzie felt cheated.

Kick him.

Yes.

He walked to the dog and gave him a mighty boot, right
into the soft part of the belly, and the dog leapt into the air,
howling with pain, legs stiff with fright at the surprise of the
attack, then went scurrying down the street, howling and
whining. Maybe that was the sound a dog makes when it
cries.

He watched it go, smiling, chuckling, and the voice said:
Nice.

But he did not answer the voice, afraid the voice might be
mad at him for losing the library woman.

He waited for old man Pinder at the mouth of the alley,
knew he would stop up here sooner or later, in the gathering
darkness, at the end of the day. Sure enough, as darkness
settled on the town like soot, the old man came shuffling up
Main Street, his feet dragging on the wooden sidewalk. As
he turned into the alley, Ozzie stepped in front of him.

"How do you do, old man?" he asked brightly.

"Ozzie, Ozzie," old man Pinder said, falling back a little, wetting his lips. Always wetting his lips, always needing a drink.

They walked into the alley, the booze smell awful, not the sweet smell of the gin his mother drank but the sour cellar smell of muscatel and a touch of vomit, to boot.

"How you been, old man?" Ozzie asked.

The old man shrugged inside his two overcoats and probably two or three sweaters. Hot or cold, winter or summer, he always dressed the same. Then he turned to Ozzie and Ozzie saw the fear in his eyes, the cringing fear that said: Don't hit me, don't hurt me.

"Hey, take it easy, old man," Ozzie said. "Nobody's going to do nothing to you. . . ."

And suddenly he wanted to share with the old man the incredible thing that had happened to him, being gone and unseen. He had kept the secret to himself until it felt like something boiling in a pot, reaching the point of blowing off the lid.

"Sit down, old man," he said. And the old man sat, crumpled to the ground, next to the rubbish barrels from Dempsey's, back against the dull brick wall. "I want to show you something." Hell, he already knew about it anyways, didn't he?

The light slanted in from Main Street and Ozzie felt like he was about to perform on a stage. Then, glancing to see that no one else was about, he pressed forward, breath taken away and then coming back, the sweep of pain and he was gone. Gone into the cold as well.

"I didn't see you do that," the old man called out, eyes blinking furiously, yellow-coated tongue darting out as he spoke. "I don't see nothing, don't know nothing." Then, still blinking but squinting too: "Where are you, Ozzie?"

"Right here," he said, shouting in the old man's ear so that he almost leapt out of his coats and sweaters.

For the next few minutes he entertained the old guy, making stuff dance in the air, crap he took out of the rubbish barrels, and then making the barrels jump and turn and crash to the ground. The old man cackled and laughed, holding his sides sometimes, but Ozzie looked at him craftily now and then, and saw something behind the laughing, and knew that the old man really was scared to death.

So Ozzie told the old man that he wasn't seeing things and he did not have the DT's. This was Ozzie Slater, all right, Ozzie who was his friend, the same Ozzie he gave shelter to in the night, who was showing off this incredible thing that had happened to him (but Ozzie did not tell him about what he did to the old fraud, of course, or the damage to Kelcey's) and the fun he had, the fun the two of them could now have.

"Fun?" The old man was bewildered, shaking from the booze or the need for booze.

"I'll show you what I mean by fun," Ozzie said. He pulled the old man to his feet and dragged him down the alley where the back windows of Ramsey Liquors looked out on a small porch.

"Watch," Ozzie said.

He broke the window near the back door, carefully removed all the pieces of glass, then slipped through. He knew the old man drank muscatel because it was the cheapest stuff he could buy, but Ozzie now sought out the good stuff, the Scotch the old man used to talk about, the sting of the Scotch the old man drank as a young man on a Saturday night down in Boston in the good times. Ozzie grabbed two bottles from the shelf, kept low because he didn't want anyone passing by

to see bottles floating in the air. He made his way out of
there, placed the two bottles on the back steps, enjoyed the
look on the old man's face. Like Christmas had come in the
middle of summer.

Back in the alley again, after the old man had settled down
but before he had swallowed too much of the booze, Ozzie
swore him to secrecy, describing the fun they could have
together, the booze Ozzie could supply him with, and all
Ozzie would require was the old man's silence and to keep
his eyes and ears open downtown and report anything he
heard, anything he heard at all, that pertained to Ozzie.

Looking at old man Pinder, who was already beginning to
dissolve with the booze, jaw loose and drooping, eyes dreamy
and far away, Ozzie was tempted simply to kill him here and
now and be done with it. But, he thought hazily, maybe the
old man would be useful, one way or another. Besides, the
fraud who was his Pa had deserved to die but certainly not
this harmless old coot.

Watch the nun.
Why the nun?
Because.
Because why?
Because. . . .

But he didn't want to listen and ran out of the convent and
through the woods, ran until his lungs threatened to burst
and his legs stung with pain. Threw himself down on the
grass, waited, afraid the voice would start again, glad when it
didn't.

Lately, the voice and the urges got together and tormented
him, stopped him from doing what he wanted to do, made
sly suggestions about what he *should* do. Like, he wanted to
go after Bull Zimmer, find out what he was doing this sum-

mer, and begin plans for his revenge. Then Miss Ball. But the voice told him to wait. Only a few weeks had gone by since the old fraud died. Better to wait.

So he waited, something he was good at, anyways. Stayed away from town except for a visit now and then to look up the old man. "Have you told anybody about me?" The old man always babbled on about how he would never tell, never tell. Ozzie knocked him around a bit to give him a taste of what might happen if he told. Bloodied his nose once, and it felt good to see blood coming from somebody else's nose. Mostly, though, he stayed at the convent, making himself useful. Busy hands are happy hands, Sister Anunciata said, handing him a bucket of water and brush or a broom or the green stuff to wash the windows. She got stung by a bee and her face swelled up, one eye closed, and she looked a little like Popeye in the cartoon and he had to cover his own face so she would not see him laughing. Later, in the fields, he saw these old yellow flowers, straggling through the weeds, flowers that were past their prime, starting to wilt. What the hell, good enough for the old nun. Nothing fancy, just right for her. He put them in a jar he found in the shed and placed them on the small table near her bed when she was out in the kitchen.

"Why, thank you, Ozzie," she said later, pleased. Her one good eye was filled with tears.

"They're just old flowers," he said, angry for some reason. Angry with himself and her.

That was a mistake.

Why was that a mistake?

Because she thinks you're trying to bribe her.

Why would I bribe her?

Because she suspects what you did to the old fraud. Be careful with her. She's watching you.

No, she isn't.

But maybe she was. Maybe she *did* suspect. He began to notice things. How that one good eye of hers was sharp, darting everywhere but most of all on Ozzie. He felt as if that eye could pin him to a wall, hold him there, wriggling. Every time he turned around, there she was. Swollen face, skin almost purple, and that sharp blue eye.

Then her face got better, the swelling disappeared, faint purple gone, both eyes open, and she seemed less threatening to him.

She's playing games.

What games?

The games of pretending not to watch you, gathering her evidence.

What kind of evidence?

Evidence of what you did. To the old fraud.

I'm not listening, not listening to you.

Yes, you are.

And, of course, he did listen and, in his own turn, *he* began to watch the nun. Watched her watching him. He found her wherever he went in the convent, whether doing his chores or just killing time. He turned a corner and there she was, busy with her own chores, but *there* just the same. Looked up from the supper table and found her eyes on him. Heard her footsteps padding by the door of his room late at night, knew it had to be her.

Know what you've got to do?

He didn't answer the voice. Hunched up in the blanket even though the night was hot.

Sooner or later, you've got to do it.

Still didn't answer, although the voice tugged at him to answer, like an itch you had to scratch.

I'm not going to do it. You said it was too soon after the old fraud to do anything.

That seemed to satisfy the voice. He waited and there was no response. He really did not want to hurt the old nun. She had taken him in, was kind to him. She was old, she would probably die soon anyways. He wanted Bull Zimmer and Miss Ball and the kids, not the old nun.

Better do something, the voice said slyly just before he fell asleep.

What he did was go on a rampage in the town. The next night. Found a hammer in the shed and raced through the woods, gone, unseen, emerging in the town, barely breathing hard, carried on waves of excitement. His body throbbed with strength and energy, as if he had swallowed a potent brew. He ran down the deserted street, swinging the hammer, breaking windows in the stores and cars parked at the curbs, then denting the cars themselves. Threw rocks at neon signs. Smashed the small panes of glass in parking meters. Spotted the library building and received an inspiration. He ran to the library, raced up the steps, broke the window, reached inside to unlock the door. Then went on a binge of wrecking, tumbling bookcases to the floor, sweeping hundreds of books off the shelves, tossing them against the window. *That'll show her*, that bitch of a librarian. He realized the voice had spoken, and although Ozzie's intention was not to please the voice, he reveled in the havoc he was creating, a thousand books spilled on the floor.

The sound of a siren drew him out of the library and back into the street, where lights had been turned out in the rooms above the stores and a police cruiser swung around the corner, the siren going ninety miles an hour, the car itself barely moving.

Ozzie frolicked on the sidewalk, laughing and dancing, jumping around, giving himself up to frenzy—God, how he

hated this town and what a joy it was to attack it like this, to
get his revenge, for himself and his Ma.

I'll show you worse than this, he vowed as the cruiser's
spotlight illuminated the damage he had created, this is nothing at all. People emerged from the buildings bewildered,
rubbing their eyes, while a young cop pushed back his cap
and shook his head as a final sheet of glass in the liquor store
window suddenly let go and smashed into a thousand pieces
of glass on the sidewalk.

Ozzie let out a whoop.

Gliding toward the alley, he saw the old man swaying,
drunk as usual, looking at the damage.

"What do you think, old man?" Ozzie said.

And the old man jumped as the voice without a body
reached him. In his high spirits, Ozzie hit the old guy.
Wanted to do to him what he did to the town. Bopped him
good on the head, which sent him reeling back against the
brick wall of the alley. Then let him have a blow to the
mouth, saw the blood spill, saw the piece of tooth fly out of
his mouth. Heard the old man's bellow of pain as he collapsed to the ground. Somebody on the sidewalk looked toward the alley, began walking toward Ozzie.

He left the old man in a heap on the ground. Enough
damage for one night. Better get back to the convent. Hated
to leave the scene of his triumph, another cruiser arriving
with siren wailing. But went anyway. Through the alley to
the woods.

That was very nice.

He waited a few days before venturing to town again, although he was impatient to see the evidence of his attack.
Caution, he told himself.

Wiping the stuff from his nose, he went down the back

steps of the convent and through the courtyard looking for a place to hide in for a while. He saw old man Pinder thrashing out of the woods and into the yard. The old man was agitated, flecks of foam at the corners of his lips, the old eyes red and bleary as usual but something else in his eyes now, something sharp and alert.

"What's the matter, old man?" Ozzie asked. He had never come out to the convent before.

"There's a stranger in town," the old man said, spit flying every which way from his lips. "And he's looking for you."

knew he was there, nearby, somewhere in the town, the instant I stepped off the bus. Something in the air, like a distant note of music only my ears could hear. An aura, a mood, which I tried to pin down but found elusive as I stood in front of a converted railroad car that obviously was a diner although it had no sign. The morning aromas of coffee, bacon, and other fried foods wafted through an open window, bringing a feeling of normality that did not quite dispel the alien atmosphere the town presented to me.

At first glance Ramsey reminded me of the cowboy towns in the old Saturday matinees at the Plymouth. Wooden sidewalks, warped boards. Iron railings to which horses had been tethered in earlier times. Slanting roofs above the sidewalks supported by wobbly posts. Only the parking meters shattered the illusion of other times.

In an encyclopedia at the Monument Public Library, I had learned that Ramsey had long ago been a prosperous resort town, famous for mineral waters that attracted thousands of visitors, including President Grover Cleveland. The springs had dried up, however, and time passed the town by. Now it was only a whisper of its former self, without industry or shopping malls, population fewer than 3,000, according to the most recent U.S. census. No motels or even a movie theater. One dubious hotel, the Glenwood, at which I had succeeded in making reservations for three nights despite the lack of interest on the part of the clerk who manned the telephone. Thus, I had been prepared for a slumbering backwater but not for the desolation and damage I observed as I walked up Main Street to the hotel.

Ramsey, in fact, resembled a town under siege. Or a town recovering from an assault. Several windows had been boarded up at a store whose sign proclaimed KELCEY'S GROCERY in faded print. Smashed streetlight globes whose broken remains had not yet been removed. The shattered tubes of a neon sign that had once advertised Dempsey's Drug Store. The small windows of the parking meters had all been smashed.

At the Glenwood Hotel I stepped into a lobby with a cracked tile floor, a sagging sofa whose color had long ago faded away. A bell stood on a small end table, the kind of bell the sisters at St. Jude's had on their desks. I rang the bell and listened to its forlorn echo.

I should not be here, I told myself. I should be back in the safety of Frenchtown. Before leaving, I had weighed all the risks. Suppose I could not control the fade in a strange town I had never visited before? Suppose the fade happened on the bus or the train or while I walked the streets of Ramsey, Maine? I finally turned my back on the fears. Finding the fader who was my nephew was more important than lapsing into the fade. The risk was small, really. Sometimes months passed without the fade occurring.

Now, in the lobby, my fears were somewhat placated. In a

few moments I would have a room to which I could flee if
the fade occurred unexpectedly, just as my tenement in
Frenchtown was always a refuge.

A middle-aged man descended an uncarpeted stairway. He
was small and thin, a few strands of hair combed to cover as
much of his bald head as possible.

"I called last week," I said. "For reservations. The name is
John LeBlanc."

Realizing that I was venturing into the unknown, into the
mystery surrounding the fade, I had withheld my real name,
feeling absurd for the moment but allowing instinct to guide
me.

"I know," he said, still uninterested. Taking a skeleton key
from his pocket, he said: "We're a residence hotel, we don't
get many transients."

I paid him in advance, doing business as we stood in the
lobby, no reservations desk in sight. As he beckoned me to
follow him, I asked: "What happened to the town? Looks like
a hurricane hit it. . . ."

"Vandalism," he said. "Young punks, probably from Bangor, tearing up the place."

The room he led me to on the second floor was surprisingly comfortable-looking, dominated by a four-poster bed
with a George Washington bedspread, a highly polished mahogany bureau, and a Boston rocker.

"Mrs. Wright's place," he said. "But she spends August in
Canada. Only room available, you're a lucky man. Nobody
comes to Ramsey anymore. No reason to. Town's gone to
pot."

He waited. I realized he had actually been asking me what
had brought me to Ramsey. My story was ready. "I'm a
writer," I said. "I'm doing a book on old resort towns. This
is a preliminary visit to check a few details. . . ."

He nodded curtly and stepped through the doorway, closing the door gently behind him. I realized that he had not once looked me in the eye from the moment he came down the stairs until he left the room.

Which I soon learned was the usual practice with strangers in Ramsey, Maine, at least on that particular day.

I spent the morning roaming the town, making small purchases in the stores—razor blades in Dempsey's Drug Store, a box of Kleenex in Kelcey's Grocery, a *Newsweek* in Dunker's Convenience Store—and no one paid me any attention. At the registers, the cashiers—middle-aged men who were probably the proprietors—barely acknowledged my presence as they rang up the sales and handed me the change.

The Ramsey Public Library and the Pilgrim Congregational Church, with a clock in its steeple, stood across from each other at the far end of Main Street. The library, a red-brick building with a sagging roof, showed no signs of life. A notice posted on the front door announced that it was closed for renovations.

Town Hall was located at the opposite end of Main Street and contained the police and fire departments. Across the street, the town common was deserted, a gazebo its centerpiece, an ancient cannon guarding the entrance.

I ate lunch in the Ramsey Diner, where patrons ordered a beer and a shot of whiskey to go with the noontime special, which that day was meat loaf. The counterman did not look at me as he took my order and later slid the plate along the tiled counter top. No one else in the place looked at me either.

In the afternoon, I struck out on foot, following a winding highway for about two miles. I finally reached a clearing where a wooden sign proclaimed *Sisters of Mercy* in faded Gothic script. Following a gravel road, I came upon an ancient stone building with a single steeple, a small gold cross at the top. Ivy clung to the building with a thousand green fingers. The windows were tall and narrow, giving away no secrets.

I rang the bell and heard chimes echoing unendingly through distant corridors. After a few moments, the heavy oak door swung open, revealing a tiny woman, enclosed in the black-and-white habit seldom seen these days. Her pink cheeks glowed like polished apples.

"Yes?" she whispered.

"I wonder—is it possible for me to attend mass in the chapel?"

"We cannot welcome visitors on weekdays," she said, voice and eyes full of regret. "Only on the first Sunday of the month. I'm sorry . . ."

She paused for a moment, as if to offer consolation, and slowly closed the door.

As I started away my flesh turned cold, as if someone had raked a fingernail across my back. I knew instantly that my fader either was here or had been here. Somewhere in the vicinity, in the convent itself perhaps. My first tendency was to ring the convent bell again. But I held back. I was not ready to see that nephew of mine who was the fader. Not yet. Somehow he was connected in my mind with the damage I had seen in the town. I did not know why I should make that assumption but there it was. The call of the blood again. The links. Between my uncle Adelard and myself. And now, myself and this Ramsey boy.

Back in town, twilight brought a chill. Until this moment the town had seemed sterile, without weather of any kind, as if under glass. My visit took place toward the middle of August, but it might have been any day of the year on a distant planet that resembled earth.

"Taxi?"

Turning, I encountered an old man wearing a faded baseball cap, RED sox faintly stitched across a dirty visor. Bloodshot eyes, face pinched and wizened, teeth broken, nose awry from an old fracture, a purple grape of a lump fresh on his forehead.

"You the cabdriver?" I asked, although I knew how ridiculous the question sounded.

"Hell no," he said. "This town, in fact, don't have a taxi. But I could arrange a ride. Tommy Pinder at your service." He had brought a variety of smells with him: alcohol and vomit and an odor I remembered from the old dump on the edge of Frenchtown. Shooting me a shrewd glance, he said: "Find what you've been looking for?"

"What am I looking for?" I asked. His eyes were red and watery, but intelligence flickered in them.

"Well, I figure you must be looking for something," he said. "Saw you all day, wandering the streets. Buying stuff you don't need in the stores. Bought a magazine in Dunker's and tossed it into a rubbish barrel without reading it. Said to myself: He's looking for something, that fellow."

"I'm a writer," I said. "Doing a book on old resort towns. Thought I might include a chapter on Ramsey."

The old man shrugged deeper into his clothes. I could see a raincoat under his nondescript topcoat and at least two sweaters.

"You from?" he asked.

"Down in Massachusetts . . ." As another drift of alcohol reached me, I asked: "Buy you a drink?"

"Is the pope Catholic?" The grin he attempted gave his face a grotesque look.

I made the writer's leap at that moment, and saw how much the old man resembled the town. Both in ruins, damaged, ancient. Behind the old man's easy manner, I sensed apprehension, nervousness, or did he merely need a drink badly?

"Let's find a bar," I said, although I had seen no bar in town, merely the Ramsey Diner where patrons drank beer and whiskey with their lunch.

"I prefer the out-of-doors," the old man said with a touch of dignity. "The gazebo there in the common across the way. If you offer me a dollar or two, I can go into Dempsey's and buy us a good bottle of muscatel. Or whatever you prefer . . ."

Taking money out of my pocket, I said: "Nothing for me. I'll meet you in the common."

The common was modest in size. The gray barrel of the cannon was covered with meaningless graffiti. Whoever had assaulted the town had ignored the common. A spotlight, spared from the vandalism, showered illumination on the gazebo. The old man and I sat on the steps, looking at Main Street across the way, almost eerie in its stillness. A few people came and went, flitting through the shadows, emerging into the light from the stores and then disappearing into the gloom.

The old man did not drink immediately and seemed to be taking pleasure from merely holding the bottle in his hands. He had neatly folded the paper bag and slipped it into an inside pocket.

"How do you like this town of ours?" he asked expansively, his hand waving in the air, as if he were offering the town to me as a gift.

"Not the friendliest place in the world," I said. "All day long, hardly anybody said hello."

"People here don't talk too much," he said, brooding, studying the bottle as he held it up to the light.

He suddenly took the cap off the bottle, raised it to his lips, and drank desperately.

"People here should have a lot to say," I said. "Look at Main Street. Like a war zone, as if it's been under attack. . . ."

"Ramsey's a hard-luck town, mister," he said. "All gone to hell. Old folks dying off and young people moving out. The springs are all dried up. And we got that convent out there in the woods. Kind of a spooky place." He grimaced, displaying the broken tooth rimmed with blood. "Maybe the town's haunted. If a house can be haunted, maybe a town can be too. . . ."

"How long's it been going on?"

"How long's what been going on?" he asked, studying the bottle, caressing it lovingly with trembling fingers.

"The haunting," I said. "Must be recent. The springs dried up years ago, before World War One. And the convent was there before that. But all this damage, the broken windows, looks like it just happened. . . ."

He did not answer but drank again, his Adam's apple dancing as he swallowed.

Across the street, two men left the Ramsey Diner and were taken up by the darkness. A young couple walked hand in hand, drifting by in the summer evening.

"That's a nasty bump on your head," I said.

Tentatively, he touched the wound. "I fall down sometimes," he said sheepishly. "Old age is hell. I'm always bumping into things too. Can't always blame the booze, either. Other day, I tripped over a loose plank in that old goddamned sidewalk. Cold sober, I was . . ."

"You must fall down an awful lot," I said, gambling a bit.

"Recently, too. That bruise on your head and that broken tooth, now. Looks like they happened yesterday. Today, maybe . . ." Fishing in the dark, following my instincts. "Guess you've got bad luck too. Like the town. Maybe you're haunted too."

Another shrewd glance as he closed one bloodshot eye, as if to see me clearer with the other.

"What are you saying, mister?"

"Just making observations," I said. "I'm a writer. I'm supposed to notice things. While you were watching me all day, I was watching the town. The damage, nobody willing to say hello to a stranger. As if everybody's afraid of something." Taking chances again. "And now those injuries of yours. It's like the town's under attack. You, along with the town . . ."

He brooded over those remarks, lifting the bottle into the air, turning it over in his hands, placing it against his lips but not drinking. "Stuff hits me fast these days," he said, words slurred a bit. "Bingo, and I'm almost gone." He belched, and I turned my face away. "Then I fall down, break my tooth—"

"I don't think so," I said, openly gambling now.

"Don't think what?"

"I don't think you broke that tooth falling down. It doesn't look like it was caused by a fall." Pushing the bluff further, I added, "I think somebody hit you. . . ."

"Who would hit an old man like me?" he asked, the bloodshot eyes alert now despite the alcohol working in his veins and spreading throughout his body. "I mind my own business, don't look for trouble."

"Maybe that same ghost," I said, keeping my voice flat and crisp, undramatic. "The same ghost that haunts the town. The ghost that isn't a ghost. . . ."

"What's that supposed to mean?"

Before I could answer, he struggled to his feet, while trying to find a pocket for the bottle.

Getting up, I placed an arm around him, tried not to breathe the sour breath and the dank odor of his clothes. "Take it easy, Mr. Pinder," I said. "I don't mean any harm." Pressuring his shoulder a bit, I got him to sit down again. "In fact, I'd like to help. If somebody's giving you a bad time, maybe we can do something about it. . . ."

"Nobody can do anything about it," he said. "Not when it's a ghost who isn't a ghost . . ."

"Who is it, then?"

"Shh . . . shh . . ." he said, raising a quivering finger to his lips, while seeming to shrink even deeper into his layers of clothing. He thrust his face toward mine and I braced myself against the assault of odors. "Terrible things are happening here in Ramsey. Best you get out of here. Out of the Glenwood and back where you belong, in Massachusetts."

"You mean something might happen to me? I might get beat up too? My tooth broken, a lump on my head?"

He drew away. "I didn't say that." His head dropped forward, his chin coming to rest on his chest. "I don't know what I said. Don't pay any attention to me." Suddenly he looked up, tilted his head, listening, tense and alert. "You hear something?"

I raised my head, squinted toward the shadows surrounding the gazebo, the dark blobs of shrubbery, trees with heavy low branches. Across the street, no one walked. A sleepy town, a town that went to bed early.

"Did you hear a footstep?" he whispered, close to my ear.

My fader? Was he in the vicinity? Lurking in the bushes?

"I don't hear anything," I said.

He nodded at my words, sighed with relief and drank again, his hand unsteady as he held the bottle to his lips. His lips hung loose now, his eyelids drooping at half-mast. I saw the danger of having him become too drunk to provide me with information. I would have to work faster.

"What did you expect to hear?" I asked, bringing my mouth close to his ear. "Whose footsteps?"

"I don't know," he said, whispering, confidential, as if we shared the same mystery.

"I do," I said, whispering back, sharing the secret. "The footsteps of a boy. Thirteen years old. He's lived here all his life. And suddenly doing things."

"Who are you?" he asked, his voice raw, his eyes wide with fear. "How come you know so much?"

"My name's not important," I said. "What's important is that I know what's going on, some of it, at least, and I can help. But you must trust me. . . ."

Again the quivering finger to his lips as he peered into the darkness, his eyes searching the grounds surrounding the gazebo. "I'm the only one in Ramsey who knows," he said, whispering. "Everybody knows *something's* going on and it's not vandalism but I'm the only one who knows what's *really* going on. . . ." He continued to study the darkness. "You see anything out there? Hear anything? He could be here, there, anywhere." Turning to me, he said: "Best we go to my place. With four walls around us. Be safer to talk there."

He was alert now, without any visible effects of the muscatel, made sober obviously by fear. As we made our way out of the park, however, he leaned against me for support, and continued to do so as we walked across the wooden sidewalks, past the Ramsey Diner to a section of three-decker houses.

"Bowker Street," he said.

A few minutes later, we descended cement steps to the cellar he called home. Linoleum covered the floor and a cot stood against a brick wall. Otherwise, no sign of habitation. No sink or stove or table or chairs. The narrow windows were covered with cardboard. "You can see why I choose to sleep outdoors," he said, with a trace of the humor he had displayed when we first met.

He bolted the door behind us and inspected the room, as he had inspected the common, eyes narrowed and suspicious.

"He's not here," I said. I was certain that I would be able to detect the presence of my fader if he was in the room or even nearby.

The old man sank down on the cot and I lowered myself gingerly, amazed at how he lived in a world of foul smells and did not seem to notice: the odor of sour wine and the smell of the dump and now the cellar air heavy with something damp and rotting.

"Tell me about him," I said. "His name. Where he lives . . ."

The old man sighed, groped for the bottle in his pocket, took it out and inspected it closely. Barely an inch of wine left. He looked at it longingly and then placed it on the floor, next to the cot.

"He'll kill me," he said. "If he finds out we talked. And he can find out easy. He comes and goes. I thought for a minute when we came in that he might be here."

I waited in silence, let him lead the way, not wanting to press too much, afraid that he might withdraw completely if I tried to hurry him.

"He used to be nice to me, you know. Buy me booze, even Scotch one time though it's too rich for my blood. Showed me tricks, too. Tricks he could do." He reached down to touch the bottle, as if touching a rabbit's foot for luck. "Then he got mean. Started doing mean things. Hit me, knocked

me down. Wouldn't buy me booze anymore. Started wrecking the town, too." He sagged, sank back against the wall, let
his chin drop to his chest. He closed his eyes and I was afraid
that I might be losing him, that the liquor had lured him into
sleep, but before I could rouse him, he said: "Then his stepfa
ther. A terrible man. Used to beat the kid up terrible. The
kid and his ma. Leonard Slater, his name. Got hammered to
death a few weeks ago. Big mystery here in Ramsey but I
know who did it. . . ."

I had not been prepared for murder, but I should have
been. Murder is the ultimate damage and I had seen nothing
but damage since arriving in Ramsey. Now I wanted to flee
this place, the cellar and the town, get away from this pathetic old man and his grisly story. I had tried to get away
from the fade most of my life and thought I had succeeded
but now saw that it was impossible to avoid it altogether. If
not in my generation, then in another. And murder in both.

"What's his name?" I asked.

"Ozzie," he said, almost dreamily. "Oscar, but nobody
calls him that. A poor kid, really. Got a nose like a rotten
tomato. Like you said, he's only a kid. He lives with the
nuns, out at the convent. Only thirteen years old but the
things he does, mister, the things he *could* do. Gives you the
willies. Thank God for the booze."

His hand reached down for the bottle and he raised it to
his lips, draining the last few ounces, neatly, no spills, those
last drops precious.

We had not talked about the fade at all, the topic silent
between us. But I had to be certain now, had to dispel any
doubts that might remain.

"What do you mean by things he does?" I said.

"You know what I mean."

"Tell me what you mean."

Flinging the bottle away, he watched it spiral through the air, bouncing against the opposite wall, not breaking, landing on the floor.

"Disappears," he cried. "He makes himself invisible." Turning to me, he said: "It's impossible what he does. But he does it. He vamooses. Into thin air. And, mister, if he can do that, he can do anything. . . ." He collapsed on the couch, out of breath, as if he had exerted himself beyond his endurance.

"When was the last time you saw him?" I asked.

His head tumbled forward. Half sitting and half lying down, he was completely still, seemed to be frozen in sudden paralysis or even death. Then his breath wheezed through his nostrils and he began to snore softly.

I shook him gently, calling his name. "Mr. Pinder . . . Mr. Pinder . . ."

No response, the snores growing louder and deeper, his chest heaving with the snores, his mouth dropping open.

I waited a few moments, listening to his snores, looking at that ravaged face, the broken tooth, the bruised flesh. I counted to a thousand, pausing between each number, and then counted another thousand. Finally, I let myself out of that dismal cellar he called home. Who was I to rouse him from whatever peace he found in his muscatel slumber?

The problem was who to kill first.

Bull Zimmer had always been at the top of the list, and Miss Ball next. Then the other kids at school. But the voice kept urging him to do otherwise. Kept urging him to kill, first, Sister Anunciata, and then the stranger. Taunting him, haunting him until sometimes Ozzie wanted to scream.

Ozzie realized that the stranger knew too much, probably knew Ozzie's secret of disappearing. But—but what? He wasn't sure. Not yet. What if the stranger was his real Pa? Ozzie had to be sure before doing what the voice wanted him to do.

Sister Anunciata was different. Killing her was the voice's idea, not Ozzie's. Besides, killing her would be a problem. The cops would come again, the crafty officer in the green plaid jacket who questioned him that night about the death of the old fraud. He would be suspicious.

Let him be suspicious.

That's easy for you to say. But he'd be suspicious of me, not you. He can see me but not see you.

*Are you daft? He wouldn't see you, either, if you didn't want him
to. You have to be smart. You have to use being unseen to kill her so
that nobody will know.*

And how do I do that?

*Simple. You kill her in front of the nuns, in front of witnesses.
Make yourself unseen and then hit her. Hard. And she'll fall down
and die in her tracks and nobody will see it was you. They'll think it
was a heart attack.*

I don't know whether I should kill her or not.

*She's looking at you funny, isn't she? Nuns have strange powers.
They know things other people don't. What if she knows you killed
your Pa?*

He was not my Pa.

Just then, Sister Anunciata came along, hurrying down
the corridor, finding him standing there looking out the window, the mop in his hand.

"Daydreaming, Ozzie?" she asked, her voice soft and
tender, almost like the voice of his Ma. Was she putting on an
act, pretending to be soft and tender?

"Just taking a rest," he said.

"You should take some time off, Ozzie," she suggested.
"Go into the town and buy some ice cream. All work and no
play is not good for you. . . ." And she touched him on the
shoulder.

He had to weigh carefully everything that Sister
Anunciata said now, had to listen to her words and then
decide whether she was saying one thing and meaning another.

"Now you finish the mopping and go along," she said,
squeezing his shoulder again, and he wondered if she was
giving him a message that way, maybe a message that the
voice could not hear.

"Yes, Sister," he said, resuming his chore with the mop as

she puttered away, her feet invisible in the long folds of her skirt skimming along the corridor.

He finished the floor and hung up the mop and changed his clothes in the small room near the kitchen.

And what about the old man?

What about the old man?

He knows too much . . .

Ah, but he liked the old man, did not *like* him exactly but liked to have him around. To cuff and tease. Once in the alley downtown, he saw a cat playing with a mouse, cuffing the mouse, the mouse trapped in a corner, toying with the mouse with its paw, until suddenly the cat pounced. The old man was his mouse. He toyed with the old man the way that cat toyed with the mouse. But the old man was also useful. The old man had told him about the stranger, staggered all the way out here to the convent early in the morning, suffering a terrible hangover, shaking all over the place, his tongue hanging out like a piece of old leather.

"A stranger asking questions," the old man said.

"What kind of questions?" Suspicious. How much did the old man tell the stranger?

The old man looked uncertain. Then his eyes got crafty. Ozzie saw that the old man was deciding how much to tell, how much that was the truth and how much that was a pack of lies.

"Questions about the town," the old man said. "He's a writer. From Massachusetts. Going to write about the old resorts. But then he started with the questions." Scratching his dirty, bristled face with a black fingernail. "About somebody who was thirteen. Somebody thirteen who has strange powers." The old man looked triumphant. "Right away, Ozzie boy, I knew he meant you. And that's when I got very

very careful, using the old noggin. He bought me booze and figured he'd get me talking that way, but . . ."

Ozzie hit him on the jaw. "You drank his booze?"

"Yes. But I didn't tell him anything." Staggering back, looking awful, scared now, too, and rubbing his jaw where a scarlet spot had appeared.

"Yes, you did." Hitting him again, a bruiser to the cheek, avoiding the nose, not wanting blood to flow here on the veranda of the convent where Sister Anunciata might stick her face out to see what was going on.

"No, Ozzie," the old man said, spittle in the corners of his mouth and his chin loose on the bottom of his face like it might drop off and clatter to the floor. "I let him ask the questions and drank the booze and fell asleep. Honest. But I knew he was looking for you. . . ."

"You told him about me," Ozzie said, not wanting to hit him anymore because he looked so pathetic.

"Bit my tongue," the old man said, doing a kind of dance on the porch, sticking out his tongue, and Ozzie saw the blood on it.

"What did you tell him about me?"

"Nothing, nothing," the old man said, whining now, loud, loud enough for the nuns busy in the kitchen to hear. "Would I come out here to warn you if I did something wrong?"

He decided to trust the old man. He had to remember that the old man did, after all, come all the way out here in his thirst and his hangover to warn him about the stranger.

He gave the old man orders. "Don't talk to the stranger but follow him. Keep out of his way but find out where he goes and who he talks to. And don't, for Christ's sake, take any booze from him, don't let him buy you any booze. I'll give you booze, I'll give you money for the booze." Which Ozzie did, taking a couple of dollars from his secret place.

"I'll be downtown later," Ozzie said.

On the street in the heat of the August afternoon and the dust being kicked up by the big sweeper from the town department, Ozzie looked for the stranger. Gone, unseen, he stalked the streets. Did not see the old man. Saw a lot of people on the streets but not the stranger. Looking high and low, he covered the whole town. He stood outside the Glenwood for a while but nobody entered or left. He stole inside, checked the lobby and lingered there, but nobody came or went.

He finally spotted the stranger at four o'clock, saw him crossing the street in front of Dempsey's, head tilted to one side as if listening to something in the air—music, voices, *something*— nobody else could hear. How did he know this was his stranger? He knew, he knew.

The stranger was not tall and not short, not fat and not thin. Squinting, Ozzie studied his face. A face not handsome and not ugly. But something familiar about him. Where had he seen that face before? In his dreams, maybe? And suddenly, like lightning striking a tree and splitting it in two, the knowledge of the stranger's identity struck his brain and it seemed to crack his head in half, the pain so intense, Ozzie gasped aloud.

And the stranger was not a stranger anymore.

Ozzie knew who he was.

I could tell he was there. That vibrancy in the air again, that distant note like music out of tune, discordant, jangled. His presence, nearby, not quite certain where, across the street somewhere. But there, no doubt at all.

All day long I had awaited his arrival, had kept myself alert for him to make himself known. I could not account for this anticipation of mine. It was possible that the old man had warned him and the fader was looking for me. I had not seen the old man during my travels that day. I had not seen any thirteen-year-old boy, either, who might have been Ozzie Slater. I realized that subconsciously I had a mental picture of him. Rose's son with her dark loveliness echoing somehow in him, in his eyes, perhaps. Despite what the old man had said, the boy was my nephew, my blood running in his veins. Before he was the monster the old man had described, he was Rose's son. And a fader, probably against his will, like myself, like Adelard. The boy who had ravaged this town was perhaps a victim of the fade, performing acts he would not otherwise contemplate.

I ate another meal at the Ramsey Diner and was returning to my hotel room when I was halted in my tracks by the certain knowledge that Ozzie Slater was nearby, his presence blazing in the air.

My eyes were drawn across the street. People walking lazily along on the wooden sidewalks. A clerk washing the window at the liquor store. All seemed normal. Yet I knew he was here, somewhere close by. Watching me. His eyes upon me.

Then I saw him. A hint of him, that is. In the full sunlight near an alley across the street, next to the five-and-ten, I saw the vague outline of a figure.

I waved at the dim figure, then beckoned with my hand: Come here, across the street, follow me. As I waved, the figure disappeared and I felt ridiculous, beckoning to empty air. Had my eyes deceived me and made me see what I wanted to see?

After waiting a few minutes, I stepped into the dismal

lobby, deserted as usual, and waited there in the silence, waited for a door to open, for footsteps to follow.

A few minutes passed. Nothing. The lobby with its cracked tile floor echoed no footsteps. I went to the doorway, looked out through the dirty window, saw nothing unusual.

As I walked across the lobby, there was a rush of footsteps behind me. Turning, I reeled from a blow to my face, staggered backward as much from surprise as from the blow itself. My cheek stung with pain. I lifted my hands to defend myself and was staggered by another blow, this time to my shoulder. I fell back against the wall, gasping, and felt the overpowering presence of him there, close to me. I heard a chuckle, low and gurgling, and footsteps moving away.

"Wait," I cried. "Don't go." Desperate to detain him, I called: "Let me help you. . . ."

The footsteps stopped, then came closer.

His voice came eerily out of nowhere.

"How can you help me?" Contempt in the voice, a snarl.

I was desperate to say the right thing and yet did not know what to say. And then decided on the truth, directness, not willing to gamble, to take chances.

"Because I'm like you. . . ."

And waited.

"Nobody's like me. . . ."

The voice, harsh and bitter, roared in my ears. And I felt his breath on my face.

"I am like you. I can do what you do—fade." Instantly, I knew that *fade* was my word, Adelard's word, a word that was probably unfamiliar to him. I quickly amended it. "Disappear. Make myself invisible. Like you . . ."

Silence again. Deep and stunning. Then:

"Who are you?" From the other side of the lobby.

"My name is Paul Moreaux. I'm a writer. I come from

Massachusetts. A small town, like Ramsey, named Monument." I spoke urgently, not wanting to lose him, needing to keep his attention. "This thing, being invisible, I call it the fade. What do you call it?" Playing for time, hoping to get him talking.

"Gone, unseen," he said, a sudden lilt in his voice, as if he were singing the words. "That's what I call it. Disappeared." The voice of a boy, bright and interested.

"What we call it doesn't matter. But it's something we share, you and me. In our blood. It makes us the same. . . ."

"If you share it, then do it."

"What?"

"Do it."

His voice like the snapping of a whip, a command that could not be ignored. But I could not possibly fade. I had vows to maintain. From years ago. From the time Bernard had died. Too many terrible things happened when I faded.

"Show me." The voice again, challenging, determined, evidently sensing my hesitancy. "Make yourself disappear. If you're telling me the truth."

I saw the trap I had sprung on myself.

And knew that I had to play for time, stall him, keep him here.

"I can't do it that easily," I said. "I need a bit of time. . . ."

"How much time?"

"How long does it take *you* to disappear?"

"Like this," he said. And I heard the snap of his fingers, a bit close to me, as if he had advanced a foot or two.

"Doesn't it hurt?" I asked.

A long pause and I waited, wondered whether my face was betraying me, whether he could read in my eyes the ploy I was using to stall him.

"It comes fast and goes fast—you get used to it," he said.

"It feels like dying," I said. "My breath goes away and then the pain comes." Keeping my voice conversational. Realizing that perhaps he wanted to talk about his strange power, the way I had wanted to talk to my uncle Adelard. "Then there's the cold."

Silence. Prolonged this time.

"Are you still here?" I asked. Dust motes danced in the air as sunlight slanted into the room, diluted by the dirty window. My shirt felt damp on my back, my armpits wet. I sensed that he was still here, but the absence of a response was ominous.

A blow took me by surprise again. This time to my jaw, snapping my head back. "Why did you do that?" I asked. "I'm trying to help . . ."

The sense of his nearness was powerful. I knew he was only a foot or two away. In the silence of the lobby, his breath was audible. Quick short breaths. Was he nervous, fearful?

"Listen," I said. "I'm not just a writer from Massachusetts. I'm more than that. I'm—"

Another blow, to my cheek.

"I know who you are," he said, his voice harsh and bitter. "That's why I should kill you . . ."

The outside door opened and I turned to see a gray-haired woman clutching a grocery bag to her chest enter the lobby, letting the door slam behind her.

Movements in the air nearby, scatterings, the patter of feet receding across the floor. His presence no longer there. An emptiness in the air, a sense of loss. He was gone.

You should have killed him. There. On the spot.
I know.

You had your chance and you blew it.

I had to find out more about him.

He was bluffing. He can't do it, be gone and unseen.

The old lady came in. He might have done it.

He was trying to trick you.

Maybe he wasn't.

Maybe he was.

And anyway—

Anyway what?

He's my Pa. My real Pa. I killed the fraud and the fake who beat me up, who beat up my Ma too. But this one's my real Pa. I wanted to see him for a minute or two. Talk to him a bit.

He left you behind. Deserted you. Didn't care enough about you to be a Pa to you.

Why is he back, then? He said he wants to help me. He says he's like me.

Says, says. He says. But did he do what you asked? No. He's a fake. He wants to use you, that's why he's back.

How can he use me?

Because he knows. About the power. What you can do about it. Once you leave this place and go into the world. All the big cities. You can come and go without being seen. Think what you can do without being seen. He knows this. That's why he came. That's why you have to kill him.

Ozzie ran. Ran from the voice. Ran blindly through the streets, not caring whether his footsteps could be heard or the breeze of his passing felt by people coming and going. Ran until his lungs burned and his legs sang with pain. The bright sun hurt his eyes. He wiped his nose he could not see with his sleeve he could not see. He slumped to the ground, rested awhile.

Later, he patrolled the streets and the stores, looking for

the old man, wondering if he had more to tell him about the stranger. Again and again, he checked out the old man's hiding places—the gazebo on the common, the alley, the empty crates behind the Ramsey Diner. No old man. Where the hell was he?

He found him at nightfall.

Emerging from the doorway of the Glenwood, reeling a bit, drunk, of course, looking foolishly around as he always did when gone on the drink and the booze, a silly look on his face.

No doubt the old man had been visiting the stranger who was his Pa, that Pa who had deserted him all those years ago. The stranger had given more booze to the old man to learn all he could about his friend, Ozzie Slater.

Oh, old man, Ozzie thought, sadly. It was possible, just possible, that he might have spared him, after all. Just might. Even now, standing across the street, watching the old man struggling as he tried to walk, as if seeking to balance himself on a high wire nobody else could see and was in danger of falling off, he almost pitied him. But he could not afford pity. Old man Pinder was a traitor and he had to die.

He killed him quickly, did not linger at the job the way he did when he killed the old fraud who was not his Pa. He struck him once with a rock to end his miserable drunken life. Funny thing, he felt sad at the end. The old man surprised him by being so tough. He did not think the old man could have survived the first blow, the whole right side of his face collapsing as he struck.

Then as he raised the stone again, the old man opened his eyes, terrible bloodshot eyes filled with tears that spilled on his cheeks and he looked right at Ozzie.

"You made me do this, old man," Ozzie said, looking down at him.

He struck him again, but this time, this time, holding back a bit with the blow, sorry as he hit the old man.

Now the stranger. He's up in his room. Knock at the door. And when he opens the door, do it.

He didn't want to kill the stranger. The stranger might be his Pa, his real Pa. Maybe the stranger really wanted to help him.

Kill him.

He did not answer the voice.

What are you waiting for? This is the night to get rid of them all.

He lingered at the entrance to the alley, nobody on the street, all the windows dark. The windows of the Glenwood were dark too.

Okay, kill the nun, then.

He drifted back into the alley, stalling, needing time to think, had to stay one step ahead of the voice.

The nun will betray you. To the cops. You can never trust the nun.

All right. He was tired of the voice, tired of arguing with the voice.

Do it, then. At the convent. Now.

Yes, yes, I'll do it. I'll kill the nun.

Nice, nice.

Trembling with the cold, in the fade, I heard a fugitive nighttime noise that beckoned me from my thoughts of Rosanna. Often, when the fade overcame me, as it did now in that forlorn hotel room in Ramsey, Maine, my thoughts turned to her and the old anguish came back.

Years had passed and I hadn't seen her or heard from her and didn't expect to anymore. She had faded from my life just as I had faded from the lives of others. The fade had not only made me invisible but had caused me to retreat from other people, even my family, in another kind of fading.

But then, isn't all of life a kind of fading? Love diminishes, memory dims, desire pales. *Why don't you get married, Uncle Paul?* my nieces (who are more romantic than my nephews) ask, teasingly. I always shrug and make jokes. *I'm saving myself for one of you girls.* For years I had tricked myself into believing that I was being faithful to that lovely ghost, Rosanna, but knew in my heart that the fade kept me solitary and remote. Or had I always used the fade as a crutch, an excuse to keep me separate from people, free to devote myself to my writing? In that hotel bed, I tried to outrun my thoughts, my guilts, realizing that life does not provide answers, only questions.

That small animal-like noise, a scratching at the dark, reached me again and I sat up in bed. At the same time, the pause, the breathlessness, announced the departure of the fade and I braced myself as the pain scalded my bones and flesh and the cold evaporated.

That sound again, which I now identified as a scratching at the door.

Slipping out of bed, I padded tentatively across the floor in the darkness, guided by instinct. Placing my ear against the door, I heard a quavering voice:

"Please . . . open up . . ."

I slowly swung the door open and saw old Mr. Pinder on the floor, bruised and battered, grotesquely perched on one elbow. One eye stared balefully at me, the other had disappeared in a tangle of flesh and blood. His mouth worked fishlike, opening and closing, but no sound came forth.

Kneeling down, I reached out to touch him but he shook his head in small desperate movements. "No . . ." he gasped. "Hurts . . . too . . . much . . ."

One side of his head was crushed, the way a melon would be crushed if dropped to the ground from a height.

"Who did this?" I asked. But did not require an answer. "We've got to get you to a hospital, a doctor . . ."

He shook his head, blood on his lips, that one eye piercing me with its intensity, while his hand clawed at the air, beckoning me to come closer. I lowered my head, placed my ear within an inch or two of his mouth.

His voice was like a whisper in a cave, echoing and hoarse and raspy, filled with a terrible urgency. "The boy . . . said . . . the nun . . . is next. . . ." His body quivered and his foul breath assailed me, the stench of death coming out of him.

His arms convulsed as he tried to grasp me. "Go," the old man commanded, blood spilling out of his mouth, as if he had brought the word up from the dark, bloody cellar of his soul.

He went limp, collapsing in my arms, slipping from my grasp, his head coming to rest gently against his elbow, the eye still open and staring but the rest of him closed, all pain and urgency over and done with.

I felt for a pulse, found none, cradled him for a moment in my arms, then closed that terrible eye.

The convent loomed in the night like a dinosaur at rest, silhouetted against a sky bright with summer moonlight. I stood in the courtyard hugging the shadows of the brick wall, blinking into the moonlight, as bright as noon in contrast to the shadows. Searching the convent for signs of light, I saw only a flickering in one of the tall, narrow windows near the center of the building: the chapel, no doubt, where nuns prayed incessantly, day and night.

I pondered my next move, whether I should ring the bell and sound the alarm, wondering also whether I might be too late. Had I done the wrong thing coming here, like this? I had telephoned the police department without identifying myself, and told them of the body in the hallway of the Glenwood. Then made my way here along the highway, keeping out of sight when occasional cars passed, knowing that I was taking a desperate, foolish chance coming alone. Yet, I felt a need to deal with the boy myself. Who else could understand him, who else could cope with the fade?

"You!"

I leapt with surprise as the voice reached me out of the darkness.

"Where are you?" I asked, looking frantically around.

"Are you my father?" The lilt still in his voice and a trembling, too.

"No, I'm not your father. Tell me where you are."

"Here," he said, his voice coming from another direction. "Who are you, if you're not my father?"

"Your uncle. Your mother is my sister. You're my nephew. . . ."

He stepped into view then, caught in the moonlight, not in the fade but visible, his figure slight, a lock of dark hair tumbling over his forehead. He drew his hand across his nose and sniffled. His eyes darted here and there and everywhere. He dropped his hand to his side and I saw his nose. Hideous and swollen, out of context with the rest of his face. I searched him for signs of Rose or Adelard or even myself. But found no resemblance and thought for one wild moment that it was all a mistake: I did not belong here, this was none of my business and I should go my way, return to Monument, turn my back on this nightmare. He moved slightly, and the light caught him differently now and, yes, I saw an echo of the Moreauxs in his stance, the slightness of his body like my cousin Jules and an expression in his eyes—soft, melting eyes like Rose's—that could not be denied.

"*I have to kill you,*" he said.

The voice was his voice and yet it wasn't. It was higher-pitched and distorted, ugly, distant, as if coming from crevices deep inside him.

"You don't have to kill me," I said. "You don't have to do anything you don't want to do."

"I know . . . I know . . ." His voice was his own again.

He was a lost, bewildered boy and I saw the fragile chin trembling.

His nose began to run. He wiped it with the back of his hand.

"But I'm going to kill you all the same," he said in that other voice, sharp, piercing. *"Then the nun . . ."*

"And then what?" I asked, masking my relief at the knowledge that the nun was safe. But what about that other voice? "Are you going to kill everybody in the world?"

"I don't want to kill anybody," he said, the boy speaking again. "All right, I killed the old fraud and I don't regret that. I'd do it again and again for what he did to me." He touched his nose. "And what he did to my Ma, who never hurt a soul in her life. I'd do it all over again . . ."

"What about the old man?" I asked, cautious, but drawing nearer to him. If only I could reach him, touch him, embrace him, show that I was not an enemy but blood of his blood, a member of his family.

"The old man led you to us." The ugly voice again. *"He had to die. Had to have his face bashed in. The nun is next."*

I saw now the dangerous contest we were engaged in, that two adversaries confronted me, not only the boy himself but another presence altogether, a presence residing within him, as if the fade itself had assumed a personality, perverse and deadly.

"What has the nun got to do with it?" I asked. "Why should you hurt her?" Was it possible to stay in touch with the boy through this other personality?

"She knows," the voice crackled. *"She pretends. She makes believe she's good, but she's not. She spies on us . . ."*

"Shut up," I cried. "I'm not talking to you. I don't want to have anything to do with you. I'm talking to the boy, Ozzie Slater. Not you . . ."

The boy looked directly at me and I realized he had kept his eyes away from mine from the beginning of our encounter, looking distantly over my shoulder. Now our eyes met.

"Are you really my uncle?" he asked.

"Yes," I said. "My sister Rose is your mother. You'd love her, Ozzie, if you knew her. She loves you . . ."

"She gave him away." The other voice, harsh, accusing.

"She had to give you away," I said, gently, reasonably, trying to ignore that voice, trying to keep the conversation between me and the boy. "She had no choice. She was young and had no control over her life at that time. She was desperate . . ."

"What kind of mother gives her baby away?"

"She wanted you to have life," I said. "She wanted her baby to live. She could have had an abortion, killed you in the womb. Instead, she went through the pain of labor, the pain and the blood. And she gave you to the nuns, to find a good home for you. Does that sound like she didn't care?"

"What's she like? Is she pretty?"

"She's beautiful. And she loves you deeply. She's the one who told me about Ramsey. I knew that one of my nephews with the power of the fade was somewhere in the world. She sent me to you. Told me about you. How she had to give you up and how sad she's been ever since. And I tracked you down. Because of her . . ."

"What do you want with me?" he asked, sounding genuinely curious.

"To help you, like I said. I know the power you have. And how that power can be a terrible thing. I have that power too. My uncle had the power before me. He came looking for me to help me the way I've come looking for you. It's handed down from uncles to nephews through the years."

"You're bluffing." The harsh accusatory voice. *"All this stuff*

about power. We've got the power. It's something you want from us.
To use it for yourself. That's why you're here."

"I don't want anything," I said. "Not for myself. But for you. I want to help you . . ."

"How can you . . . help me?" And now it was another voice altogether, a child's small voice not only lost and bewildered but confused. A child who might have been me a generation ago.

"First, you must stop what you're doing," I said. "That nun. Nothing must happen to her. You must leave her alone. Come with me . . ."

"To the police?"

"No, not the police. I'll arrange for you to see a doctor first. We'll leave Ramsey. I'll take you to a hospital in Boston that specializes in cases like yours. And then, yes, the police. But not in the way you think. There are ways to handle these things. You are not at fault, Ozzie, for what you've done. You are a victim . . ."

Was I making sense to him? Was I reaching him?

"You're a liar," he cried, his hand moving toward his belt in a swift and sudden movement. Then a knife appeared in his hand, the blade glinting in the moonlight.

Instinctively, I leapt forward and knocked it to the ground. As I raised my eyes, I saw the boy start to dissolve, like smoke dissipating in the air, so quickly that it was difficult to believe he had stood in front of me a moment or two before.

Stepping backward, I felt the wall behind me, knew that that particular avenue of escape was not possible. Simultaneously, I saw the knife rise from the ground, held by those invisible hands.

Almost hypnotized, I watched the knife slashing at the air like a miniature sword. Then it became still, suspended, knife-point directed at me. Now it began to move toward me, dangerous, deadly. I cringed, bracing myself as it came closer, closer. The tip of the blade tore my shirt, then penetrated my flesh, pausing before the final fatal plunge.

But the plunge did not come.

Instead, laughter: lewd and lascivious, a chortling of triumph.

"First, you, then Sister Anunciata . . ."

Her name leapt in my ears as I remembered Rose's voice— *Sister Anunciata, small, built like a fire hydrant*— the nun who had arranged for her son to be adopted, had helped her through the most difficult days of her life.

"Kill him."

"Wait," the boy said.

"Why wait? He has to die anyway."

"He's my blood. He's my uncle . . ."

"He's lying."

"He said he has the power like me. My uncle would have the power. It's in our blood."

"Have him prove it, then."

The knife was still at my stomach, only its tip in my flesh and the pain muted. But I knew my position was precarious, that the voice could at any moment command the boy to press deeper with the knife.

"Make him prove it," the voice demanded.

"All right," the boy said, impatient, and harsh. And then softer as he addressed me: "Prove it to me," he said. "Prove it to the voice. Make yourself gone, unseen."

"Who is the voice?" I asked, low and whispering, playing the game, desperate as it was, of postponement.

"I don't know," he said, whispering, matching my own effort at conspiracy. "But he brings the urges. And I can't do anything but obey the urges. I'm not me when the urges begin." I heard his sniffle, wondering if he was again wiping that bulbous nose, like the nose of a ruined clown. "Please disappear, prove who you are. . . ."

"I haven't used the power for a long time," I said. "I made a promise many years ago. A promise to not use it. Whenever I use the power, bad things happen. Someone dies. I don't want anyone else to die. . . ." I thought of my brother Bernard and Rudolphe Toubert and me. The murderer.

"You'll die." The voice harsh, commanding.

At the same time, the knife dug a bit deeper into my flesh and although there was only a pinch of pain, I felt something warm oozing from me and my knees grew weak.

"Do it," the boy pleaded.

I pressed forward, against the invisible wall, that small movement I had not called upon for years, uncertain after all this time whether it would work. Yet, I had no choice. I had no doubt at all that the boy, controlled by that other personality, could kill me and go on to kill the nun and who knows who else? Then the pause and the flash of pain and the cold, all of it fast, never as fast before, and I was in the fade.

I heard the fierce whisper:

"He's more dangerous now. We have to kill him."

The knife flashed forward in a swordlike thrust but I swiftly stepped aside, nimble suddenly, as if the fade had given me energy and quickness along with invisibility.

"Where are you?" Puzzlement and awe in the boy's voice.

"Here," I said, then moved away from the spot where I had spoken. "Do you believe me now?"

"Yes," he said.

He disappeared, the stranger who was his uncle. Just like that. In the winking of an eye. Becoming a vapor, a cloud of mist in the moonlight and then nothing. Ozzie had seen it happening to himself when he had practiced in front of the mirror but was shocked to see it happen to someone else. Shocked and scared because he felt at a loss, his knife pointing at nothing in the air, useless now as a weapon.

"Where are you?" he whispered again, as fear crept over him. He felt unguarded, open to attack.

No answer. Was he playing games, his uncle? Was he near or far, to the right or left?

Find him. Kill him.

That voice again. He would love to kill the voice but could not do it because the voice was himself.

You're wasting time.

The knife was suddenly struck from his hand, and his wrist leapt with pain at the blow. The knife dropped to the ground and landed at his feet.

Pick it up.

As he bent to retrieve it, the knife skittered away, glinting in the moonlight, like a fish out of water, leaping in the air and then dropping to the ground a few feet from him. He also heard the rush of receding footsteps.

"Wait," he said. "Don't go away . . ."

A moment of silence, then: "I'm right here," the voice of his uncle somewhere nearby. "I knocked the knife away because we can't talk with a knife between us. And I need to talk to you. To you, not to that voice I keep hearing. That voice isn't you, Ozzie. That voice is the killer, not you. You have to be separated from the voice. You have to resist the voice, fight it, hold it off . . ."

See what he's trying to do? He's trying to turn us against each other. And he wants to lock you up. Do you want to be locked up?

No.

That's what he wants to do to you. You have to get rid of him.

But how?
Get that knife. And stick him.

I was astonished to hear those voices in that moonlit courtyard, listening to the boy arguing with himself, the two
voices so different, the one harsh and demanding, bent on
destruction, and the other young and fragile.

As I listened a wave of sadness stole over me, the kind of
sadness that comes from loss—all the people we lose through
the years—and now I was losing this boy, my nephew, a
poor fader like myself with a savage loose inside him.

Now.

I heard the word with all its urgency and insanity, a single
vicious syllable, and saw a stirring in the air, like branches
being shaken, a sensation of movement in the moonlight, a
scurrying. And I moved, too, leaping toward the knife, half
tripping, lunging forward, hands outstretched.

The knife soared into the air before I reached it—he had
beaten me to the spot—but once more his possession of the
knife gave me an advantage and I was able to see where he
must be standing.

I straightened up and kicked, aiming for his stomach, judg-
ing its height from the ground. My shoe met the target, sank
into the softness of his stomach, deeper than I had hoped,
and he bellowed with pain. At the same time the knife fell to
the ground, loosened from his grip, and I went after it.

The instant I picked it up, I knew my mistake, knew that I
had betrayed where I stood the way he had betrayed himself
a moment before. I had also forgotten youth's capacity to
absorb and throw off pain and I heard the rush of his body
just before he crashed into me, his head butting my chest,
taking my breath away, causing me to drop the knife, to emit
my own bellow of pain. Before I could recover, his hands

were around my neck, not the hands of a thirteen-year-old boy but the steel-like hands of a deadly enemy, ageless, and mad, gaining strength from the madness. The fingers tightened around my neck, mashing my Adam's apple into my throat, cutting off air—this was how it was to choke—leaving me unable to cry out, my arms thrashing around convulsively. As I fell backward I tried to twist away from him and landed on the ground in a hard thump that sent pain shooting along my spine. My hands reached out desperately as I twisted and fought with all my strength. My right hand somehow found the knife. I managed to grasp the handle, barely aware of my movements but aware of his body pressing against mine, the sweaty cheek against my cheek, the fingers even tighter around my neck and a lassitude growing in me as the sense of suffocation took away all desire, all thought, all resistance. I felt myself fading, not the fading of invisibility but a fading away of my entire being into oblivion.

Die, you bastard, die.

The harshness of the voice lit a small fire in my diminishing consciousness. I knew that I had to resist that madman in the boy, had to make one final effort to defeat him, whether or not I gained breath again. I fought against a gathering darkness that threatened to swallow me up and obliterate me, and managed to open my eyes. Through the mist and fog of my dimming sight, I saw the glint of the knife and remembered that the knife was actually in my hand. I had only to bring the knife down into the flesh of this monster whose fingers were around my throat, who was murdering me. That was all I had to do, but it seemed impossible. I had no strength left. Do it, I told myself, do it. This one last thing. I focused on the knife, felt my eyes bulging achingly as I concentrated the final remnants of my thought processes on it.

The knife became my entire world, shining in the moonlight, poised above the madman I could not see but who was
slowly taking my life away. I willed the knife to descend,
gathered everything that remained of me and my life into
that desire. And I watched the knife finally descending
slowly, in downward thrust, and then faster, and I was no
longer aware of the fingers that had now become a part of
my throat or the blackness threatening the edges of my consciousness or the breathless world in which I was caught and
held, knew only that the knife was coming down, coming
down. When it plunged into his body, a cry of pain filled the
air, terrible in its anguish, and at the same time there was a
great rushing of air down my throat into my lungs, sweet,
sweet air that filled my life's crevices as his fingers loosened
their hold, although I still felt their imprint on the flesh of
my neck. I stabbed again and again, could not stop, did not
want to stop, my own madness taking over. He clung to me
for a moment and a sob escaped his lips, the sob of a child
crying itself to sleep at night, then he slumped against me
and rolled away.

He knew he was doomed and dying when the blade first
slipped into him, before the other stabbings, reaching a place
deep and vital inside of him where nothing had ever gone
before. He wanted to let go, let go. The voice was telling him
to hold on. But he didn't want to hold on. The hell with the
voice. *Don't let go.* I will, I will.

The pain, demanding and insistent, spread through his
body like fire eating him up. Ma, he cried, Ma. He started to
cry, opening his eyes to see if she was here but he saw only
blood, a curtain of blood, his own blood. Just before he
closed his eyes for the last time, giving himself up to the
dark, knowing he had finally overcome the voice, he heard

another voice, his mother singing to him, couldn't make out the words or the tune, her voice far away. He went toward her voice. Into the dark. Into nothing.

The boy emerged from the fade into the moonlight, slowly, in stages, his body appearing the way a film develops in a tray, my tears the liquid. His body was limp in that final fatal way of bodies after breath has gone, face slack and loose, something almost sweet in the face, in repose, as if untouched by time or pain or injury, the abused nose not repulsive now, still bruised and broken but noble somehow, like an old battle wound.

"Oh, Ozzie," I said, tasting my tears as I spoke, aware of lights coming on in the convent.

As I stood over the boy, something moved inside me, in some unknown and uncharted territory of myself, something shifting and letting go, deep beneath the surface. Standing there, I felt, impossible, that I was going away from myself, away from pain, away from loss. Not in the fade but gone in another way.

Good-bye, I said.

But did not hear my voice.

And did not, did not know to whom or to what I was saying good-bye.

SUSAN

Fiction, of course.

That was the verdict Meredith and I reached by the end of my Manhattan summer. The word, in fact, became a kind of lifeline, something to clutch and hold on to.

"You have to be slightly insane to survive in the agent business," Meredith said. Then, pointing to the manuscript, she said: "But the fade would take me way beyond the pale. . . ."

I agreed. Then.

Shit. I must agree *now*.

Despite what I have pinned to my bulletin board here in my room, what I cannot resist reading over and over again.

Although it's November outside, it's winter here in the boardinghouse. My room is not exactly the Ritz and it's impossible to heat, but it is not a dump either. (Dorm rooms seem to be a myth at B.U. and I was lucky to find this place, from which, if I stretch at the window, I can see a patch of the Charles River.)

So here I am in Boston at the typewriter writing, as Paul Roget once sat in Monument, writing. But he wrote novels and short stories and I am writing—what?

I dunno.

Trying to put my thoughts into some kind of order.

Still trying to follow Professor Waronski's dictum of getting things down on paper, between the demands of a term paper that I must start sometime if I'm to finish before the finals in December and library research I must complete for a political sci project.

The hell with all that.

Let me go back to New York and Meredith and how we came to terms with Paul's manuscript.

For the most part, I was caught up in the frenetic world of Broome & Company, twelve-and fourteen-hour days of office activity while Meredith kept up her own frantic pace.

Days passed when we barely conversed, when I collapsed in bed at nine-thirty while she was still at the office or out somewhere at a publication party. Or on the telephone in conversations that seemed endless, filled with the jargon of the trade.

At various times we surfaced and seemed to discover each other all over again. Returning from St. Pat's one brilliant Sunday morning, Meredith said: "Rose is the key, Susan." Bringing the subject up from out of nowhere. "If she were still alive, she could provide the answer. Did she or did she not have a baby out of wedlock?"

"Right," I said, wondering if either of us would have had the courage to ask her that question.

In the apartment one evening, after a late frozen-food dinner that we barely touched, both of us exhausted after a day of frenzy at Broome, she said: "I have something to say, Susan." In her best office voice.

Bracing myself, I merely said: "Yes."

Her fatigue suddenly gone, she looked me straight in the eye and said:

"Fade."

Enunciating the word so deliberately that she almost stretched it to two syllables.

I waited for more.

"Fade," she said again. Then: "Invisible. Unseen. Disappear."

Now she waited for my reaction, her eyes asking questions I could not comprehend.

When I still said nothing, she said: "See how impossible those words sound? Written down on paper, fine. In my thoughts or your thoughts, also fine. But yesterday, alone in the office for a moment, door closed, I said this aloud: 'Paul Roget had the power to make himself invisible.' And immediately, hearing those words come out of my mouth, I realized how impossible they sounded. Try it, Susan."

I tried it:

"Paul Roget faded, became invisible, unseen—"

"See what I mean?" Meredith asked.

And I did.

On paper, between the first and last pages of a manuscript, nothing is impossible. But in the reality of sunshine on a carpet, furniture you can touch as you pass, faucets that spout water, headaches, loneliness on a Sunday evening, the illusions created by nouns and verbs and similes and metaphors become only that—illusions. Words on a page. And *fade* becomes, then, just another word.

Finally, on the subway, crowded and jostled and hanging on to the straps for dear life, she said:

"I did some checking today with the help of a gal I know in the research department at *Time*. Checked on Ramsey, Maine. Which we found does not exist. And the order of the Sisters of Mercy. Which likewise does not exist." Swayed away from me as the car swung wildly entering a station. "Checked old resort towns with dried-up springs. Again: nothing." Perhaps anticipating my response, she said: "All of which doesn't mean that they don't exist elsewhere."

"Then why did he switch from a real Frenchtown to a made-up Ramsey?" I asked. "From first person with Paul to third person with Ozzie?"

"Because it's all fiction," she said. "It has to be, Susan." A kind of desperation in her voice.

"I know," I said.

We looked in each other's eyes for a long time and then looked away. As if we had called a truce there in the crowded subway car careening under the streets of Manhattan. We did not speak of the manuscript again that summer.

But that night in bed I thought of my grandfather and what he had told me one day in Monument, something I had not divulged to Meredith or even admitted to myself the day I had discovered the manuscript in her apartment.

A year ago, October, a leaf-tumbling, beautiful day, I arrived in Monument by B&M train. My grandfather met me at the depot and drove me around town, pointing out places Paul had described in his novels and stories. At one point, we pulled up in front of the public library, across from City Hall.

"Paul and I spent a lot of time there as kids," he said, indicating the ancient stone building shrouded by trees and bushes. "Paul practically lived in the place. He told me he was going to read every book in there. I wonder if he ever did." He chuckled, shaking his head. "I think he knew the library better than the librarians. I once accused him of knowing about a secret room in the building. . . ."

My penchant for drama and mystery asserted itself and, thrilled, I said: "Secret room?"

Voice tender with reminiscence, he said: "One year, when we were eleven or twelve, I received a detective kit for Christmas. We went to the library looking for books on detection. We sneaked into the adult stacks, practically tiptoeing around because libraries were quiet places in those days. I discovered a book on fingerprinting and went to look for Paul. I couldn't find him. Looked up, down, all over the building. It's as if he had disappeared.

"Finally, he showed up. Looked guilty as hell, pale, almost sick. I accused him of hiding—had he found a secret spot somewhere? He said he had felt a bit sick, sat down in the stacks, curled up, and sort of fell asleep. Sounded strange to me but I let it go because he'd been having a bad year. Fainted once or twice, lost weight, had no appetite. Growing pains, puberty probably, the doctor said, and gave him all kinds of tonics. This was before the days of vitamin pills, I guess. . . ."

At the time, the incident in the library did not make a large impression on me, and became a kind of footnote in my memory. Until that summer evening in Meredith's apartment when I read Paul's manuscript.

Why hadn't my grandfather mentioned the incident in his report to Meredith?

Had he refused to acknowledge Paul's disappearance because it would lead him to enormous conclusions that he could not accept?

Or was he keeping secrets?

Did Meredith have her own secrets?

Were we all keeping secrets from each other?

After all, I have not told Meredith about Paul's disappearance at the library, either.

Two weeks ago I visited Monument for the first time since returning from New York City and found my grandfather, weak and wan, in a bed at Monument Hospital, recovering from surgery.

"My colon," he said. "And complications."

"What kind of complications?" I asked, appalled to see this man who had never looked like a grandfather suddenly looking like one, his graying hair no longer giving off flashes of distinction but uncombed, lusterless, his face ashen.

"They don't know yet," he said wearily. "Old age itself is a complication, Susan."

"You're not old," I said. "You could never be old."

"I'm sixty-three," he said. "But an old sixty-three, my girl. More than forty years on the force, thirty of them on night shifts, walking the beat before they gave me plain clothes." Sighing, closing his eyes, he said: "Hell, it was a good life."

Speaking in past tense, as if his life were also past tense.

In Boston's North End, I found an ancient church and went inside to burn a candle for him, the way his generation did in the old days. There were no candles in the church, only an array of small light bulbs in candle holders. The bulbs lit up when you inserted a coin. I placed a dollar in the poor box instead and offered a prayer before a statue of St. Jude.

I will visit my grandfather in Monument again but won't ask him any more questions about Paul.

* * *

Meredith and I keep in touch with brief notes and late-night phone calls. She has asked me, hooray, to return to Broome & Company next summer. Two days ago I received a letter from her that contained the following:

"Had a long talk with Walter Holland at Harbor House yesterday. He's still interested in a Paul Roget collection and positively glowed when I told him about the new manuscript, fragmented though it is. Funny thing, Susan. As soon as I sent it off by messenger this morning, a feeling of—I don't know—peace? (no, too strong a word), accomplishment? (not exactly that either), came over me. A feeling that I had paid off a debt, as if I had completed a mission Paul wanted me to carry out. Crazy? Maybe. But a kind of sadness was lifted from me, sadness that had lingered ever since his death all those years ago."

Paul Roget died in his bed in a rented apartment on Second Street in Frenchtown on June 3, 1967, at the age of forty-two. The *New York Times* obituary said he died of natural causes. My grandfather told me that Paul had been the victim of a series of ailments in his final years. He had developed diabetes, lost a great deal of weight, and suffered a heart attack two years before he died.

He had become more of a recluse than ever in those last days, moving from apartment to apartment, refused to have a telephone installed, stopped writing (although he must have written the fade manuscript at that time). He did not always admit visitors when they knocked at his door. Although he never turned away his nephews and nieces, his enthusiasm for their company diminished and, sensing his growing indifference, they stopped visiting. My grandfather saw him at mass occasionally on Sunday but never saw him receive communion.

He seems to have faded away. Not the fade of his manuscript but fading the way the lights and colors of the day fail as night falls, as if he began to live his manuscript in a manner he could not have foreseen.

Thus, he became a fader after all.

That, I thought sadly, is the end of that.

Until.

Until five days ago, when I picked up *The Boston Globe* and read the following story, which is what I have pinned to my bulletin board:

MYSTERY BLAST KILLS 75:

SECOND TRAGEDY IN WEEK

SHERWOOD, N.Y. (AP)— A mysterious explosion in a chemical plant here Tuesday killed 75 workers and injured 23 others in the second major tragedy to hit this city of 11,000 in a week. On Friday night, 20 students and 3 teachers died when fire swept the Sherwood High School gymnasium during the Senior Prom.

The causes of the explosion and fire have not been determined. Police Chief Herman Barnaby said that "foul play is suspected in both cases."

"We are baffled," admitted Henry Tewksbury, plant manager of ABC Chemicals, Inc. "Because of the volatile nature of the chemicals, we maintain the strictest security in the world. Our experts tell us it was impossible for anyone to penetrate our security without being observed. That person would have had to be invisible."

Equally "impossible," according to high school principal Vito Andalucci, were the circumstances in which the students and teachers died in the gymnasium. About 100 escaped the smoky blaze, but those who lost their lives were trapped in a corridor, unable to open a door leading to safety.

"That door was under my personal surveillance the entire evening," Principal Andalucci said. "This precaution was taken because last year rowdy outsiders entered the gym through that door and disrupted the prom. I vowed that would not happen this year. Impossible as it was, someone jammed the mechanism of the lock. Thus, when I sent those students and teachers off in that direction, I was sending them to their deaths."

Chief Barnaby refused to comment on reports that the town had been plagued recently by acts of terror, ranging from vandalism in business places on Main Street to a series of break-ins in local homes.

Meanwhile, the state fire marshal's office discounted a report that a teenager had been seen in the vicinity of the plant shortly before the explosion. One Sherwood resident, who has not been identified, said the teenager "disappeared into thin air" after being spotted near the plant's entrance.

"We are looking for physical evidence and cannot be involved with rumors and hearsay," Fire Chief Martin Peters said.

I sit here in my room in Boston, safe and snug, thinking of someone at this moment in upstate New York, someone who might be a new fader, another nephew in a new generation, a madman unleashed on the world.

Impossible, I tell myself, even as I wonder if I have the answer at last to the reason why Paul wanted his manuscript held back until this year or later. Did he want it to coincide with the appearance of a new fader—as a warning or a message?

I don't know the answer to that question.

Or to some other questions, either.

I mean, I sit here and I think of the fade and that clipping on the bulletin board and I wonder if I am safe and snug after all. If any of us are.

And I don't know what to do about it.

God, I don't know what to do.